Ghosts in the Abbey

Emily L. Finch

First paperback edition June 2023

Book cover design by Bespoke Book Covers

ISBN: 978-1-7377372-1-6

www.emilylfinch.com

ONE

He lay in a pool of his own blood, his face ashen, his body thin and gaunt. As she watched, he raised his head and fixed her with a look of such intensity that his eyes seemed to fill her vision. Then he spoke her name.

"Samantha."

The awful hopelessness in his voice cut through her like a knife. Struggling to her feet, she called out to him, hoping to reassure him.

"Charles!"

She began to run towards him. Yet, somehow, no matter how fast she ran, he remained at a distance, watching her with eyes full of despair.

"Charles!" she shouted again, a sob clogging her throat.

And then suddenly, she was beside him. Falling to her knees, she tried to staunch the flow of blood, but it would not be stopped. She could feel it, warm and sticky, coating her hands as she pressed them into the torn fabric of his waistcoat.

Charles let out a shuddering sigh as he turned his head to hers. Her own heart seemed to speed up, as though determined to take on the unfulfilled beats of his, and she choked back another sob.

His lips moved, trying to form words, and she leaned closer to catch them.

Suddenly, his hands shot up and circled her throat. She could feel his fingers digging into her neck with surprising force. She clutched at them, fighting to prise them from her, but the harder she fought, the tighter they grew. Eyes wide with panic, she looked down to see Charles watching her. His expression wasn't vindictive or even angry. It was achingly sad.

Samantha Kingston woke with a gasp. For a moment, she didn't know where she was—the nightmare still lingered at the edges of her consciousness. Then she saw the familiar hangings of the four-poster bed and caught the scent of dried lavender from the sachet by her pillow, and her body relaxed.

Judging by the grey light that filtered through a gap in the bed curtains, it was morning, but early. She shivered and pulled the quilt up over her shoulders. The maid had not yet been in to light the fire, and the room was so cold she could see the cloud of her breath. She knew she ought to lie down and try to go back to sleep—Madge, her hostess, would insist on it if she were in the room—but it wouldn't do. She was too awake now and too cold.

A sense of guilty relief passed over her as she swung her feet down and slid them into the soft fabric of her slippers. She was supposed to be working to overcome her fears—reminding herself that dreams were not real—yet she could not help but be glad that the struggle, at least for that day, was over.

Samantha reached up to the bedpost and lifted down her dressing gown, wrapping it around herself before shifting aside the bed-curtains and standing up. She shuffled over to the window, tying the sash of her robe as she went, and opened the curtains. Mists rose above the wide lawn, obscuring the distant hills and making the grounds seem ethereal, otherworldly. The sight recalled her nightmare to mind, and she shivered.

He hadn't really called her name before he died—that was only her imagination—and she hadn't run to him, but the image was real. Charles lying on the ground, covered in blood, his face turned to hers, his eyes, wide with fear, never breaking contact with her own as his frantic breathing slowed and finally stopped. It was that image that had haunted her for three months. She saw it when she lay in bed at night. It was there in the darkness of the room and in the corner of her eyes every time she closed them. Whenever her mind was idle, it would creep in unnoticed until it was right in front of her.

Charles was dead. He had been her dearest friend, her confidant, her savior, her deserter, her kidnapper, her aunt's and uncle's murderer. He was the reason she spent weeks starving on the streets of London, hiding from the police. He was the reason she had been forced into a den of criminals and broken the law. Because of Charles, she had been abducted. Because of him, she had been struck so hard that she nearly lost consciousness. He had lied to her so easily and, because of him, she had lost all confidence in her own judgment.

It was that last part—the way he had made her doubt herself —that was the hardest for Samantha to move past. She could still remember the look of disbelief on his face when she told him his father and stepmother were dead and the guilt she had felt at delivering such news. To realize that—not only had he known his father was dead when she conveyed the news, but that he had been the one to pull the trigger—had shaken Samantha to her core. How could she have been so wrong about someone? How could she ever trust that she knew anyone?

The sound of the handle turning brought Samantha's focus back to the present and she watched as the door opened and a maid walked in carrying the bucket of tools she used to light the fires. She looked resigned rather than surprised to see Samantha out of bed, and she made a quick curtsy before moving to the large fireplace that took up a good portion of the wall between them.

Samantha returned her gaze to the window, trying to ignore the awkwardness of the encounter. In the normal course of things, she ought never to see the maid. It was the maid's job to be up before the family and their guests and to start their fires while they slept so that they woke to warm rooms. A guest standing awake in a cold room implied that the maid had not done her job properly. Samantha didn't mean the insult and she wished she had thought to jump back into bed before the door opened, but it wasn't the first time she had awakened early, and it wouldn't be the last.

"Shall I send Miss Forth up to you, Miss?" the maid asked as she stood and collected her tools.

"No, thank you," Samantha replied. "Let her sleep."

The maid bowed and left the room as quietly as she had entered.

It was odd to hear Alice spoken of as Miss Forth. It was the proper way to refer to her—she was a lady's maid—but Samantha had known her since she was an upstairs maid in her grandfather's house. To change from the familiar "Alice" to the less friendly "Forth" when they had become closer through her new position had seemed silly, particularly as Samantha was then only a girl and Alice not much older.

After warming herself by the fire, Samantha padded over to the wardrobe and took out the clothes she would need for the morning, including one of her plainest wool dresses and a pair of thick woolen stockings. Though she needed Alice to dress her and her hair for fashionable company, she was well able to get herself ready for a simple walk in the country. There was no need for Alice to lose sleep simply because *she* had.

Ten minutes later, wrapped in a fur-lined cloak with her feet shod in her stoutest boots, Samantha tramped through the back gardens towards the woods. The air was crisp and cold, and her feet crunched the frozen dew with every step. As she crested the first hill, she took a deep breath and turned to view the house behind her.

Bradwell Court floated above the surrounding mist, the yellow stone shining gold where the rays of the emerging sun touched it. Light reflected off the mullioned windows so that the whole building seemed to sparkle. It was a show that the house put on only for those brave or foolish enough to venture out in the wee hours of a cold December morning. Samantha felt privileged to witness it, and she smiled to herself as she watched a moment longer before turning away.

The Court, in all its Neoclassical glory, had been home to generations of Bradwell ancestors for over two hundred years and, for the past three months, it had been Samantha's home as well. After the distressing events of the summer, Lady Bradwell, who had insisted Samantha address her by the more familiar Madge almost from the first moment of their acquaintance, had brought Samantha back from London with her and installed her in one of the family suites. No word was to be spoken of her leaving. Her kindness had nearly overwhelmed Samantha, who had seen little of that virtue in her own family, much less in a relative stranger.

Wrapping her cloak more tightly around her, Samantha continued on, following the familiar trail that led through the woods and across the rolling hills. She kept a steady pace, finding comfort in the sight of a large stump or the sound of rushing water from a nearby brook, landmarks that had become as well known to her as any in London. With each breath, she felt the chill in her lungs. After a restless night of dreams, it was good to feel so undeniably awake.

When the stone wall of a ruined medieval abbey appeared ahead, she slowed her pace. There was something hauntingly beautiful about the tumbled structure, with its half-demolished cloister, flowers growing through the cracks in the masonry. Samantha could almost imagine it as it must once have been, with tall stained-glass windows and a gabled roof, but she preferred it as it was—a poetic reminder of the fragility of man's existence, as forgotten as the memories of those who had once walked its halls.

According to Madge, the locals insisted it was haunted. There had been sightings over the years of various spirits—wailing nuns, veiled ladies, amorphous wisps. For her part, Samantha had never believed in spirits, but she was grateful for the legends nonetheless because of the privacy they afforded her. She had yet to see a single person on any of her visits to the abbey.

After circling the perimeter, Samantha climbed through one of the wide openings that had once been a window into what she imagined was the great hall. She walked among the pillars that had supported the high ceiling and craned her neck to see where their tops met the grey sky above. At the far end of the long hall was the most intact of the remaining walls with its magnificent arched window. As her eyes traveled down it to the tumble of stones below, she was distracted by a sound behind her—the crunch of footsteps.

Heart in her throat, Samantha reached down into her boot and grasped the hilt of the knife she kept there, sliding it out and concealing it under her cloak. As the rational part of her mind caught up to her, she reminded herself how absurd it was to imagine someone had come to harm her. This wasn't London, after all, and Slater and Palmer, Charles' associates, were dead or imprisoned. Their boss, Skinny Jim, had no idea that the young "Sam" who had briefly worked for him was really her. No more could any of her friends from the street connect her with the "Sarah" they had known. Despite these rational thoughts, however, fear kept her hand on the knife as she stood and turned to face whoever had decided to venture so far so early in the morning.

Alice appeared from around a corner and Samantha released a shaky breath, lowering herself to a crouch as her knees threatened to give way.

"You scared me half to death," she said accusingly, taking the opportunity to return her knife to her boot before straightening again. "I told Mary not to wake you."

"I didn't mean to scare you," Alice said, her eyes traveling down to Samantha's boots before returning to her face. "I wasn't sneaking."

Samantha was sure then Alice knew about the knife, though they had never spoken about it. Explaining why she felt she needed it would have required delving into the truth of what had happened to her that summer, and she could not bring herself to do so, much as she trusted Alice.

"Mary didn't wake me," Alice said. "I was already awake."

Samantha found that highly doubtful, but before she could probe further, Alice continued.

"This is the third time in a fortnight you've been out this early." Her tone was a mixture of admonishment and concern. "Have you been taking your laudanum?"

"No," Samantha said firmly. The laudanum had been prescribed by the village doctor soon after her arrival when Madge, noting the dark circles under Samantha's eyes, had insisted she submit to his care. It had taken only a week for Samantha to grow to hate the sluggish, heavy feeling it left her with and to confine the small bottle to the depths of her wardrobe. Thankfully, Madge had agreed with her decision, asserting her belief that fresh air and steady occupation would be better than any medicine.

"You really ought to take it," Alice said. "Doctor Caruthers was sure it would help."

Samantha sighed. "Even when I was taking the laudanum, there were days I woke early. I think Madge is right. So long as I keep moving and busy throughout the day, I can usually make myself tired enough."

"I would have thought you'd've had enough to make yourself tired this past week," Alice said. "What with the house so full of guests."

In anticipation of the traditional Winter Ball hosted by Madge's husband Lord Bradwell's family since time immemorial, Bradwell Court had been host to a handful of close family and friends. Several more guests were expected to arrive that morning.

"I have been mostly avoiding the guests this week," Samantha admitted. "I feel like an interloper where the Wentworths are concerned. They are here to meet the family of their daughter's suitor, not a relative stranger. As for Lord Linwood's friends, Mr. Allen, at least, is too attentive for my comfort. Once the rest of the party arrives, I will have plenty with which to occupy myself."

Alice still looked doubtful, but she said nothing. After a few moments of uncomfortable silence, Samantha suggested they might as well return to the house.

They were passing the stables when she was hailed. She turned to see Madge, dressed in riding gear, her long, thick hair, somewhere between blond and grey, pinned up beneath a black silk hat. A groom was leading out one of her horses.

"I would ask if you were going on a walk," Madge said, approaching her with a slight frown, "but you have clearly just come back from one. When did you set out this morning?"

"I don't know exactly," Samantha said evasively. "Not long ago."

"Perhaps your maid has a better idea," Madge said. She looked to Alice expectantly.

"It was just gone seven, your ladyship," Alice said, glancing at Samantha and looking quickly away.

"You told me you were sleeping better."

There was concern in the accusation, but also a hint of exasperation.

"I was," Samantha said.

She *had* been sleeping better when Madge asked her a week ago, but not since then. She hadn't seen the point in telling Madge of the change, though. What could she do but worry? Or chastise Samantha for not working harder to overcome her difficulties? Madge, the epitome of health and vitality, with a confidence and self-possession that rivaled any Samantha had seen, could never understand why Samantha could not simply will away the nightmares and the sleeplessness.

Madge sighed, and the small cloud formed by her breath hovered for a few seconds before dissipating.

"I hope you don't mind sharing hosting duties with me," she said. "These final guests have somehow managed to stagger their arrivals to coincide with nearly every train that comes through Hope station, and I doubt I'll be available to greet everyone."

Samantha, grateful for the change of subject, smiled. "Of course. Whatever you need me to do."

"I must be going before Bucephalus freezes to death," Madge said, casting her eyes in the direction of the horse, who was stamping and tossing his head. "We can discuss this more after breakfast. If I'm not there on time, try to keep Miss Wentworth from talking Bradwell's ear off. He's too polite to stop her, but she gives him a headache, and I don't want him to use that as an excuse to retire early tonight. If I have to suffer these Wentworths, so does he."

Samantha laughed as Madge walked over to her horse and took the reins from the groom. She marveled, as she always did, at the ease with which her friend almost leapt into the saddle. The horse shifted restlessly under her as she made adjustments to her seat and then, as Samantha waved, it took off, cantering towards the open fields behind the estate.

"Mr. Wyatt arrives today, does he not?" Alice asked as they continued to the house.

Samantha looked at her sharply, hoping to gauge her motivation in asking such a question, but Alice's eyes were on the path ahead. "Yes, he does, as you well know." When Alice continued in silence, Samantha added lightly, "It will be good to see him again. I look forward to renewing our...acquaintance."

She had been on the point of saying friendship but had been unable to bring herself to do so. Were she and Wyatt friends? The first time they met, he had kissed her—by mistake and while pretending to be someone else—and she had shoved him away. When they met again, she had been the one in disguise, and she had stolen his pocketbook.

They had begun a tentative working relationship when he employed her to find information for him, but that relationship had quickly transformed when he realized she was a witness to a murder, running for her life. He had become a sort of protector to her then and agreed to assist her in clearing her name. He had brought Madge, his cousin, into her life to help preserve her reputation. She had found him frustrating, occasionally overbearing, but surprisingly trustworthy and, at times, an enjoyable companion. Though they had often argued, she had found their discussions stimulating and thought that he had grown to respect her opinion.

Then, the truth of Charles' treachery had been revealed, and the world had turned upside down. There hadn't been much opportunity for her and Wyatt to talk in that last week and, when they finally met again, it was not long before Charles was shot.

Wyatt had hurried her from the courthouse with Madge and put her on a train out of the city. There had been a moment when it seemed as though something significant had passed between them. He had been helping her into the carriage and, when he should have released her hand, he held on. Their eyes had met, and she thought she sensed a connection and a reluctance to part. It had been only a moment, though—so quick she might have imagined it. Sometimes she thought she had.

In the ensuing months, though Wyatt's friend Lord Aston had been a frequent guest of Madge's, coming in October to purchase one of Madge's dogs and twice more for weekend hunting parties, Wyatt had been absent. He had written to Madge a few times, first to inform her of what had happened after they left the city, then to tell her of the lack of progress in identifying Charles' shooter, and finally to let her know of his plans to visit France with a friend. To Samantha, he had said nothing, and she was left to wonder.

*****

V. T. Wyatt sat in an armchair by the window in one of the front rooms of Boodle's. The newspaper spread open before him was meant to discourage any attempts to engage him in conversation, but he wasn't reading it.

In the past few months, Wyatt had gone from a life of relative obscurity to one of a sort of reflected infamy. Men with whom he had been on only nodding terms now sought him out to gain his opinion on the news of the day, dowager ladies of a certain age whispered about him behind their fans, and he had never received so many dinner invitations.

It wasn't that he was unaccustomed to such attention in any form. In the character of Archie Kennedy, that trouble-making alter-ego he and his friend Lord Aston, "Bingo," had created back in their school days, he was used to drawing the eye. As the respectable V.T. Wyatt, younger son of the late Viscount Boxley, however, living on the edges of public notice had not only been his reality, it had been a great help in his investigative work. It was this work that had led to his current popularity with some members of Society and the censure of others, and it had all begun on the day he met Samantha Kingston.

It might have been more accurate to say re-met for, as he

discovered later, he had encountered her when he was in the guise of Archie Kennedy at a ball a month or so earlier. At that time, to his acute embarrassment and shame, he'd kissed her, thinking her to be a lady whose name he'd since forgotten, with whom he'd been in a prolonged flirtation. Samantha's reaction and her wit had surprised and intrigued him such that he had looked for her at every subsequent event, unaware that circumstances had forced her into hiding.

When they met again, she was dressed like a street waif and was picking his pocket. When he caught up to her, he'd been distracted by a familiarity in her hazel eyes. She'd taken advantage of this, surprising him once more as she temporarily incapacitated him and ran off with his pocketbook.

Surprise continued to be the theme of their encounters as she first turned up on his doorstep the next day to return the pocketbook (without the money it had held), then discovered the identities of the very criminals he'd been seeking for weeks and, particularly, when he realized that she was the runaway witness to the infamous murders that had held the city spellbound.

It had taken her time to trust him with the whole truth. In fact, he'd had to come upon most of it himself before she gave him a full explanation. When she did, in spite of his frustration with her lack of cooperation, he had felt a growing respect for the intriguing young woman. She had escaped being abducted by the men who were blackmailing her uncle. When her aunt and uncle were then tracked down and murdered, she had avoided being arrested as a suspect and successfully hidden on the unforgiving streets of London for weeks. She had been reluctant to accept Wyatt's assistance in proving her innocence and, even once she did, had insisted on helping, something he was forced to admit she had done quite successfully.

All told, Samantha Kingston was the most fascinating, intelligent, stubborn woman Wyatt had known. That she was beautiful, too, had only increased the challenge he'd had in avoiding her over the past three months, but avoid her he had, for her own good.

Though they had worked to hide the reality of the time Samantha had, of necessity, spent under his roof during their investigation, the fact that they had spent a good deal of time together away from the prying eyes of Society could not be altogether avoided, and it had caused a lot of speculative whispers. With the support of Wyatt's cousin Madge, Lady Bradwell, they were only whispers, but even whispers could destroy a reputation. Wyatt had hoped, by distancing himself from Samantha for as long as he could, to dispel the whispers. So far, this had failed to prove effective.

A loud, brash laugh drew his attention back to his surroundings, and Wyatt snuck a glance over the top of his paper. The club was filled with members, unusual for that time of year, but an emergency cabinet meeting had been called a little over a week ago, and many prominent citizens had arrived in London to express their views on what was being referred to as "the Trent affair." Among those prominent citizens was Wyatt's brother, Tom, the current Viscount Boxley, who was, at that moment, playing cards with three other men at a table near the fire.

"But where was the sense in it?" one of the men, Lord Penn, was saying. "Seizing two Confederate ambassadors from a neutral British ship? They must have known it would provoke action on our part. Why start a war with another country when they are already fighting one with their own people?"

"It's like the *Chronicle* said," Tom put in. "Senseless egotism. That's what the Americans have always had. Lyons said from the beginning that Seward was a dangerous foreign minister, enhancing his political capital by displaying violence towards us."

Wyatt smiled behind his paper at the familiar way Tom referred to Lord Lyons, British minister to the U.S., as though they were more than passing acquaintances.

"He also said he didn't think Mr. Seward would ever consider actually going to war with us," Lord Sterling said in his calm, measured voice. "And I must say I agree. I find it incredible that any country run by intelligent men should, in the midst of civil war, choose to increase the number of its enemies and, especially, to make an enemy of such a powerful nation as England."

"Immensely foolish," the fourth member of the group, Lord Alcott, agreed with a snort. "Particularly when it should have been clear to anyone that the ambassadors' mission was doomed to failure from the start. Having stated her policy earlier this year, Britain was hardly likely to change it in favor of supporting the Southern interest. And what would be the point, I say, in committing our money and troops to a cause whose success has been inevitable from the beginning? If we couldn't keep America from seceding, what makes them think they can keep the Confederacy from doing the same?"

Lord Alcott was merely repeating a position shared by most of his peers, but Wyatt still fought the urge to roll his eyes. Though he might not consider the Union's success likely, he at least recognized the differences between a country trying to retain a colony across the ocean and a country trying to mend a rift within its own borders.

"I agree with all of that," Lord Penn said dismissively. "But it remains that the ambassadors *were* taken, and saying that it was foolhardy to do so doesn't change the fact that it was done. What I want to know is why?"

"To provoke war," Tom said simply. "Whatever their motivations for doing so, it's the only reason they could have had for breaking Britain's neutrality so brashly."

"I wish the prince hadn't opted for such soft diplomacy," Lord Alcott said. "I'd like to bash the lot of them. We can't stand for such an insult."

"Hear, hear," said Lord Penn.

Wyatt checked his watch and folded his paper. He needed to get going if he was to make his appointment and still catch his train. As he stood, Tom looked over at him and frowned.

"Leaving already?" he asked.

"As a matter of fact, I am," Wyatt said. "I bid you gentlemen a good day."

He nodded to the other three, who nodded back, but Tom stood. "I'll walk you out. Excuse me, gentlemen. I'll be just a moment."

"There's no need," Wyatt said as they made their way to the door and out into the hall. "I can find my own way, you know."

"I've been asked to convey a message to you," Tom said, ignoring him. "From Mother."

Wyatt raised his eyebrows. "Left it a bit late, haven't you?"

Tom's lips thinned, but he pressed on. "She and I disagree—"

"For the first time in your life," Wyatt said under his breath.

Tom had almost certainly heard him, but he acted as though he hadn't. "—about Miss Kingston. I continue to believe that staying away from the entire mess is the only way to mitigate the scandal and restore our name. She, however..."

He stopped speaking and Wyatt looked over to see his jaw clenched and a muscle twitching at the corner of his left eye—a sure sign that he was working to master his emotions.

"She, however," he continued, "would like me to convey her hope that you will 'not be a gudgeon and waste the edge you have on every fortune hunter in England.'"

"What?"

They had reached the entrance to the club, and Wyatt's exclamation echoed through the front hall, causing several heads to turn their way.

"What are you saying?" Wyatt asked in a lowered voice, turning away from the onlookers to fix his brother with a piercing stare.

"Mother believes that the scandal will have blown over completely by the start of the Season," Tom said. He spoke quickly, no doubt in a hurry to rid himself of his unpleasant task and return to his friends. "Especially if we end up at war with America. She says that, by then, all anyone will remember is that Miss Kingston is one of the richest heiresses in Britain. She thinks your...previous interactions with Miss Kingston should be viewed in a positive light, giving you an advantage in the competition for her hand."

"She does, does she?" Wyatt said, fuming.

"Yes. As I said, I do not agree. I think you should steer as far from Miss Kingston as possible. Every time people see you together, it will remind them of the scandal. It's why I wish you were not going to our cousin's house today."

"It's the Winter Ball," Wyatt reminded him, privately irritated to hear his own concerns coming from his brother's mouth. "I go early every year. Wouldn't it be stranger if I stayed away this time? Wouldn't that give rise to speculation as to why?"

Tom huffed. "I suppose you're right, but I beg you would ignore Mother's advice."

"I don't plan to heed her advice any more than I do yours or anyone else's," Wyatt said. "And I'll thank you to stop speaking of Miss Kingston as though she were some wanton pariah. None of this was of her doing."

"I never said it was. That is not the issue."

Wyatt checked his watch. "I have to go now or I'll miss my train. I'll convey your best wishes to our cousin."

"Do that," Tom said. "But think on what I said."

Outside, Wyatt considered hiring a cab, but meetings with Tom always left him irritable, so he decided to walk off some of his frustration. He hadn't been at it more than five minutes when he sensed that he was being followed. A glance behind him told him he was right. It was the thin-faced Irishman, again. Ever since

Wyatt had returned from his extended visit to France, he'd found himself followed, either by the Irishman or a brutish, heavily tanned sailor.

Wyatt paused in front of a costermonger's cart and could see, out of the corner of his eye, that the Irishman had stopped as well. He stood in the middle of the pavement with his eyes on Wyatt, not even trying to hide his intentions.

If his errand had been less important, Wyatt might have allowed the game to continue—to see how far he could push the man—but he couldn't risk it. Not today.

After selecting a package of walnuts, Wyatt handed over a few coins and strolled into the nearest shop. It was a stationer's. He pretended to peruse the shelves of paper and ink as he kept an eye on the window. Outside, the Irishman walked past the shop, then stopped, leaning against the wall as he pulled out a cigarette.

"Excuse me," Wyatt said, approaching the counter. The shopkeeper, a middle-aged woman with flyaway hair, gave him a polite smile. "Is there a back door to your shop?"

The smile slid away as her eyes narrowed. "Why do you ask?"

Wyatt pulled his pocketbook from his coat and extracted a shilling. "Would you allow me to leave by it?" She hesitated, frowning. "There's someone out front I'd rather avoid."

Understanding lit her eyes. "Creditors onto you? I wish you luck. There's none outruns 'em forever."

She took the coin, however, and motioned for Wyatt to follow her. He did so, after glancing out the window one more time to assure himself that the Irishman remained in his lounging position.

"Thank you," Wyatt said to the shopkeeper as he slid out the back door.

When Wyatt entered The Hanged Man some ten minutes later, it was as crowded as ever. He found himself jostled from all sides as he moved through the tables to the back of the pub. He hadn't been lying when he told Tom he had a train to catch, but he did have another appointment first.

Inspector Whicher, immediately recognizable by his thick side whiskers and pockmarked face, sat at a table in the corner, staring absently at the chalkboard menu as he nursed the pint in his hands. He looked up when Wyatt took the chair across from him, and there was a grim set to his features.

"More good news, I assume?" Wyatt asked sardonically, picking up the tankard in front of him. "Thanks for this, by the way."

"You bought last time," Whicher said, taking a swig and setting his tankard down. He let his gaze wander around the pub for a moment before adding, "Fletcher's disappeared."

"I was afraid that was what you were going to say."

John Fletcher was a porter at the Old Bailey courthouse who had been on duty the day Charles Prescott was shot to death.

"His mother's had a letter from him saying he's gone off to make his fortune in South America," Whicher continued.

"Do you think that's true?" Wyatt asked.

"That she's had a letter or that what it says is true?" Whicher sighed and took another drink. "I don't know. It could be. It makes no difference either way. That's the third witness we've lost."

"You're sure it's Skinny Jim, then?" Wyatt asked, lowering his voice as much as he could and still be heard above the noise. Skinny Jim was the most powerful criminal in London, with a network of thieves, housebreakers and murderers. In all his years operating from the city's east end, he'd never been caught. It was one of Wyatt's biggest regrets that it was partly his own fault that Samantha had ended up working for the man, however briefly; though she had, thank heavens, been in disguise at the time.

Whicher nodded. "It's how he works. Even killing Mr.

Prescott—or, Sir Charles, or whatever he was meant to be called —was his style. Prescott was set to testify. We've never gotten anyone to testify against him before, but Prescott had nothing to lose. Whether he actually would have or not, it's enough that Skinny Jim thought he might. It's my guess the actual shooter was one of his lackeys, but he's made sure we can't get to him, either." Whicher leaned forward and lowered his voice. "I can't trust my own men on this one. He's got informants in the police force. I've never tracked down who, but they'll be the ones letting him know which witnesses we're pursuing."

"What are you going to do?"

"Nothing left to be done," Whicher said dourly. "I'm dropping the investigation."

"You can't be serious?" Wyatt asked incredulously. Whicher gave him a warning look, and he lowered his voice. "You're going to let him get away with murder?"

"What do you suggest I do, Mr. Wyatt?" Whicher raised an eyebrow. "Track down every witness until they're all dead or vanished?"

"Surely there's something—"

"There isn't. Some battles aren't meant to be won."

Wyatt sat back heavily in his chair. "What are you going to tell the press?"

Whicher looked down at his pint and frowned. "That's out of my hands."

"What does that mean?"

He was silent for a moment before saying, slowly, "It means that I was not part of that discussion, and if what you read tomorrow differs from what I've told you, I trust you'll keep that to yourself."

"In other words, Skinny Jim will get away with murder and the British public will rest easy, thinking the matter has been resolved." Wyatt scoffed. "All hail the Metropolitan Police Force."

The corner of Whicher's lip twitched. "As I said, some battles aren't meant to be won."

"What do I tell Samantha?" Wyatt asked tonelessly.

"That's up to you. You know her better than I. Can she handle another disappointment?"

Wyatt was unsure how to respond. While he hesitated, Whicher stood.

"You did help catch a murderer," he reminded Wyatt as he replaced the hat on his head. "It's not all bad."

TWO

The first of the new houseguests arrived just before noon. Madge was busy discussing the menu with the cook, so it was Samantha who welcomed Lord Bradwell's elder sister, Lady Chesterton, her daughter, Miss Fanshaw, and her daughter's school friend, Miss Thorpe.

"Where is Margaret?" Lady Chesterton said peremptorily as a footman helped her down from the carriage.

It took Samantha a moment to realize that she was referring to Madge. She had never heard anyone call her hostess by her full Christian name, not even her husband.

"She has been tied up with a domestic matter," Samantha said diplomatically. "She asked me to ensure that you were comfortably situated. I am Miss Kingston."

"Are you indeed?" Lady Chesterton's eyebrows raised, deepening the lines in her forehead and drawing attention to her overuse of pearl powder.

A noise of interest issued from one of the young ladies who had stepped down behind her. The two were of a similar height, but otherwise as different as night and day. Samantha had no trouble determining the dark-haired one to be Miss Fanshaw. She was a smaller, thinner copy of Lady Chesterton, without the powder. Her clothes were impeccably tailored and the height of fashion, though she seemed to shrink in them beneath the shadow of her imposing mama. By contrast, Miss Thorpe's outfit showed signs of having been made over, though her somewhat haughty demeanor defied anyone to notice. Her light blonde hair and wide blue eyes would no doubt draw the attention of many a gentleman.

It was Miss Thorpe who had made the sound of interest, a fact that was made clear by the way she studied Samantha with unabashed curiosity, though Samantha sensed calculation behind her eyes. She felt her stomach twist. She was not used to drawing attention, and she did not like it. Knowing she would be subject to even more such scrutiny as the months wore on did not make it any easier to bear.

"Your usual rooms have been made ready," she said to Lady Chesterton, "and a room has been made up in the guest wing for Miss Thorpe."

"Not the Blue Room, I hope," Lady Chesterton said brusquely. "The chimneys are drafty. If I've told Margaret once, I've told her a hundred times, that she ought to give that room a thorough going-over. Hasn't been updated since my grandfather's time, and it shows."

"The Peacock room, actually," Samantha said quickly when Lady Chesterton stopped to breathe.

"Hmm. I suppose that's alright. Has she made any plans for the Blue Room?"

"I couldn't say."

"No, I suppose you couldn't. Very well. We'll take tea in the Gallery when we've freshened up."

"Lady Bradwell had tea set up in the drawing room," Samantha explained, fighting to hide her amusement at Lady Chesterton's proprietary attitude towards her childhood home. She couldn't imagine it went over well with her sister-in-law.

Lady Chesterton snorted. "Of course she did. Quite like Margaret to overlook the details. That room has full sun this time of day. We'll take tea in the Gallery. It will give Lavinia the opportunity to show her friend the family portraits if nothing else."

Without another word, she swept off towards the house. Miss Fanshaw gave Samantha an apologetic look as she followed in her mother's wake, but Miss Thorpe smiled. It was an enigmatic smile and left Samantha feeling uneasy.

Her business with the cook concluded, Madge was on hand to greet the next arrival, Lord Bradwell's widowed niece, Lady Stuart-Lane. Samantha passed a peaceful hour in the library in company with Lord Bradwell. Madge's husband preferred silence to idle chitchat, and Samantha was happy to oblige him.

It was late afternoon when the carriage bringing Wyatt's friend Lord Aston pulled into the front drive. Samantha hurried out to greet it. Wyatt himself was expected to arrive last, and she was hopeful that Madge would be on hand to welcome him. Now that the moment was upon her, she was ashamed to discover in herself a deplorable sense of trepidation at the thought of meeting him again. She did not like to be at a disadvantage but, not knowing where they stood, she was unsure how to speak to him or even whether she should.

A footman jumped down and opened the door. Samantha smiled as Lord Aston stepped out. She held out her hands as he approached, and he took them, leaning forward to kiss her cheeks.

"Miss Kingston, how good to see you again," he said warmly.

She started to respond in kind, but her gaze was drawn by movement at the carriage. Her heart stopped as, ducking his head to clear the door, Wyatt jumped down. As he straightened, brushing soot from his coat, he looked up and their eyes met.

She had only known him a matter of weeks, really. They'd spent more time apart since then than they ever had together. And yet, as she looked into his deep brown eyes, she was overcome by a profound sense of familiarity, as well as a surprising relief.

Wyatt's eyes widened. "Samantha! That is," he corrected himself, casting a glance at his friend, "Miss Kingston, I—"

"No need to be formal on my account," Lord Aston said, a glint of humor in his eyes. "We're co-conspirators, after all, are we not?"

It wasn't entirely true. Only Wyatt knew the whole of Samantha's activities over the past summer, with Madge slightly less informed. But, they had invited Lord Aston into part of the secret before it had been revealed to the world at large, and he had proved himself a friend.

"I wasn't expecting to see you yet," Wyatt said, ignoring his friend. "I thought Madge—"

"We're sharing hosting duties," Samantha explained. "I thought you were meant to come later."

"I was, but my business concluded sooner than I expected, and I caught an earlier train. Bingo and I met in Sheffield and took the train into Hope together."

"Are we the last to arrive?" Lord Aston asked.

"Yes," she said, turning quickly back to him. "Dinner isn't for a few more hours. Until then, I believe several of the gentlemen are in the billiards room if you're interested."

"Excellent." Lord Aston clapped his hands together. "I'll wash up and join them."

He followed the footmen carrying his baggage into the house, leaving Samantha alone with Wyatt. That sense of trepidation settled over her shoulders. She forced a smile.

"How was your journey?" she asked at the same time he said, "How have you been?"

She laughed and felt some of the tension ease.

"I beg your pardon." He grinned. "You go first."

She repeated her question.

"Long," he replied. "And dirty. Nothing new. How have you been?"

"I've been..." She hesitated, wavering between a pat answer and a truthful one. She had a sudden urge to confide in him, to unburden herself in a way she hadn't with either Madge or Alice. After all, he could understand more than anyone why she might feel as she did. And yet, three months of silence between them stilled her tongue.

He looked down at her with concern, and she knew she had waited too long to answer. She shrugged and said, "We should head inside."

Wyatt offered his arm, and she took it.

Inside the front door, Headley, Madge's stoic butler, greeted them. With his usual calm efficiency, he took Wyatt's hat and cane. Then, when he moved to close the door behind them, Wyatt nodded his head towards the music room, which lay just off the front hall, and Samantha preceded him inside.

"I thought perhaps we could steal a minute or two to talk without servants or other guests listening in," he said, closing the door behind them.

Samantha had been hoping for and dreading such an opportunity in equal measure, but all she said was, "I would like that."

He led her to a sofa and took a seat in the chair across from it. From that position, he scrutinized her carefully and she did the same to him. In all the particulars, he was much as she remembered. Tall, broad-shouldered, with dark, wavy hair that always looked disheveled. Yet, he was also different, and she could not put her finger on how.

"What do you think of Bradwell Court?" Wyatt asked, gesturing around them.

"I love it," she said. "It's perfect. The house is lovely and the grounds...even in winter, the grounds are beautiful. I could get lost in them. I have, actually. Twice."

She laughed and he smiled.

"And Madge?" he asked.

"The perfect hostess."

"She hasn't recruited you to help her redesign the estate cottages, has she? Or to plan the Winter Ball?"

She shook her head. "I am helping with the ball, but I have been well looked after, I assure you."

"Good." He hesitated, then leaned forward. "You would tell me if anything were wrong, wouldn't you? If you needed help in any way?"

He held her gaze for a long moment, and she was surprised by the intensity in his eyes. Eventually, she was the one to break the connection, looking down as she considered his words. Why would he think something might be wrong? Had he seen the shadows around her eyes? She had been more diligent than ever to disguise them with powder that morning.

She considered telling him about the nightmares but immediately dismissed the idea. After all, nightmares were understandable in children, for whom the lines between reality and fantasy were blurred, but an adult who allowed them to plague her could only be thought ridiculous.

"Nothing is wrong," she said, hoping repetition had added conviction to that oft-repeated phrase.

He seemed to scrutinize her a moment more before leaning back in his chair with a sigh. "If there ever is anything..."

"I'll know whom to come to," she assured him, surprised to realize, as she said it, that she meant it. She hesitated, then added softly, "Wyatt, I...I know I said something before, but—"

"Don't," he said firmly. She looked up at him, surprised by his tone. He grimaced, then continued more gently. "Please, don't thank me again. I hardly did anything in the end." When she opened her mouth to protest, he shook his head. "A roof over your head was the absolute minimum of decency, especially after I pushed you into getting tied up with Skinny Jim. You never would have met him if not for me."

"And if I hadn't, I never would have learned who killed my aunt and uncle," Samantha insisted. "I would never have found Slater and Palmer. I would have reconnected with Charles with no way of learning the truth. I might have..." She broke off abruptly, pressing her lips into a firm line.

She had been about to voice aloud something she had only thought to herself, a realization that had come to her not long after moving to Derbyshire with Madge, something that filled her with both fear and shame.

"You might have what?" Wyatt asked quietly.

"I might have married him," she said finally, in a voice barely above a whisper.

Charles had been her first love, her only friend when she moved in with his father and her aunt when she was fourteen. Until she met Wyatt, she had planned to find Charles and gain his help in solving the murders and clearing herself as a suspect. No doubt, he would have thrown suspicion on her cousin Cyril, as he had done, but without the investigating by herself and Wyatt into Slater and Palmer, Charles' accomplices, she wouldn't have known any better. He would have gotten away with murder and, she, grateful for his help and thinking him the same honorable man she had once known, might have fancied herself still in love with him. The vision of that parallel life, that world of what if, terrified her.

"Would you have, though?"

She looked up to see Wyatt watching her with skepticism.

"What do you mean?"

He shrugged. "I may have been wrong, but I was under the impression you were less than enamored of him even before I shared Palmer's confession with you."

She frowned as she considered his words. He may have been right, though she thought her point still stood. To her surprise, his face broke into a grin.

"What?" she said defensively.

"After the number of times you have caused that exact reaction in me when you turn one of my long-held convictions on its head, it's good to know I can do the same to you, if only occasionally."

A reluctant smile spread across Samantha's face. Before she could reply, however, the sound of footsteps echoed in the hall beyond, a reminder that they were not alone in the house.

"I should go," Wyatt said. "I need to change for dinner."

"As do I," she agreed, getting to her feet.

She started for the door, but he caught her arm.

"I nearly forgot," he said, lowering his voice and glancing at the door as another set of footsteps hurried past. "It's late, I know, but I didn't want to risk it getting lost in the post." Letting go of her arm, he reached into the inner pocket of his coat and pulled out a small package wrapped in brown paper, handing it to her. "Happy birthday."

Samantha stared at the package. It was so unexpected, not to mention unnecessary, for him to have remembered her birthday, and yet she was foolishly pleased he had.

"It's nothing, really," Wyatt said, looking uncharacteristically self-conscious. "I just thought—I knew you had Madge, of course, but, with your parents gone, and your aunt and uncle and—"

"Thank you," Samantha said, taking the package from his hands. She smiled as she added, "That is quite thoughtful."

He gave a quick bow and exited the room.

When she got back to her room a few minutes later, Samantha leaned against the door and closed her eyes. Her birthday that year had been a day of mixed emotions. She had still been in mourning for the uncle she hated and the aunt she had tried to love, so there had been no big celebration, not that she would have wanted one. It had been a significant birthday, however. It marked her independence, and it was the day she came into her inheritance.

Madge had made a point of ordering a special cake from her cook, importing a pineapple for the occasion. There had been a dinner with all of Samantha's favorite dishes, which she, Madge, and Lord Bradwell had eaten on the family's best serving ware. And yet, though Samantha appreciated her new and dear friend's efforts, that quiet dinner had been a reminder to Samantha of how alone she was.

Opening her eyes, Samantha looked down at the package in her hands—a birthday present. No one had given her a birthday present in years. With shaking fingers, she unwrapped it carefully. A piece of paper fell out. She bent to pick it up, unfolding it as she stood. Wyatt's handwriting was nearly illegible, but after a moment, she was able to decipher the cramped letters.

So you never need take mine again. -W

Curiously, she reached into the brown paper and pulled out a red leather rectangle—a pocketbook.

With a gasp that turned quickly to a laugh, she flipped it open, examining the elegant stitching. When she turned it over, tiny gold letters along the bottom edge caught her eye.

S. S. M. A. K

She puzzled for a moment as to their meaning and then the answer came to her.

"Is this it, though?" he had said to her, all those months ago when the full truth had finally come out between them and he had learned who she was. *"The final name I am to call you? After all, first, you were Sarah, then Miss Avery, then Miss Kingston. Is Samantha official? You don't have another name I might be asked to use in future?"*

"I do have a second name," she had said, *"but I've never liked it, so,*

yes, Samantha it is."

"*Very well, Samantha. And you may call me Wyatt if you wish.*"

She shook her head, the corner of her mouth lifting in a reluctant grin. The two S's were for Sarah and Samantha, then, the A for Avery, and the K for Kingston. The presence of the M meant he'd somehow discovered her hated second name, Maud.

Running her fingers over the delicate embossing, Samantha smiled to herself. It wasn't an expensive gift, nor even a typical one, but it was thoughtful. It was a reminder of what she and Wyatt had shared, and it proved that, whatever the reason for their silent separation, he hadn't forgotten. Setting the pocketbook on the bedside table, Samantha crossed the room to the bell and rang for Alice. It was time to get ready for dinner.

*****

In the room he typically occupied when visiting his cousin, Wyatt cleaned the soot of train travel from his person and changed into the dinner jacket his valet had pressed for him. As he adjusted his cuffs, he replayed his meeting with Samantha in his mind. He had been surprised to see her so soon. He had imagined their reintroduction would be in the semi-public setting of the pre-dinner gathering. They would have been formal and maintained the boundaries he had placed on their relationship when they parted ways. Instead, she had thrown him off his guard, both in her unexpected timing and in the way she had made him feel.

He'd managed to convince himself in their time apart that he had built her up to be more than she was—more fascinating, more intelligent, more beautiful—yet the moment he saw her, he knew he'd been wrong. If his memory were at fault, it was in undervaluing her. She captivated him with her vibrant eyes and dark, silky hair, and when she spoke, he was transported back to the evenings they'd spent together in his house, almost as though no time had passed.

Time had passed, though. He could see it in the tightness around her eyes and the way her smile didn't quite reach them. She had suffered and he, in his desire to save their names, had left her to do so on her own. Guilt, and a wish to ease some of her pain, had led him to give her the gift he had bought the month before. He had gone back and forth about the wisdom of buying it in the first place and then of giving it to her, but now that it was done, he found himself wishing he could take it back, or at least replace it with something simpler, like a book.

When he had finished getting ready for dinner, Wyatt went in search of Bingo. As he descended the stairs, he saw a short, corpulent man standing at the foot of them, shifting from one leg to the other and looking around as though waiting for someone. When he saw Wyatt, his eyes lit up.

"Mr. Wyatt!" the man said, coming to meet him as he reached the bottom. "You are Mr. Wyatt, are you not?"

Wyatt nodded slowly. The man was impeccably tailored. A gold watch chain showed beneath his jacket when he moved his arm to shake Wyatt's hand. In appearance, he was the picture of a wealthy English gentleman. Yet, something about his forward manner and the energy he exuded screamed new money. Adding into consideration the strong northern accent, Wyatt felt confident that this must be the father of the young woman Madge's son Lord Linwood was courting.

"You must be Sir Rupert," Wyatt said, shaking his hand. "A pleasure to meet you."

"I met your brother this past spring at Henley," Sir Rupert said. "Fine chap. Quite a career ahead of him, I shouldn't wonder."

Wyatt made a non-committal noise. If the man was hoping to ingratiate himself, he was going about it the wrong way. As though he sensed his error, Sir Rupert abruptly changed tact.

"I hoped I might have a private word with you," he said, lowering his voice. "Now, if possible."

Wyatt almost refused him. After all, he didn't know the man, but his curiosity was piqued. It was clear now that Sir Rupert had been waiting for him, and he doubted it was to discuss the week's upcoming entertainments.

For the second time in an hour, Wyatt found himself ensconced in the music room, though with far less pleasant company. He sat in the same seat he had earlier, and Sir Rupert arranged himself on the settee. He unbuttoned the lowest button of his waistcoat and splayed his hands over a somewhat expansive belly, looking up to fix Wyatt with a penetrative stare.

"Men I trust have assured me that you are a man of discretion," he said.

"I seem to have developed that reputation," Wyatt agreed.

A smile spread across Sir Rupert's face, and he nodded approvingly.

"Careful to commit yourself, too, I see. That's good. I'm not going to beat about the bush—that would be a waste of your time and mine. Suffice it to say, I've come up against some difficulties, and I hoped you might be able to help."

"Difficulties?"

"I'm not sure if you're aware of my business interests, but aside from several mills and various smaller businesses, I run a shipping company. Nothing too large. It's mostly a way of cutting out the middleman. I distribute all my products via my own ships.

"Recently, I sent a shipment of cargo to South America along with some money, in gold, that was part of a new investment—Colchis Enterprises. However, when the ship reached port and the crate with the gold was unloaded, the top layer was all that remained. The rest had been replaced by rocks."

Wyatt raised an eyebrow, interested in spite of himself.

"The captain of my ship wrote to me immediately. They had made no other stops since leaving England, and I personally witnessed the gold loaded into the crate the day before the ship set sail, which means it must have been stolen at some point between then and when the crate was taken on board."

"Have you notified the police?" Wyatt asked.

Sir Rupert shifted his position and cleared his throat.

"No, I haven't," he said. "You see, I haven't yet informed the other investors of what happened."

"They have a right to know."

"I'm aware of that. And they will know, if nothing can be done, but I would much rather recover the gold first. You must see that, as the owner of the shipping line, the fault will be laid at my doorstep. I have a reputation to uphold."

"What is it you expect me to do?"

"I had hoped you might make discreet inquiries for me—to find the gold or, at least, to learn what happened to it."

It was an extraordinary request and one Wyatt was not sure he was equipped to carry out. After all, he had few connections in the north, and a missing crateful of gold was quite different from a pearl necklace or a packet of letters or any of the other things he had found for people.

"You would be handsomely rewarded, of course," Sir Rupert said, watching him closely.

Wyatt bristled. "I am not a detective-for-hire. I do not work in anyone's employ. I may have done a few favors for friends in the past, but I've never stooped to paid work."

"I've offended you," Sir Rupert said, looking disgruntled. "I meant no disrespect."

Of course he hadn't. Whatever title he may have earned or purchased for himself, Sir Rupert was not a gentleman and could not be expected to understand the rules governing such a class. Still, Wyatt barely contained his irritation as he accepted the man's apology.

"I'm afraid I have yet to greet our hostess," he said, standing. "I will see you at dinner."

"Will you think on what I said?" Sir Rupert asked, moving to stand as well.

Wyatt dipped his head in a quick, polite bow and left the room. As he re-entered the hall, he spotted Madge crossing in front of the stairs. When she saw him, she smiled and came to greet him.

"There you are! I heard you'd arrived. I thought you'd be with Aston, but he said you parted ways on arrival."

She took his hands and kissed both his cheeks.

"How was the journey from London?" she asked, stepping back and looking him over. "It seems an age since I saw you last. Did you eat on the train? We have a little left over from tea if you can't hold out till supper."

Wyatt laughed. "I'm fine. The journey was unexceptional; Mrs. Plummet packed me a lunch for the trip; and I will be alright till supper. Is there anything else?"

"Actually, there is." Madge looped her arm through his. "Come take a walk with me."

She led him to the long hall where generations of her husband's family were immortalized on canvas. Candles had been lit throughout the house and cast eerie shadows across the portraits. The view through the tall windows along the other side of the hall was obscured by darkness—the sun had set completely now.

"I told you, did I not," Madge began, her voice lowered conspiratorially. "About Linwood and Miss Wentworth?"

"You said he was pursuing her and that the courtship had become serious."

Madge nodded. "Which is why I invited her parents to this family affair. I thought it was best we get to know them before things progress too far."

"A wise decision. Do you think he will propose soon?"

"I don't know." Madge wrinkled her brow. "I know he was

looking for a good dowry—which she has—for repairs to his property, but I must say I'm still surprised at his choice. I wouldn't have thought they would suit. But then, I'm only his mother. What do I know?"

"And how do you find Sir Rupert and his lady?"

She passed a hand over her brow and sighed. "Unremarkable so far, although, they've only been here a week and, naturally, they've been on their best behavior. Now, however, with so many people in the house, it will be hard to focus on two."

"Why did you invite so many?"

"I didn't intend to. I've been trying to keep it to close friends and family since Samantha joined us. She'll be facing enough scrutiny next Season, poor dear. But, the Wentworths brought their eldest son as well as the daughter, and then Linwood asked to be allowed to invite a couple of his friends. They arrived the same day as the Wentworths. Constance expected to be invited for the ball, of course, and she brought her youngest, Lavinia, who pressured her mother and, thereby, me into being allowed to bring a friend of hers. Then, there was you, of course, and Aston and Samantha, and I invited Bradwell's niece to make up the numbers."

"Is Lavinia the one with the prominent front teeth?"

"No, dear. You're thinking of Millicent. You've never met Lavinia. She's only just come out. She hasn't even been presented yet."

"Quite the party you've arranged."

"Indeed, which is why I want to talk to you." Madge stopped walking and turned to face him. "I need your help."

"Anything you need. I am at your service."

There was a twinkle in her eye as she said, "You may regret agreeing so quickly when you hear what I have to say. I need you to befriend Sir Rupert."

Wyatt frowned.

"I don't want to hamper your enjoyment of the party," Madge

said, speaking rapidly. "You needn't spend every moment with him —just learn what you can about him. If you have any acquaintances who might know anything about him or his business dealings, that would be appreciated as well."

"You want me to investigate him for you," Wyatt said.

"Yes." She paused, then went on more slowly. "It's not that I object to the connections to trade, necessarily, and I would have no reservations if there were a strong affection between Miss Wentworth and my son, but I must necessarily be cautious and conscious of the inequality of the match."

"I understand."

Wyatt thought back to his conversation with Sir Rupert. If what he said was true, Sir Rupert would soon be in a good deal of trouble, and that trouble would affect his future relations as well. Wyatt grimaced. It seemed he would be assisting the man after all.

THREE

Samantha stood in the hall outside the drawing room for several minutes as she steeled herself for what was to come. Most of the guests had assembled, judging by the rumbling of voices coming from within, and she knew that the moment she stepped through the door, she would be on display. It wasn't a new sensation—it was what happened at every event she had attended since the period of mourning for her aunt and uncle had ended. Yet, Wyatt's presence this evening made everything more acute. People wouldn't just be watching her—seeing whether she lived up to their expectations of the sensational Miss Kingston with her misfortunes and her fortune—they would be watching Wyatt, too. They would be looking for signs that there was more to the relationship between the two of them than they claimed—anything to fuel the gossip.

At least she could be confident that, however she might feel inside, she did look well. She wore a new gown, which she'd had made up especially for the occasion. It was burgundy silk taffeta with gold trimmings—the sort of dress she had always wanted to own but had never been allowed to. Her aunt had insisted on dressing her in pale colors. Taking a deep breath, she schooled her features, put on a smile and stepped forward.

A quick sweep of the room told her Wyatt had yet to arrive. She was unsure whether to be relieved or not, but focused on keeping all true emotion out of her face as she greeted the ladies nearest her with politeness.

"How are you this evening, Miss Wentworth?" she asked, addressing the petite auburn-haired young woman.

"Very well, thank you." Miss Wentworth spoke in high, affected tones, likely adopted during her time at the finishing school to which her father had sent her and which she had only just left.

"You must be Lady Stuart-Lane," Samantha said, turning to the woman beside Miss Wentworth. Lady Stuart-Lane's dark hair, not too dissimilar from her own in shade, though much tamer in texture, was crafted into an elegant chignon. She looked to be in her late twenties and carried herself with a refined grace Samantha could only hope one day to emulate.

"And you must be Miss Kingston," Lady Stuart-Lane said in a pleasant alto. "Madge has told me so much about you, I feel we know each other already."

"Has she?" Samantha was taken aback. She hadn't been aware that Madge discussed her with anyone. She hadn't explicitly asked her not to, but she would have thought her desire for privacy was assumed.

Lady Stuart-Lane nodded. "I believe she hopes we will become friends. Or rather, she insists that we will, and we both know how persistent she can be when she gets an idea in her head."

Samantha must not have been quick enough to disguise her alarm, because Lady Stuart-Lane smiled and added, "Do not worry. Much as I love my aunt, I would not allow even her to force my company on someone who did not wish it. But I do hope we may become friends, irrespective of her wishes. Society in my part of Cornwall is rather limited, and I could use a friend."

Samantha felt some of the tension leave her and found that the smile she gave in return was almost natural. Wyatt appeared then at the entrance to the room, accompanied by Sir Rupert, and the tension returned. The older gentleman wore an expression of satisfaction. He turned as Wyatt said something to him in an undertone, nodded, and then joined his wife by the fire. Wyatt made his way over to Lord Aston, who stood near Samantha. He moved automatically, his thoughts clearly far away and, judging by the furrow of his brow, troubling.

"I wasn't aware you knew Sir Rupert," Lord Aston said as Wyatt joined him.

"We just met today," Wyatt said. Then, turning to Samantha, his brow cleared and he gave a short bow.

"Miss Kingston," he said.

"Mr. Wyatt." Samantha dipped her head in acknowledgement. It took all her willpower to keep her focus on Wyatt as she felt the draw of half a dozen eyes trained on the pair of them. "I hope you are well."

"Tolerably, Miss Kingston. May I enquire as to your own state of health?" Though he spoke in a polite, but disinterested voice, there was a spark in his eyes and the hint of a smile.

Samantha fought the sudden, overwhelming urge to laugh. She felt as though she and Wyatt were performing a play, one their audience was pretending to be too polite to watch.

"I am well, sir," she managed to say, her voice uneven. She turned to indicate the ladies beside her. "Have you met Lady Stuart-Lane? And this is Miss Wentworth."

"Lady Stuart-Lane and I are acquainted," he said inclining his head in her direction. "Miss Wentworth, it is an honor to make your acquaintance."

He bowed to Miss Wentworth, who giggled as she curtsied. "Likewise, sir."

"If you'll all excuse me." He bowed again and walked away.

"That was well done, my dear," Madge said, appearing at Samantha's elbow. She gave Samantha's arm a quick squeeze and turned to address Lord Aston. "I hope you won't mind, but, for this first dinner, I've made Sir Rupert and his wife the guests of honor, so they will be taking your place in the procession to the dining room."

"I don't mind at all," Lord Aston said breezily. "Who will I be taking in?"

"Ah. As to that..." She turned as Lady Chesterton came walking purposefully towards them.

Samantha heard Lord Aston swear under his breath.

"Nothing to be done, I'm afraid," Madge said apologetically. "She is the highest-ranking lady and my sister-in-law. I couldn't very well slight her for your convenience." She turned to Samantha. "You will be entering with Mr. Allen."

Samantha felt she hid her own chagrin better than Lord Aston had. Mr. Allen had made his interest in her clear from the moment of his arrival and seemed both blind and deaf to her attempts to express her own disinterest. As Madge led her to him, she looked back to see Lord Aston greeting his dinner companion with a pained look and bit back a smile.

When they had all been paired up according to their relative ranks, Headley came in to announce dinner. Samantha and Mr. Allen lined up behind Miss Fanshaw and Lord Godwin. Directly behind them, Wyatt and Miss Wentworth joined the queue. Samantha reflected that, if Madge had not made the Wentworths guests of honor, she and Wyatt would be walking in together. She wondered if that had factored into Madge's decision.

The dining room of Bradwell Court was always beautiful, with its high ceiling, gilt fixtures and crystal chandeliers, but that evening, decorated for a full party, it was breathtaking. The mirrors that lined the walls reflected the candles so that the whole room glowed with light. In the absence of flowers, lush greenery and holly sprigs made festive centerpieces.

Samantha sat between Lord Aston and Mr. Allen. Besides being persistent, Mr. Allen was dreadfully dull. His conversation had been limited to a recital of his opinions on the state of the train service from London, so she was happy when courtesy dictated he turn his attention to the lady on his other side as the second course arrived.

"Is that relief I see in your eyes?" Lord Aston asked as they turned to speak to each other. "Or am I merely seeing a reflection of my own?"

Samantha gave him a quelling look. He shrugged. "I wouldn't worry. Lady Chesterton is partially deaf in one ear. She could barely hear me when I was facing her. As for Linwood's friend there, I wouldn't mind if he did hear. Man's a complete bore, and it's time somebody told him. But, setting that aside, how have you been? I haven't seen you since the hunting party last month. How have you been occupying yourself lately? Not in target practice, I hope. I still aim to best you at the next opportunity."

"At the risk of injuring your sense of pride, my lord, I must inform you that I see no necessity in practicing only to best you."

"Touché, touché," Lord Aston chuckled. "We must find another contest, then. Perhaps a race? When next I bring my favorite mount, we shall have one."

"In that, I am certain you would triumph, as I have never been fond of riding and would no doubt fail from the start."

"Not fond of riding? Nonsense. I thought Lady B said you were a country girl at heart. Whoever heard of a country girl who didn't ride?"

Samantha shrugged. "I've always preferred to walk."

Lord Aston continued to look baffled at her admission, but he pressed on gamely. "I suppose there are some lovely gardens here for walks."

"I'm sure there are," Samantha said with a smile. "But as it's winter, they are hardly picturesque. I generally walk over the hills. There are some interesting ruins nearby that I often visit."

"Which ruins are those?"

The question did not come from Lord Aston. Samantha looked across the table in surprise. Miss Wentworth had abandoned her conversation with Wyatt and was leaning forward, addressing Samantha, having apparently been eavesdropping. Samantha glanced at Wyatt, who raised his eyebrows but said nothing.

"There's an old abbey," Samantha explained when it was clear she needed to respond. "It sits atop a hill—"

"Donwell Abbey?" Miss Wentworth asked eagerly. "It's within walking distance, then?"

"It's a bit of a long walk, but yes."

By now, their conversation had drawn the interest of several people. Miss Wentworth flushed but continued. "I heard it's haunted."

"Haunted?" On Mr. Allen's other side, Miss Thorpe leaned forward with interest. "Haunted by what?"

"By nothing." Sir Rupert's voice cut across the table before his daughter could answer. "There are no such things as ghosts."

All heads turned to him, a mixture of surprise and disapprobation on every countenance. Miss Wentworth looked down at her plate, her cheeks reddening. Samantha felt a sympathy with her. At times, Sir Rupert reminded her of her uncle, though her uncle had been too aware of his own consequence to embarrass his family in public.

"I, for one, love a good ghost story," Madge said. "I do think they lose something in the telling if the atmosphere is not correct. Perhaps, Miss Wentworth, you will regale us this evening by the fire? I'll be sure to tell the staff to douse most of the candles in the drawing room. That should serve."

Samantha hid her smile behind her napkin. Across the table, Wyatt raised an eyebrow at her, the corner of his mouth curving up in a surreptitious grin.

"Now," Madge said, turning back to the young Mr. Wentworth who sat beside her. "What were you saying about your mare?"

Taking their cue from her, the rest of the guests resumed their private conversations.

*****

After the ladies had retired to the drawing room, Lord Bradwell called for port. Wyatt took the opportunity, as a footman laid out the glasses on the sidebar, to study his fellow guests. Linwood he'd known from boyhood, though his cousin was several years his junior, but he hadn't spent much time with him over the years. Of average height and looks, he lacked the charisma of his mother and had never, to Wyatt's knowledge, bestirred himself to show an interest in anything beyond the care of his small estate in Leicestershire. It was a surprise, therefore, when Wyatt noted the animation with which he spoke to his potential father-in-law.

"But he's been ill before," he was saying, "and there's never been much cause for concern."

"He's never been this ill," Sir Rupert replied with a supercilious air. "They're saying it's Bertie's fault. That embarrassing matter of the actress. The prince traveled up to Cambridge to talk to him about it and came back sick as a dog."

"If he dies," Linwood said, with a quick glance at his father, "how much of an influence will that have? Insofar as the Trent Affair is concerned."

Wyatt also stole a glance at Lord Bradwell. Madge's husband was a great friend of Prince Albert's. Sure enough, he was frowning at his son's cavalier dismissal of his friend's life, but, predictably, he said nothing. Wyatt had known Lord Bradwell all his life and, while he could be a pleasant conversationalist when the mood struck him, it rarely did. No doubt he was counting down the minutes until he could reasonably send them all to the drawing room and take himself to bed.

"It remains to be seen," Sir Rupert said in response to Linwood's question. "He was the leading advocate for peace. As I understand, he practically rewrote the letter to the Americans on his own."

"Did he indeed?" Linwood's expression was eager, and Wyatt found himself wondering what had struck a spark of life in his normally dull cousin. Was it love for Miss Wentworth? Madge did not seem to think so, but she had been wrong before. Rarely, but it did happen.

"Do you mind if I sit here?"

Linwood's friend Lord Godwin had pulled back the chair beside him and sat down before Wyatt could reply. He then removed his jacket and leaned against the back of the chair with a cigar clenched between his teeth.

"So, you and Miss Kingston?" he asked, raising an eyebrow suggestively.

Wyatt reached for his glass and took a long, slow drink before replying. He had hoped, among family and friends of family, to avoid the sort of probing questions he'd become accustomed to in London.

"I was happy to have been able to render her a service," he said discouragingly.

"Come now, man," Lord Godwin said. "You spent all that time with her and that's all you can say?"

"It's all I mean to say."

"You could make it an even contest. Offer some advice to those of us without the advantage of familiarity." He gestured to Mr. Allen, who sat across from them. "Or have you decided not to pursue her? Tired of her already? One hundred thousand pounds not enough to keep you interested?"

Wyatt didn't need the hand on his shoulder to keep him in his seat. He'd been expecting a provocative remark and steeled himself for it. He was still grateful for Bingo's support, though.

"Perhaps he's merely being a good friend," Bingo said lightly.

"Not you, too!"

Mr. Allen's outburst startled Wyatt and he supposed, from the way the other two men looked wide-eyed across the table, it had startled them, too. Mr. Allen flushed to the roots of his thinning, faded brown hair.

"I beg your pardon," he said, resuming his placid manner, "but is it your intention, my lord, to pursue Miss Kingston as well?"

"As well as half of London, do you mean?" Bingo asked lazily.

"Can you blame us? It's an incredible sum."

Wyatt felt a flash of anger at the mercenary way in which Samantha was being discussed. Bingo appeared to have read his mind for he said, "I put more weight on the merits of the lady than her pocketbook."

"And well you can," Lord Godwin said dryly. "No doubt a hundred thousand would hardly register with you. Would it be too much to ask that you step aside and let those of us who need the money have a chance?"

"Do you need me to step aside?" Bingo asked. "Haven't you had a whole week with her to yourselves already? If she can't yet see your merit, I doubt my standing down will do you much good."

"Allen's been annoying her to no end," Lord Godwin said, earning a gasp from that quarter. "I had planned to use that to my advantage."

Wyatt saw Bingo's lips quirk at this, but he decided he'd been quiet long enough.

"I can't imagine you have much chance," he said, "if you are merely preferable to a constant irritation and cannot stomach a creditable rival."

Lord Godwin shrugged. "It's not a matter of stomaching anything. I simply prefer to hold all the cards. Wentworth understands, don't you, Wentworth?"

Wyatt had forgotten all about Sir Rupert's son, who sat at the far end of the table, staring morosely across at his father., who was still deep in conversation with Linton.

"Did you say something?" he asked, sitting up straighter as he noticed them all looking at him. "Sorry. I wasn't attending."

"I said you understand the advantage of holding all the cards. You're not a risk taker."

Oliver Wentworth frowned. "What makes you say that?"

Lord Godwin laughed. "I've played with you. I've never seen a more timid player in all my life."

"I suppose that's true," Wentworth said vaguely. His gaze had drifted back to his father.

Lord Godwin laughed again and stood up to refill his glass, asking if anyone else would like more port. Wyatt shook his head, noting, as he did, how adroitly Lord Godwin had shifted the conversation away from himself.

*****

When the ladies retired to the drawing room, Samantha made her way directly to the piano, where she remained until the gentlemen, finished with their port and cigars, joined them. It wasn't much more than a half hour, but it was a respite from smiling and making forced conversation, and she appreciated every minute of it.

When Wyatt entered with the other gentlemen, he caught her eye and nodded politely before moving to sit beside Miss Fanshaw. It felt wrong, after their shared intimacies of the summer, to now be little more than a stranger to him, in public at least. Less than a stranger, really, when she considered how they could not develop an acquaintance for fear of fanning the flames of malicious rumors. This realization caused a pang of loneliness that only grew stronger as she saw that Madge and Lord Aston were also engaged in conversation and that Mr. Allen was making his way towards her with a determined air.

As the evening wore on, Samantha began to think Madge had forgotten the ghost story recital. Miss Thorpe, who had succeeded her at the piano when the gentlemen entered, was encouraged to play an encore, after which Miss Fanshaw followed up with two sonatas. As she stepped away from the instrument, however, the door opened and several footmen entered with candle snuffers. They moved around the room, dousing the candles until the sole source of light was the fire crackling in the grate of the large, ornamental fireplace.

Slowly, the guests made their ways to the couches in front of the fire. The ladies seated themselves while the gentlemen stood behind them. Samantha watched Miss Wentworth and Madge as the latter led the former to the chair nearest the fire. While she knew Madge had been defending the poor girl against the insult of her father's rude interference, she couldn't help wondering if putting her in the spotlight was the right response.

"This is quite exciting," murmured a low voice near Samantha's ear.

She turned to see Lady Stuart-Lane beside her, arranging her skirts as she watched Miss Wentworth.

"I've never been to a ghost story recital before," Lord Bradwell's niece continued, turning to look at Samantha. "Have you?"

Samantha shook her head. "I hope that it lives up to expectations."

Miss Wentworth cleared her throat and smoothed her skirts.

Sir Rupert had followed Lord Bradwell's example and not come to the drawing room with the younger men. In the absence of her father, Miss Wentworth's confidence seemed to have returned in full.

"Many years ago," she began. She spoke softly so that her listeners were forced to lean forward to hear. "In a small village not far from here, there lived a young woman called Evelyn. She was known far and wide for her beauty, and many a man sought her hand in marriage, but she would have none of them. She was determined to marry for love."

To Samantha's right, she heard Miss Fanshaw sigh. She felt more like rolling her eyes.

"Unfortunately, Evelyn's father did not support his daughter's decision, so when a wealthy but cruel man called Damian came from the south promising to pay an extravagant bride price, Evelyn's father agreed. Evelyn overheard the agreement and, fearing what would become of her in the hands of such an evil man, she fled. She sought sanctuary with the nuns of Donwell Abbey, determined to take holy orders to save herself from Damian and any other man her father might consider for her hand. The nuns took her in and promised to protect her.

"Though he searched high and low, for five whole days, Damian could not find Evelyn, and she began to hope she might be safe. But then, one stormy night, he arrived at the abbey. The nuns denied him entrance, but he would not leave. He began to shout Evelyn's name and to say that he would see her wed to him or dead."

Miss Fanshaw gasped. Lord Godwin, who stood behind her, placed a hand on her shoulder. Miss Wentworth's face betrayed a small smile before returning to its former serious expression. Samantha felt a grudging respect for Miss Wentworth's storytelling abilities. The way she altered her tone and cadence made a relatively simple, predictable story much more interesting.

"As he stood yelling and cursing at the entrance to the abbey," Miss Wentworth continued, "Evelyn herself came to him. She stood by the gate in her novice garb and told him that he was too late. She was on the path to sisterhood and was pledged to Christ. She begged him to cool his anger and plead God's forgiveness for his evil words. In response," she paused for effect, scanning the room to ensure they were all riveted, "he spat in her face.

"He jumped on his horse and rode away, calling curses down on the woman who had spurned him and the nuns who had hidden her from him. They thought they had heard the last of him, but they were wrong." She paused again, and when she continued, she spoke slowly and deliberately. "When he returned, later that night, while all the sisters were asleep inside...he burned the abbey to the ground."

Miss Fanshaw screamed. The sound made Samantha jump. She looked up to see Wyatt watching her with an amused expression. She frowned at him, trying to convey silently that it wasn't the ghost story that had startled her. When her frown merely produced a wider smile, she rolled her eyes and looked away.

"Really, my dear," Lady Wentworth said in scandalized tones. "Wherever did you hear such a story?"

"Did anyone escape?" Miss Thorpe asked eagerly.

Miss Wentworth shook her head. "They all perished, even the beautiful Evelyn. It's said that the ghosts of the nuns continue to haunt the ruins of the abbey. Unable to accept that they could not protect her, they attack any man who looks like Damian."

"And what did he look like?" Wyatt asked, an amused tinge to his voice.

Miss Wentworth looked up at him. She smiled slowly as she tilted her head. "He was tall, with brown eyes and dark, curly hair."

Lord Godwin snorted, then pretended to cough when Lady Chesterton fixed him with a glare.

"I shall be on my guard then," Wyatt said. "If I ever happen that way."

He caught Samantha's eye and started to smile but, glancing to her right, stopped abruptly and looked away. Samantha turned to see Miss Thorpe, one seat down from her on Miss Fanshaw's other side, looking between her and Wyatt with a greedy interest. Samantha's amusement at the ghost story evaporated.

"Did you say it's near here?" Miss Fanshaw asked breathlessly, oblivious to what was happening on either side of her. "Do you think we might be able to see the abbey?"

"Do you want to see it?" Lord Aston asked. "After that scream you just gave?"

As Miss Fanshaw's cheeks turned a lovely shade of pink, Miss Thorpe's gaze left Samantha to jump between Lord Aston and her friend. Her brow furrowed.

Miss Fanshaw's enthusiasm was not dampened. "There's no risk in going during the day, surely. We could have a picnic."

"In midwinter?" Lady Wentworth asked.

Lady Chesterton shuddered. "Whoever thought of a picnic in December?"

"Not a picnic, then," Miss Fanshaw pressed. "We could take carriages there and walk around. If we're bundled up sufficiently, I daresay no one will freeze."

"I'm game," Lord Godwin said cheerfully. "What do you say, Linwood?"

Lord Linwood looked to Madge, who smiled in amusement, and shrugged. "We could organize a small expedition if there's the interest in it. How many would come?"

The older ladies refused. Madge, because she'd seen the abbey plenty of times, and the other ladies out of fear of being cold. Lady Wentworth tried once more to dissuade them from the scheme, but the younger ladies eagerly agreed to it, and the gentlemen said they would go to please the ladies. Samantha would have joined the naysayers if it would have made a difference. She didn't quite like the idea of a large group roaming all over what she had come to think of as her abbey. However, there was nothing she could do. The expedition was set for Tuesday afternoon, in three days' time.

Early Sunday morning, Samantha found herself once more at the ruins of the abbey. She'd had another restless night, punctuated by dreams of relentless pursuits through London streets and a shadowed figure with eyes of a deep, piercing blue. Slater was dead, as she well knew, having seen his corpse lying in the morgue, but that did not seem to prevent him from living in her nightmares.

Walking to one of the arched windows of the great hall, Samantha leaned against it and looked out at the river below. It wasn't long before she heard the crunch of footsteps behind her. She sighed.

"You needn't come, you know," she said without turning around. "It's too early for anyone to even notice I'm gone."

"'S that so?"

Startled by the unfamiliar voice, Samantha whirled around. Before her was a young man in the slightly battered clothes of a labourer, standing with his hands in the pockets of his oversized coat, a crooked smile on his face.

"I beg your pardon," she said, opting for an appearance of civility in the hopes that he would follow suit. "I thought you were my maid, Alice. She tends to follow me when I go for walks, whether I ask her to or not."

The man made a show of looking all around, craning his neck in each direction as he took in the deserted abbey. When he returned his gaze to Samantha, his smile widened. "I don't see her. It looks like we're alone."

Samantha felt her chest tighten at the sinister undertones of his words.

"Well, I should get back, anyway." She looked up at the grey sky. "It's much later than I thought it was. They'll be missing me soon."

"You're from the Court, ain't you?" He nodded his head in the direction of Madge's house. "Visiting? Only I never seen you before."

"I haven't seen you, either," Samantha said, starting to edge away. "And I've been here long enough to know you aren't part of the grounds staff, which means you're trespassing right now."

He snorted. "Trespassing. And who gives anyone the right to own the land? It's been here 'fore they come, and it'll be here long after they've gone."

"In the case of the Bradwells, I believe it's been their family's for quite some time. Good day." Dropping all pretense, she gathered her cloak around her and strode away.

She didn't get far. A hand snagged her upper arm, holding her in a firm, unyielding grip.

"Where do you think you're going?"

Heart hammering in her chest, Samantha responded with an attempt at acerbity. "I should think that was obvious."

"Bet you wouldn't be running if I was a gentleman or some lord or other."

"Your rank is of much less concern to me than your manners. Unhand me."

He chuckled. "Give us a kiss and I will."

Samantha froze, staring at him with incredulity. "No."

"It's only a kiss. No need to be so priggish. As you said before, no one will even know you was up here."

Samantha made an effort to twist away from him. He didn't let go, but she was able, by shifting her weight to her left leg and bending her right left back, to reach her ankle and remove her knife from its sheath.

"I said, let go of me." His eyes widened at the sight of the blade inches from his chest, and he dropped her arm. She took a step back, still aiming the knife in his direction. "Now, go back wherever you came from and leave me alone."

He took a few steps back, his arms bent at the elbows with his hands up in a placating gesture. When he hit a wall, he stopped, and the crooked smile returned.

"The question is," he said, lowering his hands, "do you know how to use that?"

"I'm fairly certain the sharp end goes into the other person," Samantha said with an effort at bravado.

He chuckled and began to walk slowly towards her. She took an involuntary step back before standing her ground.

"I'm afraid it's a bit more complicated than that. You have to ask yourself, are you fast enough to stick me 'fore I take it from you? 'Cause I'll tell you right now, I don't mind a nick or two. I've had my fair share in my time."

Samantha's grip on the knife tightened. Despite the cold wind that swirled around her, she could feel sweat sliding down her back. She was starting to doubt the wisdom of the knife. If she weren't fast enough—if he took it from her—she'd have provided him a weapon to use against her.

He stalked closer, the smile on his face showing how much he was enjoying himself and how little he feared her. Then, just as Samantha was beginning to wonder if she should drop all pretext and run, Alice appeared from behind a crumbled wall to her right. She moved so fast that the man, his attention focused on Samantha, barely had time to look round before she was beside him, a moss-covered stone in her hand, swinging with all her might.

He crumpled to the ground, blood oozing from a spot near his temple. Alice turned to Samantha, her chest heaving as she dropped the stone beside her. Samantha gaped at her.

"I...told...you," Alice gasped, bending over with her hands on her knees, "to send...for me...when you...get up." She straightened and frowned at Samantha. "What were you thinking?"

Samantha looked from her to the fallen man and back. "Is he dead?" Alice paled. Together, they approached the body. Using the toe of her boot, Samantha prodded his shoulder and he rolled onto his back. To her relief, she could see the rise and fall of his chest. "Should we...do something?"

"I don't know. I was only trying to stop him. I don't want to be responsible for..."

Samantha could see that the energy of the moment was beginning to wear off, and Alice was starting to realize what she'd nearly done. "I know you were," she said consolingly. "And I thank you. I don't know what I would have done if you hadn't come along." Then, speaking briskly in an attempt to buoy Alice's spirits, she added, "We'll send someone to check on him. There's no sense in us staying here waiting for him to wake up. Let's go home."

Alice nodded, her eyes fixed on the body until Samantha took her arm and dragged her away.

FOUR

By the time they got back to the house, Alice looked ready to faint. Samantha sent her to the kitchens for some tea and went upstairs herself. She had fully intended to speak to Madge but, as she passed Wyatt's room, a few doors down from her own in the family wing, she stopped and turned back. Before she could rethink her intentions, she raised a fist and knocked lightly on the solid wood door.

After the second knock, she heard movement from beyond and she waited. A few seconds later, the doorknob turned and the door opened inward. Wyatt's hair was more rumpled than usual, sticking up in odd places, and his dressing gown exposed enough of his chest to make her blush and look away, regretting her hasty decision. He held a hand over his mouth as he yawned. When he finally blinked down at her, his eyes widened.

"Samantha!" he said in a hoarse whisper, pulling his dressing gown tighter. "What are you doing here?"

"It's Alice," she said hastily. "She was only trying to help me, but she may have seriously injured someone. I need you to see if he's alright."

Wyatt blinked at her. "Can you say that again?"

Lowering her voice, Samantha gave him a brief summary of the past hour. By the time she finished, all signs of sleepiness had gone from his eyes and he was frowning at her.

"You went walking on your own?" he asked. "All the way to the ruins?"

"Yes," she said with irritation. "It's not that far, and there's never been anyone about until today."

"Until today? How often do you go out walking alone?"

In his incredulity, he had raised his voice. She flapped her hands in a shushing gesture.

"That is not important right now," she whispered. "There is a man out there with a head injury, and we need to make sure he's well."

"Give me five minutes."

Less than five minutes later, he was back out, fully dressed and buttoning up a thick woolen coat.

"Explain to me again where you left him."

She followed him downstairs as she described the part of the abbey where Alice had knocked the strange man unconscious. When they reached the entrance hall, he turned to her.

"I'll be back as soon as I can. Tell Alice not to worry. If he was breathing when you left, he's probably well enough, though with a rather large headache."

She tried to smile at this but found she couldn't. Worry clutched at her insides. He took her hand in his and squeezed it briefly before hurrying out the door.

*****

Wyatt's first stop was to the stables where he had Gringolet, Lord Bradwell's beautiful white stallion, saddled for him. It wasn't just that speed was of the essence—if the man needed medical attention, having a horse would make it easier for him either to fetch the doctor or transport the patient, depending on his condition.

Thanks to Madge's habit of early morning riding, the groom had been up for hours. He had Gringolet ready in no time and soon Wyatt was thundering across the fields, the cold air like ice on his face. When they reached the outer edge of the abbey, he dismounted. He didn't bother to secure the horse—all of the Bradwell horses were well trained and Gringolet was particularly docile, despite his massive size.

Wyatt had visited the abbey often as a child, intrigued by the stories of hauntings and keen to prove his bravery. It had terrified him then, but he'd expected to find it woefully mundane now. However, as he stood facing its jagged outline, noting the irregular shadows cast by the weak morning sun, and listening to the wind whistle through the gaps in the stones, he was surprised by the prickling of unease that ran down his spine.

Leaving the horse behind, Wyatt began slowly to pick his way across the field of fallen stones, heading for the place Samantha had described. He still couldn't believe that she had been reckless enough to walk so far from the house on her own, especially after all that had happened that summer. He was thankful that her maid had defied her wishes and followed her. He didn't want to think about what might have happened if she hadn't.

The abbey was eerily quiet. The wind had died down and the crunch of Wyatt's boots against the pebbled ground was the only sound to break the stillness. He had been certain the man would have regained consciousness by now. He'd expected to hear moaning or cries for help. It was with a sense of growing dread that he increased his pace. Was he too late?

Wyatt had run past the place Samantha described twice without realizing it. After all, he was expecting to see a body. When he didn't—when he'd gone through every archway and looked around every pillar—he slowed to a walk.

He found the stone first. It lay in a circle of dirt and dead grass. On one side, three or four dark hairs were stuck to it by a small quantity of tacky, not-fully-dried blood. As Wyatt bent to examine the ground around it, there was a loud thump behind him.

He shot to his feet and spun around. There was no one there. Nothing moved. Slowly, he reached into his coat and pulled out the pistol he'd carried with him since Charles' murder.

"Who's there?" he asked, his voice sounding odd in the stillness. "Come out slowly. I'm armed."

There was no response. After several tense moments, Wyatt began to doubt himself. He scanned the area around him. There were a lot of fallen stones. Might one have shifted? The thump could have been a stone hitting the ground.

With the pistol still in his hand, Wyatt turned back and knelt down again. The ground around the stone had been recently disturbed. There were a lot of boot prints, most of them only partial and quite of few of them his own. He found what looked to be a man's boot print near the outer edge of the space. When he went in the direction it pointed, he found more prints in a patch of dirt a dozen or so feet away. This continued until he reached the edge of the abbey, where rocks and dirt were swallowed up in the meadow.

It seemed that Samantha's attacker had regained consciousness and left without assistance. The boot prints led in the direction of the village—his home, no doubt. As relieved as Wyatt was to discover that Samantha's maid was not a killer, he couldn't help but worry what would happen if the man chose to bring some sort of legal action against Samantha and her maid, seeking restitution for his perceived wrongs. If he did, Wyatt hoped he might be more successful in persuading him against it than he had been in persuading Sir Rupert to seek police assistance.

After his conversation with Madge, Wyatt had swallowed his pride and told Sir Rupert he'd changed his mind. They'd spoken at length and Wyatt had extracted from him a list of the investors in Colchis Enterprises in descending order of their involvement. He'd also received a description of the missing gold bars which included the names of the assayers—Sawyers and Collins—as well as the number missing and their equivalent value in pounds sterling. It was a truly staggering amount—hence Wyatt's attempt to persuade Sir Rupert that the police would be better equipped to recover it. He found Sir Rupert's insistence on exhausting every other avenue first as frustrating as it was foolish.

The sound of crunching pebbles behind him set Wyatt spinning round again. Gringolet was utterly unfazed by the pistol pointing at him. He trotted forward and nuzzled Wyatt's pockets, looking for a treat. Wyatt let out a shaky laugh.

"I haven't got anything for you boy," he said, patting the horse's neck. "I think you have the right idea, though. Let's head back."

Holstering his pistol, Wyatt swung himself onto Gringolet's back. He cast a final look at the abbey, still and silent as ever, before they cantered away.

*****

Breakfast was underway before Wyatt returned. Samantha had given up her vigil by the door and joined those members of the party who had not requested breakfast in their rooms. Lord Bradwell sat at the head of the table with Madge on his right, both with newspapers spread before them. Neither looked up when Samantha entered, but Lady Stuart-Lane sent her a smile and invited her to take the empty seat beside her.

"I always find it interesting," she said once Samantha had filled her plate and joined her, leaning over and speaking in a whisper, "to take note of who comes down to breakfast and who does not. For example, one would hardly imagine Miss Thorpe or Miss Fanshaw to be early risers, yet here they are."

Samantha followed her gaze to where the two young ladies sat at the far end of the table, picking at their food and yawning. Grateful for the distraction, she said, "I see that they have positioned themselves to be in view of the door. Do you suppose they hoped certain gentlemen would join us?"

Lady Stuart-Lane grinned. "It is a shame that only two of the young men are here, and one of them practically engaged."

"Poor Mr. Allen," Samantha said, adding milk to her tea. "They seem to have dismissed him entirely."

"I am sure you are wishing he would do the same to you."

Samantha shot a glance at Mr. Allen, who had returned to the sideboard for second helpings. "I confess I am."

"Is there any news on the prince's health?" Lord Linwood asked his mother.

Madge folded back her newspaper and set it aside. "The palace says he's taken a turn for the worse."

"How awful," Lady Wentworth tutted sympathetically.

"Indeed," Sir Rupert agreed. "Of course, we all hope for his swift recovery, as before, but I could almost wish the turn had happened some weeks ago."

"What do you mean?" Lord Linwood asked.

"Well, if he'd been this ill then, he likely wouldn't have been able to rewrite that letter to the Americans. It's my opinion that he severely mishandled the whole affair."

Samantha saw Lord Bradwell's eyes lift from his paper for the first time, to fix narrowly on his guest. "Do you?" he said evenly. "And how would you have gone about it differently?"

Either Sir Rupert missed the undertones in his host's voice or he was too impassioned to care because he went on doggedly. "From the moment that American captain boarded a British ship, it ought to have been seen for what it was—a declaration of war. We shouldn't be tiptoeing around, trying not to upset anyone. We should be fighting back."

"You would advocate for war with America?" Lord Bradwell asked. "Again?"

Sir Rupert sat forward. "I would advocate for the quickest end to this rebellion possible. The result is inevitable—the rebels will win. All that comes of drawing it out is disruption to international trade."

"And what about the disruption that war brings?" Lord Bradwell asked. "And the loss of lives? British lives, in an American conflict."

"How many British lives will be lost to starvation when whole industries fall?"

"As you are a member of one of those industries, I can hardly take your opinion as objective."

"Personally," Lord Linwood spoke up, "I see Sir Rupert's experience as a positive. He gives a perspective that is needed." His father shot him a brief, irritated look, which he ignored. "The current state of British politics—"

"I'm afraid," Madge interrupted, "that I have not sufficiently prepared myself to hear a lecture on the current state of British politics this morning. Perhaps another time." She turned to the footman who stood by the door. "Thomas, you may begin to clear the dishes. I believe we have finished with breakfast. We shall be leaving for the church soon."

Samantha half-wished Madge had not put a premature end to the discussion. She enjoyed political discourse and resented how often it was confined to men-only regions, like gentlemen's clubs. She was also curious to hear how Sir Rupert would continue to defend his position, if for no other reason than it was a welcome distraction from her worry about Wyatt's prolonged absence.

She didn't have much longer to worry, though. As Thomas gathered up the servingware, Wyatt entered the room. His hair was windblown and his nose and cheeks were red with cold, but he seemed otherwise unharmed.

"Good heavens," Madge said, looking him up and down. "Where have you been?"

"Good morning, Madge," Wyatt said cheerily. He turned to Lord Bradwell and inclined his head, "Sir." Grabbing a plate, he hastened to fill it before Thomas carried off his first load, calling over his shoulder. "I went for a ride."

"In this weather?" asked Mr. Allen, speaking for the first time that meal.

Wyatt shrugged as he sat down.

"Cold weather is good for health," Lady Wentworth volunteered. "I am fond of a brisk walk myself."

Sir Rupert speared a bite of sausage. "With the amount of time you spend walking through the gardens at home, you ought to be the healthiest woman in Britain."

Samantha thought she detected an acrid note in his tone.

"I do enjoy gardening," Lady Wentworth agreed placidly.

Yet again, in observing Sir Rupert, Samantha was reminded of her uncle, though this time it was his wife's placating manner, so reminiscent of her Aunt Victoria, that sparked the memory. As her mind traveled down an all-too-familiar path, one that she knew ended with two lifeless bodies, she sought to rein it in. Fortunately, Wyatt was watching her curiously, and she recalled why she had been so eager for his return.

"Did you see anything interesting on your ride?" she asked.

He shook his head. "Sadly, no."

"Nothing?" She could not keep the incredulity from her voice, earning her a few curious looks.

"Nothing." Then, after taking a bite of eggs, he turned to Miss Fanshaw and asked her what she planned to do that morning.

Samantha wasn't sure whether to be relieved or not that Wyatt had found no trace of the mysterious stranger in the abbey. If he was missing, surely that meant he had regained consciousness and gone back to wherever he'd come from. Yet, the fact that he had disappeared meant she couldn't know for certain what had happened, and she didn't like it. She wondered if she might make inquiries in the village on her next visit, or perhaps send Alice to ask around. Without a name, though, would a description be sufficient? And what would she do if she ran into the man himself?

The next morning, Samantha sat sifting discontentedly through her basket of embroidery, looking for a dropped needle. The gentlemen of the party had planned an afternoon of pheasant shooting, and she found herself envying the variety of outdoor activities available to them. When she said as much to Madge, she was surprised by the response.

"Why should you be jealous? By all means, come along."

Samantha looked around the drawing room where the other ladies of the party sat in groups of two and three, talking quietly.

"I thought," she said, lowering her voice, "that we were working to bolster my reputation. Wouldn't it be rather a step back if I were to flout convention now? You didn't suggest I do so at any of the hunting or shooting weekends this autumn."

"You shot against Lord Aston the last time he was here."

"That was only the two of us, and it happened well before the other guests arrived."

"I didn't know you wanted to participate in the shooting," Madge said. "I wish you would have said as much, for I only stayed behind for your sake. If I had known you wanted to come —but that is neither here nor there. If you have need of a shooting costume, I have half a dozen I could lend you. And as for flouting convention, I do not think this will signify. If anything, people will say it is my influence on you, which can only strengthen our connection in the eyes of Society, and that must be a good thing. What do you say? Will you come?"

Burying her doubts under the strength of Madge's convictions,

Samantha felt a growing excitement as she nodded in agreement.

The clouds above were heavy and grey as Samantha, Madge, and the rest of the shooting party spread out across the wide meadow. Wind gusted through the bordering trees, stirring anticipation. Madge's favorite retrievers wound in and out of people's legs, barking happily.

There had been only a slight murmur when Samantha came out the front door with Madge, dressed simply in wool and carrying a shotgun in the crook of her arm. Most of the gentlemen hid their surprise in a flurry of sudden activity—checking guns, adjusting jackets and knocking mud from their boots. Wyatt acknowledged her with a smile and a nod, but Lord Aston grinned broadly as he came to join her, switching his gun to the other arm so he could offer himself as her escort.

Now, as they waited for the beaters to do their work, Lord Godwin appeared at her side, dressed in a checked jacket with a cap covering his sandy blond hair.

"I wasn't aware you enjoyed shooting, Miss Kingston," he said. "Do you do it often?"

"Not in years," she admitted. She hadn't shot game since she lived with her grandfather, but she wasn't worried. The shotgun was familiar in her hands and she could almost feel her grandfather adjusting her hold.

"If you would like some assistance, I could offer you a few pointers," Lord Godwin said smoothly.

"No, thank you." She smiled at him because she did not doubt he meant well, but added sweetly, "Would you mind stepping away? I would like to be ready as soon as the birds appear."

"Of course," he said. "Let me know if you need anything."

He retreated to where his valet stood some feet away.

As the first birds came over the tops of the trees, Samantha planted her feet, lifted the gun to her shoulder and breathed out slowly. Then she took aim and fired. High above her, a small, dark form recoiled and began to spiral to the ground.

"Good shot, miss," said Philip, the footman Madge had provided for her.

"Thank you." They exchanged guns and she settled the loaded one into her shoulder. She followed the progress of a bird above her, anticipating its path, then fired again. Another hit. She smiled. It was good to know she hadn't lost her skill.

Philip was ready for the switch, but the flock had disappeared over the hill. Samantha lowered her gun and watched in amusement as Madge's dogs bounded across the meadow towards the fallen birds.

"That was impressive," Lord Godwin said, coming up beside her again. "I can see why you didn't need my help."

"Thank you."

Samantha looked to the other side of the meadow. Wyatt and Lord Aston were laughing together while their valets gathered up their things.

"I hadn't realized you knew Aston," Lord Godwin said.

She turned to see that he had followed her gaze.

"Did Wyatt introduce you?" he asked. "Or did you know him before?"

It was a perfectly innocent question, but something about the way he asked it—with an almost calculated casualness—put Samantha on her guard.

"Why do you ask?"

If he noticed the edge in her tone, it didn't show.

"I just wondered how long you had been friends," he said with a shrug. "You seem very close."

"I wouldn't say we were close. Lord Aston has an ease of manner that makes it hard not to enjoy his company."

He smiled. "Very true. He does have an ease about him."

He bowed and left her to join Lord Linwood, his valet trailing behind him. Samantha wondered if she had misjudged him. Her experience with Charles had left her worried that she was blind to evidence of malice in others. Was it possible that she was now inventing evidence where there was none?

"Are you ready, miss?" Philip asked.

Samantha looked around and realized that she was the last to move. The rest of the shooting party was beginning to disappear over the crest of the hill, headed for the next location.

"Yes, of course," she said.

They started off, but they hadn't gone more than a few feet when movement in the trees to her left caught her eye. She turned to see a flash of something dark, moving fast. She stopped where she was and watched the trees. There it was again. This time, she was able to make out a shape—a hooded figure.

"Miss?"

Phillip was watching her with concern.

"Did you see that?" she asked.

"See what?"

Samantha looked back at the woods. There was no sign of the hooded figure.

"Nothing," she said, shaking her head.

She was being paranoid. Her encounter with the strange man at the abbey had her jumping at shadows. The dark shape had probably been nothing more sinister than a deer.

It was several hours later, with the light fading and the rising wind indicating an oncoming storm, that the shooting party returned to the house. Samantha, walking between Wyatt and Lord Aston, could hardly contain her excitement. There was something about the moments before a storm broke, when the world was filled with a tangible energy and a sense of possibility, that she had always liked. To be outside, surrounded by it and accompanied by people she had come to consider friends, filled her with a giddy joy she hadn't felt in years.

"How many did you bag, Val?" Lord Aston asked cheerily, using his nickname for Wyatt.

"Three," Wyatt said comfortably. "You?"

"Ha! I got four."

"Well done," Samantha said.

"How many did you get?" he asked, raising an eyebrow at her.

"I'd rather not say."

Lord Aston rolled his eyes and looked over Samantha's head to Wyatt. "She's trying to protect whatever sense of pride I have left."

"I didn't realize you had any," Wyatt said.

"How many did you get then?" Lord Aston asked. "A dozen?"

"Not nearly that many," she said with a grin. "Only seven."

"Only seven, eh? I'm disappointed in you, Miss Kingston. I felt sure you would have bagged at least ten."

"Next time."

It struck her in that moment that there would, indeed, be a next time, because the choice was entirely her own. She had come shooting of her own volition, and she hadn't had to answer to anyone in making that decision—not her father nor her uncle. She had wanted to come, and she had. True, she might have ruffled a few feathers among the ladies present, but she would bear those consequences, if there were any.

It wasn't the first decision she had made since gaining her independence, but it was the first of which her uncle would most definitely have disapproved. She smiled at the thought.

FIVE

The eagerly anticipated trip to the abbey ruins took place on Tuesday, after the midday meal. Lord Linwood took Miss Wentworth and her brother in his carriage, while the rest of the party distributed themselves between two of the Bradwell carriages. Samantha was kept from joining Wyatt and Lord Aston by a very determined Miss Thorpe, who dragged an apologetic Miss Fanshaw with her. That left Samantha to join Lady Stuart-Lane and Lord Linwood's friends in the final carriage.

"How far is it to these infamous ruins?" Lord Godwin asked as the carriage started off. "Does anyone know?"

"Not far at all," Samantha assured him. "We could have walked were it not for the cold. In a carriage, I would estimate ten minutes at most."

Mr. Allen's narrow face fell at this and he seemed on the point of addressing her, no doubt to make as much use of the time as he could, so Samantha turned to Lady Stuart-Lane, who sat beside her.

"Madge said that you live in Devonshire, near the sea. I've never been to the sea. What is it like?"

"Vast," Lady Stuart-Lane said. "Endless. Terrifying, but

beautiful. It's impossible to describe the feeling you get as you stand on the edge of a cliff with the smell of the sea and the feel of the spray in the air."

"It sounds wonderful."

"You wouldn't say that if you were in it," Lord Godwin said with a chuckle. "On a ship, tossed about like a child's toy, holding on for dear life, unable to keep food down."

"Godwin!" Mr. Allen sounded scandalized. "I hardly think that an appropriate topic to bring up around ladies."

"I wouldn't worry, Mr. Allen." Lady Stuart-Lane said serenely. "I daresay we ladies have experienced as many unpleasant bodily sensations as you gentlemen. Considering what we go through to bring children into the world, hearing stomach bile mentioned so obliquely is hardly likely to overset us."

Mr. Allen turned beet red, and even Lord Godwin looked surprised. Samantha couldn't help smiling.

"Have you been to the abbey before?" Lady Stuart-Lane asked, turning to Samantha as though nothing had happened.

"Yes, many times. I'm afraid Miss Wentworth will be disappointed. I've never once seen a ghost."

"Not even a glimmer of something strange and mysterious out of the corner of your eye?"

Samantha's mind flashed to the dark figure in the woods. However, she merely shook her head and said, "Not even that."

"How very disobliging. We shall have to contrive to hear an otherworldly whisper at least, or the whole trip will be wasted."

When they reached the bottom of the small hill on which the abbey stood, the carriages drew to a stop and the whole party alighted.

"Ooh!" Miss Wentworth exclaimed. "It's even grander than I imagined it. Look! That must be the chapel. How high it is!"

Lord Linwood held out an arm and she took it, but her eyes

never left the abbey as the party ascended the hill and her stream of observations continued. "It's so beautiful. Imagine how it must have appeared with all the stained glass intact. Are those the cloisters? I hope we may be able to tell where the living quarters were. That is what I am most excited to see. To imagine Evelyn in her room, her haven..."

"I wonder that Linwood can stand it," Lord Godwin said in an undertone as he took Samantha's arm, out-maneuvering Mr. Allen in the process. "I know I couldn't. Five minutes with her, and I'd want to tear my hair out."

"Why is he pursuing her, do you think?" Samantha asked, hoping to gain insight for Madge.

"She's got quite the dowry."

"She isn't unique in that," Samantha said.

Lord Godwin shot her an amused look. "Want him for yourself, do you?"

"No!" Samantha spoke with more vehemence than she meant in her surprise. She grimaced as several heads turned their way, including Wyatt's.

Lord Godwin laughed. "No, he's far too serious for you. As to Miss Wentworth, though..." He lowered his voice conspiratorially. "I think it's more her father than her lovely self that Linwood's interested in. Sir Rupert is something of a rising star, politically, though in the Commons, of course, not the Lords, and Linwood imagines himself a politician."

"I see."

"I've tried to dissuade him. I've told him, 'It's not Sir Rupert you'll have to listen to across the dining table every day,' but he is determined."

They ascended the hill in the same groups they had ridden in, but once among the tumbled stones of the abbey, the young people began to mingle. Samantha had hoped finally to join Wyatt and Lord Aston, but the latter had slid away from Miss Fanshaw to join Lord Linwood and the Wentworths, and Miss Thorpe had attached herself so firmly to Wyatt that she seemed in danger of cutting off the circulation to his arm. Samantha did not think he looked particularly happy with his situation, but neither did she feel up to rescuing him. Seeing Mr. Allen making his way towards her, she looked for an escape, but he was intercepted by Lady Stuart-Lane.

"Might I have the use of your arm, Mr. Allen?" she asked, steering him away. "The ground here is so uneven. I am afraid of turning my ankle."

Samantha mouthed a silent "thank you," and Lady Stuart-Lane smiled back before turning to Mr. Allen and asking his opinion of the edifice. Left to herself, Samantha wandered away from the group to the far end of the chapel and turned down an ancient corridor. The corridor, which was more of a bordered garden path as most of the walls had long since gone, led to the great hall. Here, the walls were mostly intact, and the outer wall boasted several tall, narrow windows. Looking through these, Samantha could see down the hill to the river Derwent that lay a quarter of a mile away. She watched the water for several minutes, dazzled by the way the sun glinted off the surface.

When she reached the courtyard of the cloister, with two of its walls still standing, Samantha looked around to see that she was, indeed, alone. That confirmed, she lifted her skirts and climbed onto the sill of one of the windows, turning to face the courtyard with her legs dangling over the edge. Adjusting her skirts, she leaned against the cold stone of the window frame and let out a sigh. Sitting there, with the walls around the courtyard in her vision, she could almost imagine, as Miss Wentworth did, what it must have looked like hundreds of years before. She imagined the sisters passing between the windows opposite her on their way to vespers. It was a beautiful place to be isolated. She could see the appeal it must have had for Evelyn, if there ever was such a person.

She was staring idly at a spot on the opposite wall, thinking about abbeys and nuns and marriage, when a voice spoke suddenly behind her.

"There you are."

She shrieked and would have fallen out of the window if a pair of strong arms had not caught her waist and held her back.

"Wyatt!" she snapped reproachfully when she had her breath back. "You scared me!"

"I noticed." His voice held laughter.

"You shouldn't sneak up on people. I might have been seriously injured."

"I wasn't sneaking," he said. "You weren't paying attention."

She turned to argue with him and found that he was standing quite close behind her. His hands, which had steadied her on the window, were still at her waist and their faces were inches apart. To her embarrassment, she felt heat rising in her cheeks.

"Yes, well, thank you for stopping my fall," she said, and she shifted around. As she had expected, he removed his hands from her waist, but he didn't step back.

"Do you need help getting down?" he asked, a glint of amusement in his eyes.

"No, thank you," she said primly, arranging her skirts so that they covered her ankles even as she twisted, lifting her legs onto the window sill. "Though it would be easier if you turned around."

He said nothing to this but continued to watch her with a half-smile as she struggled. Finally, she gave up trying to be ladylike and jumped down, landing with a thump beside him before taking a step back.

"Where is your shadow?" she asked pointedly.

"Do you mean Miss Thorpe? She managed to capture the attention of a much better prospect, and I was released."

"Oh?" Samantha was amused in spite of herself. "I hope you

don't mean Lord Aston."

"No, no," he assured her. "Bingo would never go within ten feet of a girl like that. It was Lord Godwin she hooked."

"It's a shame it wasn't Mr. Allen."

"Isn't he one of your suitors?"

She sent him a withering look. "You must know, even if I were ever to marry, I should never consider a man like Mr. Allen."

"What do you mean 'if' you were to marry?" He sounded taken aback.

She shrugged her shoulders, feeling suddenly uncomfortable. She hadn't meant to say "if." The word must have floated up from her subconscious. She was not as careful in what she said to Wyatt as she was with other people. She somehow felt she didn't need to be.

"Do you not mean to marry?" he pressed. "Why?"

"For any number of reasons," she said, resigning herself to the conversation. "But, I suppose, chiefly, because, with my inheritance, I don't have to." He seemed unsure how to respond to this, so she added, "Tell me, do you know anyone who is happily married?"

"Madge," he replied promptly.

"That is true," she said, considering. "Or it seems to be, in any case. But, apart from your cousin?"

He shrugged. "How should I know what goes on behind closed doors?"

"But you do," she insisted. "We all do. It feeds half of Society's gossip—who's sneaking behind whose back. Who is too friendly with whom. There's a reason names are printed on doors at house parties."

"What of it?" he asked.

"Well, it's not the most encouraging endorsement of marriage. Though, when one marries for title or wealth, what else is to be expected?"

"Some people marry for love."

"And even they often end up miserable. How much worse to have been in love with one's husband only to learn of the opera singer he keeps in some London apartment."

Wyatt coughed, and Samantha narrowed her eyes. "I know it isn't the thing for a lady to mention the subject of mistresses. We're meant to endure them, not to speak of them."

"Not every man keeps a mistress," he said. "There are honorable men, Samantha."

"Perhaps," she conceded, "but the risk of marrying the wrong one is too great. In which case, where is the benefit of marriage? At least for the woman. If I were to marry, I would lose any right to my money, my home, even my person. I wouldn't be free to make my own choices. And if he were to be unfaithful, I would be forced to turn a blind eye. Because, if I left him, he would have rights to everything. I would have nothing."

"When you put it that way, I suppose you are right," he said slowly. "Yet, to be alone...

"But I won't be alone," she said earnestly. "I'll have my friends. I'll find a companion to keep me company at home."

"A paid companion?" His tone was laced with disdain.

"Is that not what a husband would be for me?" she asked. "He would be even better paid than my companion and less agreeable, I am sure. Less grateful, too, I shouldn't wonder."

She laughed bitterly. Wyatt didn't laugh. He seemed to be considering how to respond, but she had no wish to prolong the depressing conversation, so she sought a change of subject.

"Wyatt," she said. "While we're alone for a moment, may I ask you something?"

He must have heard the alteration in her tone, because his focus seemed to sharpen, and he regarded her seriously as he nodded.

"Have you learned anything more about Charles' death?"

If she hadn't been watching him, she might have missed the

way his nostrils flared and his jaw clenched. He looked away quickly. She wondered at his reaction. Was he upset she had mentioned Charles? Why?

"Have you not been keeping up with the news?" he asked.

She shook her head and then, realizing he couldn't see her reaction, she said, "No. I was at first, but it was...difficult. Madge and I don't discuss it anymore, either. Have there been any developments?"

He nodded absently and ran a hand over his jaw.

"What is it?" she asked, anxiety rising in her chest. "What happened?"

He looked back at her, and his eyes seemed to search her face before he spoke. "Scotland Yard announced that they found Charles' killer. They tracked him down, and there was a shootout. He was killed before he could escape."

Her eyes widened. "How did they know it was him? Did he say why he did it?"

Wyatt looked away again, shoving his hands into the pockets of his coat. "A porter who was there during the shooting testified to it—that's how they say they found him. As to why he did it, they say he claimed Charles had stolen from him, ruined his business, and that he'd become unhinged because of it, wanted revenge."

Samantha's mind reeled. She walked away from Wyatt and leaned against the stone wall, crossing her arms under her cloak.

"Are you alright?" Wyatt came to stand in front of her, looking concerned.

"I don't know," she said. "I don't know. I suppose I thought I'd have some sort of relief from learning who'd killed him—that there would be a sense of completion, of understanding." She looked up at Wyatt. "But I don't understand. It wasn't even related to everything that happened? It was only a man he once knew who decided to kill him right before he was about to be sentenced to death?"

Wyatt's jaw twitched and, when he spoke, his voice was oddly flat. "If he wanted revenge, he likely wanted to do it himself."

"I don't understand," Samantha repeated. "It's so senseless. And this is the reason for my nightm—" She broke off, flushing as she looked down.

"The reason for what?" Wyatt asked.

"Nothing," she said hurriedly. She straightened and made to leave, but he was blocking her way.

"Why don't you want to tell me?" he asked, his expression a mixture of hurt and frustration.

"It's not your concern."

"Well, I am concerned," he insisted.

"Why?" Samantha asked recklessly. "You haven't been for months."

As soon as she spoke the words, she regretted them. They sounded so petty, not to mention needy, and she was neither of those things. It would have been strange if Wyatt had written to her. After all, correspondence between the sexes was frowned upon unless the correspondents were engaged or married. Neither should she have expected him to visit. He had his own life, which he had put on hold for her that summer. He didn't owe her anything.

"I'm sorry," she said quickly. "That was—"

"Don't apologize," he said, shaking his head. "You have every right to be upset with me. I should have written. I should have made sure you were alright. After what happened with Charles—"

"No. There was no need. You introduced me to Madge. You got me out of the courthouse. You've done plenty."

"I could have done more. I should have done more."

She was struck by the regret that filled his tone and the earnestness in his eyes. She felt she ought to say something, but she couldn't think what. The seconds stretched to a minute as they stared at each other. Then, something shifted in his expression. He reached out a hand and brushed back one of her curls, which had come loose, his fingers lingering on her face a moment longer than was necessary. She felt her breath catch.

The sound of footsteps echoed from the direction of the great hall. Wyatt dropped his hand and turned to look behind him just as Miss Wentworth came around the corner, her head down, her hands clutching what looked like a letter.

She looked up and, seeing them, gasped. "Oh! Excuse me. I didn't mean to intrude."

A blush suffused her cheeks, and she hurriedly folded the sheaf of paper, stowing it in the folds of her cloak.

"You're not intruding," Samantha said hurriedly, stepping away from Wyatt.

"Are you lost?" Wyatt gave no indication that he had noticed Samantha's movement. "Where's Linwood?"

"Oh!" Miss Wentworth said again. "No, I'm not lost. Lord Linwood is in the chapel, I believe. I wanted to explore more on my own. That's all. Isn't it beautiful?"

Her tone, as she asked the question, was distracted and held none of the wonder she had spoken with earlier. Samantha wondered what was in the letter that had her so discombobulated. She glanced at Wyatt, who raised an eyebrow and gave a slight shrug.

"Are you feeling well, Miss Wentworth?" Samantha asked.

"Oh, yes. I feel fine. Or, rather, no. Perhaps I am not. I think I will return to the carriages until everyone is ready."

"Would you like us to accompany—"

"No!" Miss Wentworth exclaimed. Then, blushing, she added, "Forgive me. I thank you for the offer, but I don't wish to keep you from your...from enjoying the abbey."

With that, she turned and hurried away.

"What was that about?" Samantha asked, watching Miss Wentworth disappear down the side of the hill.

"It was certainly odd," Wyatt said. "But then, that seems to be the norm for Miss Wentworth, so perhaps it wasn't so very strange."

Samantha turned a frown on him. "You can't think that. She's clearly hiding something."

He opened his mouth to respond but shut it again as Lord Aston appeared with Lady Stuart-Lane on his arm.

"Just who we were hoping to find," Lord Aston said. He glanced between the two of them, and his smile grew.

"Had your fill of the ruins yet, Bingo?" Wyatt asked in a quelling tone.

"The ruins, yes. Practically from the moment we arrived. Interesting conversation, however...It looked as though you were having some just now. Please don't stop on our account."

Samantha could not help but be glad he hadn't arrived when Miss Wentworth had. She felt sure he would have said something even more provoking then—something that would have made it impossible to pretend that whatever had passed between her and Wyatt hadn't happened, which was exactly what she intended to do. Instead, she would focus on what had happened after and Miss Wentworth's strange behavior.

"Miss Kingston," Lady Stuart-Lane said as she detached herself from Lord Aston's arm and came to stand beside Samantha. "I noticed there is a beautiful view of the river beyond the abbey. Perhaps we might take a walk in that direction and leave the gentlemen to amuse each other?"

Happy for an excuse to leave, Samantha said, "I would like that."

"If you will excuse us, gentlemen." Lady Stuart-Lane linked her arm with Samantha's and they walked away, down the hill.

*****

When they were out of sight, Wyatt fixed Bingo with a piercing stare. "'Interesting conversation'? What precisely were you hoping to accomplish just then?"

Bingo shrugged, grinning. "I thought you might appreciate some help. I know it's been a while, but the usual aim when you steal a moment alone with a woman is to leave her smiling, not frowning at you like thunder."

"Don't be an imbecile. You know that wasn't what was happening."

"Do I?"

Wyatt rolled his eyes heavenward. "You sound like Tom."

"Oh? He's talked to you about Miss Kingston?"

"Yes, he cornered me before I came up here to tell me of our dear mother's wishes that I throw in my hat for her and his own that I publicly denounce her."

Bingo threw back his head and laughed loudly. "What a dilemma for you, my friend. I suppose you'll have to decide whom you hate more."

"I would never be so childish as to allow spite to influence my pursuit of a young lady," Wyatt said irritably.

"So you are pursuing her?"

"You know what I meant."

"I don't, actually," Bingo said placidly. "But if you are pursuing her, you're going about it entirely the wrong way. You've hardly seen her since August."

"I *haven't* seen her since August," Wyatt corrected him.

Bingo looked surprised. "At all?"

Wyatt sighed. "I've kept myself away from her and even from Madge so that these rumors about us will die down. If people see us together, there will be talk, and that's the last thing Sa—Miss Kingston needs right now."

"If you had only asked, I could have told you what an asinine plan that was," Bingo said, not attempting to hide his amusement.

"What do you mean?"

"To begin with, there was always going to be talk, whether you were there or not," Bingo said superciliously. "This is London Society, after all. If you avoid her, people will speculate as to why. If you want my advice, I'd tell you to be seen around Miss Kingston as much as possible. The more people see you together, the more ordinary and dull the sight becomes, until you all but fade into the background."

Wyatt pinched the bridge of his nose, recognizing the wisdom in Bingo's words and mentally chastising himself for not having thought of it before. He could have saved himself a lot of worry, and he might have been supporting Samantha all along, rather than leaving her to hide out on her own.

"Of course," Bingo said slyly, "my advice only works if there is no evidence to be seen—if you have no feelings for Miss Kingston to be witnessed."

Wyatt wished he could respond with a firm denial and put to rest all of Bingo's irritating though well-meant insinuations. In the privacy of his own thoughts, however, he couldn't deny that what he felt for Samantha was something more than mere attraction nor that he often wondered if she felt the same.

*****

Samantha found Lady Stuart-Lane to be a pleasant companion and, after they had discovered a mutual love of novels, they passed an enjoyable quarter-hour discussing their favorites until Lady Stuart-Lane was insisting Samantha call her Eden, Samantha was returning the favor, and their friendship was sealed. They had just decided to return to the abbey on the assumption that the others must be ready to leave soon when Eden pointed to something on the riverbank.

"What is that?"

When Samantha turned to look, she thought at first that the

dark shape some thirty feet ahead of them was an oddly shaped rock, then, as she stepped nearer, a large coat laid aside and forgotten by a local fisherman. It wasn't until she was close enough to touch it that she realized the shape was a man.

The coat concealed most of his body, and his hair was so matted with dirt and mud that she had not at first distinguished it from the ground around him. With mounting trepidation, Samantha knelt beside him.

"I'm not sure that's wise," Eden said hesitantly when Samantha put out a hand to touch his shoulder. "He won't thank you for waking him, not if he's sleeping off the drink."

But Samantha had already taken note of the stillness of his form, the lack of rise and fall in his chest. Grasping his shoulder, she turned him over.

Eden gasped. Samantha let out a shriek herself, clapping her hands over her mouth. Lying beside her, glassy eyes open but unseeing, was the man from the abbey.

SIX

I've killed him. God forgive me, I've killed him.

They were Samantha's first coherent thoughts after the initial shock, and they played on a repetitive refrain in her head as she stumbled to her feet. Why had she ever left him on his own? He must have come to consciousness after she and Alice left only to be overcome by a wave of dizziness, falling into the river and drowning.

Samantha felt bile rise in her throat as she considered how her choices had led to a man's death—and she had pulled Alice into it with her. He wouldn't have fallen if he hadn't been hit, and he wouldn't have been hit if she had just run as soon as she saw him or, better yet, not gone to the abbey alone in the first place.

"I'll go get help."

Samantha heard Eden's words as through a haze, and her new friend had taken her first steps towards the abbey before she had the wherewithal to grasp her arm and hold her back.

"Wait," she said hoarsely. "We don't want to cause a panic. Find Mr. Wyatt. He'll know what to do."

Eden nodded and hurried off, leaving Samantha alone by the riverbank. When she closed her eyes, she could hear the rush of water beside her, the twittering of the birds and the scuffling of small animals as they scurried through the underbrush. She could feel the sun on her face, the chill in the air and the whip of wind through her hair. Yet, through it all, the presence of the body loomed large in her mind and it brought the memories of those other bodies, the ones from the summer, sharper into focus.

The squelch of footsteps on the soggy ground heralded Eden's return with Wyatt. Lord Aston was with them as well, gallantly escorting the lady while Wyatt strode ahead of them.

"Are you alright?" he asked, stopping in front of her, his eyes searching her face. She thought for a moment he might take her hands. His left hand did reach briefly towards her, but then he clenched it and it dropped to his side. She tried to ignore the disappointment she felt as she focused on answering his question.

"I...I don't know," she replied, her eyes flicking to the body beside them. She lowered her voice so that Eden and Lord Aston, drawing nearer, could not hear. "It's him, Wyatt. The man I told you about—the one Alice struck. He's dead."

Wyatt stilled. She wished she knew what he was thinking, then decided it was best she didn't. She felt bad enough as it was.

This time, Wyatt did take her hand. He squeezed it briefly before turning to the others.

"We'll need Lord Bradwell," he said briskly. "He's the local magistrate. Most likely the man was merely drunk, but we ought to do things properly. He'll know how to contact the constable and whomever else we need."

"I can fetch him," Lord Aston volunteered, releasing Eden's arm.

"I think it would be better," Wyatt said firmly, "if the ladies were to return to the abbey and encourage everyone to leave. The outing has gone on long enough that it will seem natural. Then," he turned to Eden, "when you get to the house, you might send him back on his own. That way, no one is the wiser, and we can keep things quiet, at least for now."

"Are you and Lord Aston staying?" Eden asked. "Won't that seem odd to the others?"

"Tell them we've decided to walk to town. We'll hire a carriage back."

Eden nodded and looked to Samantha expectantly. Samantha nodded back, but she made no move to leave. Her legs had become like lead, and a weight was pressing into her chest. She struggled to breathe.

"A moment," Wyatt said to Eden. As he turned to Samantha, Lord Aston tactfully drew Eden's attention to a bird up on the hill.

"I've killed him," Samantha said in a hollow whisper, her eyes staring, unfocused, at a point beyond Wyatt.

"No, you haven't," Wyatt insisted. "Look at me."

Samantha focused on his face with difficulty. He was watching her earnestly.

"You did not kill this man," he said, emphasizing each word. "At this point, we can't even be sure how he died. He may well have been drunk. He may have come back in the dark and tripped."

Samantha knew he was only trying to calm her down. He must know as well as she what the most likely scenario was. Still, she forced herself to breathe deeply and nodded.

"Very well," she said. "I'll send Lord Bradwell as soon as I can."

Samantha barely spoke during the ride back to Bradwell Court. The intrepid Miss Thorpe had organized herself and Miss Fanshaw as partners for Lord Godwin and Mr. Allen, leaving Samantha and Eden with a carriage to themselves. Samantha was happy not to have to make small talk with the gentlemen and happier still when Eden did not attempt to fill the silence.

After informing Lord Bradwell of the tragedy on his land, she retired to her room. Though she hadn't asked for her maid to be sent up, the efficient Alice was by her side within minutes.

"What is it?" she asked as soon as the door had closed behind her. "You look as though you've seen a ghost."

The trite comment was so near the truth that it was a moment before Samantha could respond with composure. Her mind flashed back to the sight of the man's bedraggled corpse, his distressingly familiar face turned up to hers, and she shuddered.

"We found a body, Alice," she said. Then she added, hesitantly: "It was the man from the abbey."

The color drained from Alice's face. "Dead?" Samantha nodded. Alice gripped the doorknob behind her and said faintly, "If it's alright, miss, I think I might need to sit down."

"Of course." Samantha rose quickly to her feet and gestured for Alice to take her place on the bench in front of the vanity. Then she settled herself into the settee by the fire. They faced each other, and Samantha thought that in Alice's expression she could see all the dismay, regret and fear she had been feeling since she recognized that half-frozen body on the riverbank.

"Lord Bradwell is on his way there," she explained. "He'll ensure the body is identified properly and the...cause of death is determined. Mr. Wyatt will let us know what he finds."

Alice merely blinked, and Samantha wondered how they would bear the interminable period before Wyatt's return.

*****

Wyatt felt uneasy as he watched Samantha walk back up the hill, her arm linked with Lady Stuart-Lane's. Though less pale than when he'd arrived, she still looked quite ill, and no wonder.

"Is he really dead?" Bingo asked, drawing Wyatt's attention back to the body on the riverbank.

Wyatt bent down. He hadn't had the opportunity to examine the man yet, but the blank, staring eyes had been indication enough of his state of being. "Yes, he's really dead."

"Poor Miss Kingston."

Wyatt looked up sharply. "What do you mean?"

"Finding another dead body," Bingo said, seemingly unable to look away from the corpse below them. "After everything that happened this summer, I mean."

"Ah, yes." Wyatt nodded.

"She'll have to give evidence at the inquest, too. One can only imagine what the London press will make of that."

"Nothing, if I can help it," Wyatt said firmly.

Bingo turned to him, looking amused. "Still fancying yourself her protector, are you? Or is there something more to your concern?"

"Lord Bradwell won't want a fuss made, either," Wyatt continued, ignoring his friend. "He'll make sure it stays out of the papers."

"I hope you're right," Bingo said. "I've grown to like Miss Kingston quite a lot. I'd hate to see her hurt."

Wyatt narrowed his eyes, sure Bingo was goading him, but Bingo's gaze had drifted to the fields beyond them, seemingly lost in thought. Wyatt felt an odd twist in his gut that he reluctantly recognized as jealousy. Samantha had spent a good deal of time with Bingo while he'd been keeping himself away from her. Had she grown to like him as much as he did her?

They didn't speak for some time after that. Wyatt finished examining what he could of the body without moving it. He had seen the wound on the temple where Samantha's maid had struck, but nothing else to give him a clue as to how the man had died. Attempting to distract himself from the implications of that knowledge, he searched the space around the riverbank. Unfortunately, heavy rain the previous night had washed away any footprints or other useful evidence.

It was only a little more than half an hour after Samantha and

Lady Stuart-Lane had left them that Lord Bradwell crested the hill. He dismounted his broad stallion in one fluid motion and strode towards them, the many capes of his greatcoat flapping with every step, his expression grave.

"What's this about a dead body?"

Wyatt gestured to the riverbank. "Your niece and Miss Kingston found him. It's not clear how he died, but I thought you ought to be informed."

"Anyone else see it?" Lord Bradwell said brusquely, moving around Wyatt and bending to examine the body.

"No, we thought it best to keep it quiet for now."

"Quite right. No telling what some of them might've—" He stopped abruptly and reached to brush aside some of the mud that caked the man's face. Then he grunted and rose swiftly to his feet.

"What is it?" Wyatt asked.

"I know him," Lord Bradwell said, brushing off his gloved hands. "Jeremy Jones. Odd-job man from the village. He's done work for us before."

"Had he any reason to be on your land now?" Wyatt asked.

"This part of the river is popular for fishing. It's close to the village and I allow the villagers access."

"Fishing in midwinter?" Bingo asked.

"If it's mild enough," Lord Bradwell said. He sighed and rubbed a hand over his face. "We'll need Smithers—he's the local constable—and the doctor will need to examine him. I expect he'd rather not do that out here."

Leaving Lord Bradwell to guard the body, Wyatt and Bingo hurried to the village—Wyatt to fetch the constable and Bingo, the doctor. Mr. Smithers, who was also the blacksmith, had been hard at work in his forge, but when he heard what Wyatt had to say, he hastily removed his apron and called in his apprentice to take over.

Naturally, the small village had no morgue, but an abandoned barn on the outskirts served well enough once Wyatt and the constable had moved the body there using a quickly fashioned stretcher. Stiff with cold, the body had been difficult to extricate from the river bank, and Wyatt knew he would not soon forget the unpleasant task of transporting it across a rickety bridge and over a field. The thin blanket that concealed it kept slipping off, exposing blank, staring eyes that silently watched their progress.

They'd been careful to skirt the village, not eager to alert the villagers to the presence of the dead body of one of their own. After they had settled themselves and their macabre burden, Bingo arrived with the doctor.

Doctor Caruthers was a thin, bespectacled man with a clipped, business-like manner of speaking. He took in the sight of Jeremy Jones, half-frozen and sodden, without blinking an eye and knelt beside him.

"There is a wound to the temple," he said, lifting wet hair from the area he was examining. "It's not serious enough to have been fatal, and it looks as though it had begun to heal, so I'd say he received it a day or so before his death." His hands moved swiftly and meticulously over the face and around the head. "Ah. If you would..." He gestured for Wyatt and Bingo to help roll the body over. "Yes. That's it. See here?" His fingers moved through hair matted with dried blood, pressing and prodding. "This is what killed him. A heavy blow to the base of the skull. Death would have been instantaneous."

"Would the blow have come from a fall?" Wyatt asked. "As he fell into the river?"

Doctor Caruthers shook his head. "Unless he fell from a great height, and I see no indication elsewhere on his body that he did, he is unlikely to have received so heavy a blow by accident. Also, the dried blood indicates that there was a period between when he was struck and when he entered the water. At least a half hour, if not more."

There was a moment of uncomfortable silence as they all came to the same realization.

"Are you saying he was murdered, Doctor?" Mr. Smithers asked.

The doctor shrugged. "I would not swear to it, but it seems the most likely conclusion. If I had to guess, I'd say he was hit on the head, then carried to the river and thrown in."

"How long has he been dead?" Lord Bradwell asked.

"It's difficult to say. These cold temperatures slow the processes of death. Hours at the very least, but possibly a few days."

"We can narrow it down," Wyatt said. "Since we know who he is, we can ask around, learn when he was last seen."

"After we inform his mother," Lord Bradwell said wearily. "And find out what she wants to do with the body."

Wyatt left Lord Bradwell to his unpleasant tasks, after promising to help with the investigation once it was possible to move forward. Eager to ease Samantha's conscience, he returned to the house and was informed that she was in the library.

When he entered the elegant, high-ceilinged room moments later, she was sitting on one of the velvet-cushioned window seats, gazing out at the back garden. On hearing his footsteps, she turned, and he was sorry to see the anxiety that lined her face.

"Well?" she prompted, getting to her feet as he approached.

"It was a blow to the back of the head," he said. "Nothing to do with you or Alice."

A strangled sound from the corner distracted him as Samantha collapsed back onto the seat. He turned to see her maid with one hand clasped over her mouth, her eyes squeezed shut, chest heaving.

"You may go, Alice," Samantha said, drawing in a shaky

breath.

The two women exchanged a look as Alice curtsied. Wyatt presumed the dismissal was Samantha's way of allowing her maid a moment of privacy to relieve her emotions. He wondered if he ought to leave Samantha to do the same, but before he could suggest as much, she spoke.

"What else did you learn?" Her voice was determinedly strong and there was a stubborn tilt to her chin.

"His name was Jeremy Jones," he said. "A local odd-job man. The doctor believes he was taken to the river after he was hit and thrown in."

"Murder." Samantha breathed out the word, staring, unfocused, at the window. He thought she must be remembering her aunt and uncle. Then her eyes snapped back to his and she said, "I suppose Lord Bradwell has asked for your help looking into it?"

"He has."

"I want to help, too."

Perhaps he shouldn't have been surprised, after her determination to help him investigate over the summer, but he was. After all, those murders had been personal to her, and her innocence had been at stake. Why should she concern herself with a complete stranger?

"No." In his surprise, the word came out harsher than he had meant it, and he saw her frown. In what he hoped was a gentler tone, he said, "There really is nothing you could do. Besides, aren't you helping Madge prepare for the Winter Ball?"

"Only for three more days. She does most of the work herself. And you are quick to dismiss the assistance I gave you before."

"I do not dismiss it. I was grateful for it. But you must see that the circumstances are different. You had unique knowledge then. You were the only one who could connect Slater to the murders."

"Knowledge can be acquired."

"And I will acquire it. It would be impractical for me to bring you along. Even were it not for the rumors surrounding us, you are a single lady and I am a single gentleman. We cannot travel about the country together."

"How good of you to explain our circumstances to me," Samantha said with mock sweetness. "I was not, however, proposing that we go anywhere together, merely that I be permitted to assist you in whatever capacity I could. Do I take it, then, that you refuse my offer?"

"I believe I already did."

SEVEN

Samantha left the infuriating *Mr.* Wyatt to amuse himself in the library. She was determined, with or without Wyatt's consent, to solve the murder of Mr. Jeremy Jones. Her relief that she had not turned her maid into a murderer was slightly dampened by the fear that she might still, in some way, have contributed to his death. Perhaps the blow to the head had left him woozy and less quick to react. Perhaps, in full possession of his faculties, he might have been able to fight off his attacker or run away. Whatever the truth, she could not rest until she had discovered it.

How could she discover it, though? Much as she hated to admit any merit to Wyatt's arguments, she was limited in her investigating opportunities. Unlike the men of the party, the unmarried women could not simply disappear to attend to vague business.

After some consideration, Samantha hit upon a plan. Under the guise of shopping, she could conceivably take a quick trip to the village accompanied by Alice and one of the footmen. Once there, she could speak to the villagers about Mr. Jones and see what they might know.

Madge, as Headley had informed her, was in the stables,

feeding carrots to her favorite horse. When Samantha approached, she glanced up.

"I was just about to go looking for you," she said, patting Bucephalus' neck.

"Oh?"

"Yes. I need to visit the village tomorrow. A few final purchases for the ball. I'd like you to accompany me."

"Do you need my help choosing something?" Samantha asked doubtfully.

"No. In fact, feel free to wander about as you like once we get there."

Though this fit in quite fortuitously with Samantha's own plans, she felt the need for clarification. "Then why—"

"I promised Lady Wentworth and her daughter I would take them with me in my carriage."

"Ah. I see."

"It's not a particularly long journey," Madge said, "but if I have to listen to Miss Wentworth's chatter for the length of it, it will feel eternal."

"You could engage Lady Wentworth in conversation."

"No, I couldn't. That's why I'm bringing you." When Samantha looked confused, she sighed. "I have tried to engage her. We have no friends in common. She doesn't hunt or shoot, and I don't garden. She hates dogs. She doesn't even read novels. I thought fashion would be a safe bet, with her husband in cotton, but after she told me she could not see much point in altering her gowns to fit a style that would be obsolete in a few years' time, there seemed little point in pursuing the subject. In short, I have run out of ideas."

"I don't know that I could do much better," Samantha said.

"Perhaps not, but you could do the same again. You two haven't spoken much, so you can rehash all of the topics I covered without it seeming strange."

Samantha laughed.

"Let us say ten o'clock, then," Madge said. "We shall return in time for luncheon."

The next morning, Samantha traded her practical woolen cloak for an elegantly tailored *pardessus* coat with wide trailing sleeves, her hands warmed in a French sable muff. She climbed into the silk-lined Bradwell carriage and settled into the seat beside Madge. Across from them, Lady Wentworth and Miss Wentworth sat slightly apart. It suddenly occurred to Samantha that it was the first time she had seen mother and daughter together since their arrival. She wondered at the reason for their distance. Was it Lady Wentworth's decision or her daughter's?

"Lady Wentworth," Samantha said, preparing to take on the task Madge had assigned her. "I believe I heard you say you like gardening. I've never done any myself. Have you always liked gardening, or is it a more recent pastime?"

"I have always enjoyed it," Lady Wentworth said in a manner somewhat less stilted than Samantha's had been. "When I was a girl, our gardener was very generous with his time. He taught me a great deal, and his enthusiasm was infectious."

"He sounds very kind." Silence descended on the carriage. Samantha waited to see if anyone else would break it. When no one did, she said, "Do you do the planting yourself or just the planning?"

"I do some of the planting when I can, but I trust Mr. Jeffords to do most of it."

"He was Mama's gardener when she was a child," Miss Wentworth said, leaning forward. "The one she was just talking about." She laughed. "Most people find that strange."

"There's nothing strange about it." Lady Wentworth fixed her daughter with a repressive stare. "My father planned to let him go, and I offered him a position."

"That was very generous of you," Madge said.

"It was the least I could do."

"He never taught *me* anything about gardening," Miss Wentworth said.

"He would have if you'd shown an interest."

"I like flowers. I saw a white cotton with red roses in a shop only last month that was absolutely breathtaking." She turned to Samantha. "Of course, Mama said I didn't need another gown, but I reminded her that I'll need some new ones for the spring if I'm to go to London. You were there last spring, were you not? How many ladies would you say follow the fashion plates?"

Miss Wentworth continued to prattle on about London fashion the rest of the way to Lower Bradwell while her mother stared out the window. Samantha sent an apologetic look Madge's way. Madge grimaced.

When the carriage stopped in front of the haberdashery, a footman opened the door and all four ladies alighted.

"I won't drag you all along with me," Madge said brightly. "Feel free to go where you like. We can meet here in, say, two hours?"

They agreed and went off in different directions. Samantha decided to start with the draper's shop but, just as she was stepping across the threshold, she felt a tug at her arm and turned to see Miss Wentworth holding her back.

"Might I have a word?"

She looked so earnest and so worried that Samantha didn't hesitate to agree. Looping her arm through Samantha's, Miss Wentworth led her away down the street.

"I've been meaning to speak with you ever since the abbey," she said, her light tone undermined by the determined way she held onto Samantha's arm. "You must have thought it odd, my coming across you and Mr. Wyatt as I did, on my own." When Samantha didn't respond, she added, "You must have wondered what I was doing."

Samantha could feel Miss Wentworth's eyes on her and sensed that she was trying to gauge her reaction, so she kept her face neutral.

"Why would you think that?" she asked evenly.

"Oh, I don't know." Miss Wentworth gave a little laugh. "Of course, I considered you might have even forgotten the incident, but I did not want you to think I was doing anything untoward, wandering off on my own—not that I wandered, of course. But, after my excitement to come to the abbey, to abandon the others...Though, naturally, I was more curious than they were to see it, knowing the stories."

"Naturally."

"Nor did I want you to think I meant to interrupt you and Mr. Wyatt. I know how important it is to take advantage of any unchaperoned time one can."

Having no desire to travel down that line, Samantha steered the conversation back to Miss Wentworth. "I did not think you meant to interrupt us. In fact, I was sorry that we seemed to have disturbed your solitude. I know I prefer to be alone when reading my correspondence."

Miss Wentworth's hand tightened on Samantha's arm. "Oh! The letter. Yes, I received it that morning and hadn't had time to read it, so I brought it along to read at the abbey. Speaking of letters, I see the stationer's ahead. Would you mind if we stopped there? I am in need of paper and more ink."

Samantha followed Miss Wentworth into the stationer's, allowing the latter's prattle to roll over her. Though she had found the young woman's behavior at the abbey odd, she had completely forgotten about it in light of all that happened after. Now, Miss Wentworth's transparent attempts to find out what Samantha had noticed and to convince her of its insignificance had her curiosity roused. What was in that letter? Whom had it been from? And why was Miss Wentworth so keen to hide it?

They were not alone in the shop. A pair of middle-aged women stood near the window, sifting idly through a bin of wax seals as they chatted animatedly, and a stout, older gentleman stood at the counter while the shop assistant lifted down boxes of paper for him.

Something of the conversation between the women by the window caught Samantha's attention, and she drew nearer to listen on the pretense of examining a display of fine pens.

"...hit over the head," one of the women was saying, picking up a seal and examining it by the light coming through the window. "That's what Mary Wilkes said, and she heard it from the doc himself. Of course, I always knew he'd come to a bad end, that one. Always scheming, hardly an honest day's work in his life."

"You think someone did him in then?" the other woman asked in a voice laced with fearful excitement. "Someone he knew?"

"Not someone from here, I'm sure," the first woman said. "If anyone he'd angered in the village had a mind to do him in, he'd've been killed long before now. No, this were a stranger, mark my words. One of them men what comes round the pub every now and again. He's only gone and tried to fool the wrong man."

"But he was found by the old abbey, wasn't he?" Samantha risked a glance and saw that the second woman's eyes were wide as she spoke in a hushed whisper. "And it was sometime in the night he went missing. Don't you think..."

The first woman snorted. "Don't tell me you've been listening to those old wives' tales."

"There's been plenty enough's seen the Grey Lady over the years. They're not just stories."

"She's never killed anyone, though, has she?"

"That's because folk round here aren't mad enough to disturb her rest. But that Jeremy Jones, he was a fool if ever there was one. He was just the sort to go where he had no business being, angering a poor spirit."

"Jeremy Jones?"

Samantha jumped. She had not heard Miss Wentworth come up beside her. The two women also started and turned to her companion. Their matching expressions of surprise and indignation morphed into confusion as they beheld Miss Wentworth's ashen face.

"Did you say Jeremy Jones?" Miss Wentworth repeated faintly. "He's dead?"

The first woman, quickest to recover her wits, nodded. "Found him yesterday, they did, by the river. Did you know him?"

"I...no...I...that is..."

She collapsed in a dead faint.

Samantha's arms went out a second too late to catch Miss Wentworth, but she dropped to her knees and lifted the young woman onto her lap. Golden curls spilled out as she untied her bonnet. Miss Wentworth's face was devoid of color except for twin, very faint, spots of rouge on her cheeks that Samantha was quite certain Lady Wentworth knew nothing about.

"Is she alright?" the shop assistant asked, coming to join them.

"She will be," Samantha assured him, rubbing Miss Wentworth's wrists. Then, turning to the two women, she added, "Would one of you open my reticule? There is a tin of smelling salts in there."

It was the second woman, a look of concern on her weathered face, that handed her the tin. The effect of the salts was swift, and soon Miss Wentworth was sitting up on her own, apologizing to the onlookers, a tinge of embarrassment deepening the rouge on her cheeks.

The women showed signs of wanting to stick around, most likely to learn the reason for Miss Wentworth's strange reaction to their news, but Samantha assured them she would accompany the lady home. Miss Wentworth herself said nothing, but allowed

Samantha to help her to her feet and guide her out of the shop.

"How do you feel?" Samantha asked once they were out in the cool air of Main Street.

"Not well." Miss Wentworth's voice was still weak even if her steps were more assured. "I think I ought to go back."

"Of course," Samantha said. "I'll go find your mother and—"

"No!" Miss Wentworth grabbed Samantha's arm. "There is no need to disturb her or Lady Bradwell."

"We cannot leave them stranded without the carriage," Samantha pointed out. "How else do you propose we return?"

"You're right." Miss Wentworth sighed. "I suppose I can wait here."

Samantha led her to a bench but, as they sat down, she saw a familiar figure striding up the street. Telling herself it was merely relief that made her feel so unaccountably happy at the sight of him, she stood up.

"Perhaps we might be able to return after all," she said.

*****

When Wyatt was summoned to Lord Bradwell's study not long after breakfast, he was surprised but pleased to find his host had company.

"Mr. Smithers came to inform me of his progress," Lord Bradwell said, gesturing to the constable, who stood to one side of the large mahogany desk. "I asked him to wait until you could be here. Figured you'd want to hear it, too."

"Thank you, sir," Wyatt said, coming to stand on the other side of the desk.

"Sit, sit," Lord Bradwell said impatiently, gesturing for them both to take the upholstered chairs that flanked the fireplace. "Bring them over here. It's dashed uncomfortable to be the only one seated. I don't want to have to crane my neck up at you, Smithers."

The chairs did not move easily, and there was a scraping and banging as Wyatt and Mr. Smithers maneuvered them to the desk. Once they were settled, Lord Bradwell gestured for Mr. Smithers to begin.

"Mrs. Jones confirmed the body is that of her son, Jeremy," Mr. Smithers said, sitting forward, as though desirous of making as little contact with the chair as possible. "She was quite upset, as you might expect, but she did convey her wishes to Doctor Caruthers. He'll be interred tomorrow."

"Tell her Bradwell Court will cover the expense of the funeral," Lord Bradwell said.

"That is most generous of you, my lord."

Lord Bradwell dismissed his thanks with a wave of his hand. "His death happened on our land. Until we learn what occurred, I feel somewhat responsible."

"Did she have any idea who might have done it?" Wyatt asked.

Mr. Smithers shook his head and sighed. "She's always been a bit blind about Jeremy. She insisted he was a lovely boy without an enemy in the world."

"Were you able to confirm when he was last seen alive?" Lord Bradwell asked.

"Half the village saw him in the pub around half past eight last night. He was going on about how his ship had come in and he was about to be richer than...well, than you, my lord."

"He'd come into money?" Wyatt asked, intrigued.

Mr. Smithers shrugged. "Jeremy was always bragging about one scheme or another of his, claiming it was going to make him rich. Everyone assumed it was more of the same."

"Would you mind," Wyatt asked, looking between Lord Bradwell and the constable, unsure whose permission he should request, "if I took a look around his house? To see if there's any hint that he wasn't just bragging this time? It could be related to why he was killed."

Mr. Smithers looked to Lord Bradwell, who nodded. "If you like," he said, turning back to Wyatt. "I'd suggest you do it soon. There's no telling when Mrs. Jones or some other relation will go in there and pack up his things."

"I'll come back with you now if you don't mind."

"Let me know what you find out," Lord Bradwell said, getting to his feet.

Wyatt and Mr. Smithers rose as well, and when the constable took his leave, Wyatt followed him out.

Jeremy Jones lived with his widowed mother and three younger siblings in a small, two-bedroom house near the greengrocer's. The exterior was unprepossessing, but the interior was swept clean, with fresh flowers on the hall table and a handful of framed photographs of a happy family. The photographs were several years old, and the late Mr. Jones featured prominently in them.

Wyatt and Mr. Smithers were let inside by a young girl with pigtails and a sprinkling of freckles who informed them that her mother was out visiting and she didn't know when to expect her back. The girl seemed to know Mr. Smithers and began to describe to him animatedly and at length the new doll her brother Jeremy had bought her the day before. After sending Wyatt a long-suffering look, the constable gestured for him to continue alone.

Jeremy's room, which he shared with his two younger brothers, was at the back of the house. Wyatt hesitated on the threshold, taking in the half-made beds of the younger boys, feeling a bit of an intruder. He wondered if he ought to have waited to secure Mrs. Jones' permission.

Reasoning that she would be happy enough when he solved her son's murder, Wyatt stepped inside. Jeremy's side of the room was cleaner than that of his brothers—the bed neatly made, no clothes lying on the floor. Wyatt moved as quickly as he could, not sure how long he had before one of the boys returned or the girl came to see what he was doing. He looked under the mattress and inside the clothes chest, running his fingers along the edges in search of a hidden catch that might open a secret compartment. He found none.

Then, as he shifted the bedframe back into place after checking beneath it, he felt the floor move slightly beneath his boot. Kneeling, he discovered a loose board which, when he prised it up, revealed a small cavity containing a rectangular package wrapped in rough cloth. Wyatt reached in and lifted it out. It was heavier than he expected and quite solid. When he unwrapped the cloth, he sucked in a sharp breath.

In his hands, he held a solid gold bar.

EIGHT

At first, all Wyatt could do was stare. Then, he registered the words stamped across the top of the bar: *Sawyers & Collins, Assayers*, along with one of the numbers Sir Rupert had told him to look out for.

Moving quickly, Wyatt, re-wrapped the bar and slid it into one of the deep pockets of his coat before replacing the floorboard. He was just getting to his feet when Mr. Smithers entered the room.

"Find anything?" the constable asked.

Not wanting to lie to the constable and equally unwilling to involve him in the mystery of the missing gold until he'd had time to sort things out, Wyatt opted for distraction.

"I expect by now you could reproduce that doll completely if called upon."

Mr. Smithers chuckled. "I don't mind. She's a good girl, Sally."

"It's time I headed back," Wyatt said, casting a final look around the room. "I'm sorry to have taken up more of your time."

"My son Johnny's handling the forge," Mr. Smithers said with a shrug. "He's used to stepping in for me when I'm needed as constable. Not that we've ever had a murder before."

They said goodbye to Sally and came out to the street, where their paths diverged.

"I meant to tell his lordship when I was up at the house," Mr. Smithers said, holding out a hand to stop Wyatt as he made to set off down the street. "There's been a stranger seen round here recently. An older man, none too tall, wears a green cap. He stops for a pint from time to time but never stays long and don't talk much."

"Do you think he might be involved in Jeremy's death?"

Mr. Smithers sighed and looked up at the sky, squinting in the noonday sun. "I don't know. But I've known most everyone in this village all my life. I'm not saying as they're all saints, but I can't imagine any of them killing anyone. Leastways, I don't want to imagine it. Do you see what I'm saying?"

Wyatt nodded. "I'll see what I can find out."

They shook hands, and Wyatt turned onto Main Street while the constable went in the opposite direction, farther into the village.

He hadn't gone more than a few steps when he heard someone call his name, and, turning, he saw Samantha hurrying towards him.

"I didn't expect to see you here," she said when she caught up to him. "What are you doing in the village?"

"I was here with the constable," he said. "What about you?"

"Helping Madge. I don't suppose you came in a carriage?"

"No, I came on horseback. Why do you ask?"

Samantha sighed. "It's Miss Wentworth. She's come over faint and insists she wants to return to the house, but I didn't want to strand Madge and Lady Wentworth by taking the carriage."

"Send her on her own, then," Wyatt suggested. "Tell Matthew to return with the carriage after he drops her off. You can assure Madge yourself when she arrives." When Samantha looked doubtful, he added, "Or do you fear for her health if she is left alone?"

"It isn't that. It was something she said—something I meant to ask her about. But I suppose she won't be up to answering at the moment in any case."

When Samantha returned after helping Miss Wentworth into the carriage and explaining the plan to the coachman, Wyatt asked, "What was it she said that concerned you?"

Samantha did not immediately answer. Instead, she watched him thoughtfully before saying, slowly, "I think she knew Jeremy Jones." His eyebrows rose and she continued, "When she heard some of the village women talking about his death, she seemed shocked. That was the cause of her faint."

Wyatt's mind raced with the revelation. Miss Wentworth, Sir Rupert's daughter, had known Jeremy Jones. That was the second connection between Mr. Jones and the stolen gold he'd found in an hour.

"That means something to you."

It wasn't a question. Samantha was watching him through narrowed eyes. He checked his ruminations and focused on her.

"It does," he admitted.

"Before you explain to me why you won't share the reason for its significance," she said tartly, "allow me to point out that I have, once again, provided relevant information to your investigation. Not only that but, if you wish to learn more from Miss Wentworth, I am much more likely than you to be successful in gaining her confidence."

Wyatt smiled in spite of himself. She was right, again, and she knew it.

"Very well," he said resignedly. "You have won your point."

He hadn't put up much of a fight. He hadn't even wanted to. He probably ought to consider why that was, but he didn't have the luxury now. She was watching him expectantly. He sighed audibly, a final token resistance, before launching into an explanation, starting with Sir Rupert's proposition.

By the time he had described his discovery of the gold bar in Jeremy Jones' house, they had walked from Main Street to the outer edge of the village and had begun the return journey.

"Do you really think Miss Wentworth stole that gold from her father?" Samantha asked when he finished speaking.

"She may have been an unwitting participant," Wyatt suggested. "Jones may have ingratiated himself to her and wheedled the necessary information from her."

Samantha shook her head. "I don't believe that. I don't think this Mr. Jones could have ingratiated himself with someone like Miss Wentworth. I met him, remember? He was arrogant and demanding. And he had a strong dislike of the upper classes."

"Miss Wentworth is not exactly of the first order," Wyatt pointed out.

"He wouldn't have made the distinction."

"And yet she did know him. She fainted when she heard he was dead."

"I will grant that she knew him in some capacity, but I cannot believe they were friends or that he had somehow sweet-talked her. Besides, what would have been the point of his doing so? You said this investment was something of a secret. How would Mr. Jones have heard of it in the first place? Why would he imagine Miss Wentworth to know anything of it? I can't think that her father would have shared such information with her."

"She may have overheard it." Wyatt ventured. "Perhaps she wanted the gold for herself and reached out to Mr. Jones to do the actual stealing."

"But she and her family came to Bradwell less than a fortnight ago, and the gold was stolen more than a month before that. How would she have known him to involve him?"

Wyatt sighed and ran a hand through his hair. "I don't know. It seemed such a solid connection—finding the gold bar in Jones' house, then learning that Miss Wentworth knew him."

They were silent for a moment, then Samantha spoke.

"If there's one thing I am certain of, it's that Miss Wentworth was shocked to learn of Mr. Jones' death. She could not have faked that pallor, and why would she have? If she and Mr. Jones were involved in the disappearance of the gold, they cannot have been the only ones. After all, he is dead, and if she didn't kill him, someone else did—someone who knew about the gold."

"That must have been why she was so frightened," Wyatt said. "She must know who killed Jones and be afraid for herself."

"Who could it be? You don't think Sir Rupert..."

"No." Wyatt shook his head. "He asked me to help him find the gold. If he were searching on his own, why ask me? And if he did find Jones, he would have been better served leading me to him than risking so public a murder, knowing I might discover the connection and expose him. It must be someone else."

"It might be anyone," Samantha said dispiritedly. "If Miss Wentworth is one of the conspirators, the others need not necessarily be connected to Sir Rupert or Colchis Enterprises. It could be a friend of Mr. Jones or someone else entirely. However will we find them?"

Her use of the word "we" struck him, and he found that, despite his earlier objections to her help, he was glad of it. He liked that they were a "we."

"I think it's time I made a trip to Liverpool," Wyatt said. "I may learn something at the warehouse where the goods were stored before they shipped out. Perhaps someone saw something and, with the theft unreported, doesn't understand its significance."

"Good idea," Samantha said. "I'll see what I can learn from Miss Wentworth. It may be that, frightened as she is, she will appreciate a sympathetic ear."

She smiled at him then, and he couldn't help but smile back.

When Wyatt returned to the house, he visited Lord Bradwell in his study, aware that his host would expect him to report back after his visit to the village.

"Find anything?" Lord Bradwell asked, unconsciously echoing the constable's question.

"I did, actually," Wyatt said. "I'm not entirely certain of its significance, but I do know there was truth in Jones' boasts about coming into money."

"What did you find?"

Wyatt hesitated. As little as he liked Sir Rupert personally, he had promised him discretion. Of course, if the death of Jeremy Jones proved to be linked to the missing gold, he'd have no choice but to tell Lord Bradwell and involve the authorities, but until then, he thought he ought to keep his promise.

"I've been searching for some missing items of value," he said finally. "I think I may have found one in the Jones house."

Lord Bradwell frowned. "Are you saying he was a thief?"

"He may well have been. I'm not sure to what extent he was involved in the theft, only that he is tied to it in some way."

Lord Bradwell regarded him thoughtfully, absently stroking his beard. "The inquest will need to be scheduled soon. Do you have any definite information that might shed light on who killed Mr. Jones?"

"Nothing definite, no."

"If you do learn anything significant, you will tell me?"

"Of course, sir."

"Then I see no reason why you cannot keep your own council in this matter. I trust you, Wyatt."

"Thank you, sir."

"You are no longer a boy in short trousers, Wyatt. I think we may dispense with the 'sir' now, don't you?"

"Yes, sir," Wyatt said, as Lord Bradwell threw him a quick frown. "That is, yes. I think we may. Before I go, I should tell you,

I know how Jones received the other wound. The one the doctor said had begun to heal?" Lord Bradwell nodded his understanding. "It was Miss Kingston's maid, Alice, who hit him."

Lord Bradwell's eyebrows raised. "Miss Kingston's maid?" he repeated. "I was not aware she even knew him."

"I don't think she did. Miss Kingston met him while she was out walking one morning, and when he refused to leave her alone, Alice hit him over the head. He was knocked cold. The ladies came back to the house, and Miss Kingston asked me to check on him, but by the time I got to where she said she left him, he'd gone."

Lord Bradwell, never one to let the old school down by unseemly displays of emotion, barely blinked at what Wyatt considered to be a fairly shocking story. He hummed under his breath and then said, "I don't think anything need be said at the inquest. It's hardly relevant to Jones' death, after all. Unless you think this Alice went back to finish him off?"

"No s——. No, I don't think it's relevant."

"In fact," Lord Bradwell went on contemplatively. "I don't think we need involve Miss Kingston at all. My niece was with her, was she not? She can give testimony about discovering the body. There's no need to involve Miss Kingston's name in this unfortunate affair, don't you agree? Not after all that happened over the summer."

"That's very generous of you, s——, my...my lord." Wyatt grimaced with annoyance at himself for sounding such a fool.

"Bradwell, my boy. Call me Bradwell. And it's not generosity. It's practicality. Don't want a mess of reporters descending upon us and making a great to-do over such a small thing. You know they would, too. Make out that Miss Kingston is some sort of evil omen, bringing death wherever she goes."

Wyatt was sincerely thankful Samantha had not been around to hear that comment.

NINE

Brisk salty air blew across Wyatt's face as he stepped down from the hired carriage onto the crowded streets of the Liverpool docks the next morning. He adjusted his thick woolen scarf and pulled the brim of his hat down to keep it from blowing away as he turned to pay the driver.

It was not difficult to find the particular warehouse he sought. A few coins tipped to a helpful dockhand had been all it took, and before long he found himself standing before a substantial brick building with the name *Wentworth Shipping* printed boldly over a set of tall double doors. The doors stood open as dozens of dock workers hauled large, heavy-looking crates to and from the building on the backs of wooden carts. Wyatt took advantage of the confusion of noise and people to slip inside.

The inside of Wentworth Shipping was even more impressive than its outside. Four stories high, it was completely open, as though someone had carved out its insides, leaving the building an empty shell. Unobscured by walls or floors, sunlight filtered down through a line of narrow windows just under the roof. On the far wall, a set of rooms constructed of steel and glass sat on a platform where the second story might have been, a narrow set of metal stairs leading up to them. Otherwise, there was nothing but row upon row of crates stacked two, three, and even four high, separated by wide pathways along which burly men pushed wheeled trollies, loaded with cargo.

Wyatt made his way casually along one row and then another, noting the markings on the crates that proclaimed their destinations and the ships that would carry them there. The sheer number was overwhelming, and Wyatt realized how difficult it would be to find a single crate among the hundreds unless one already knew where to look. He could think of only two possibilities. Either the thief, or thieves, had spent several hours scouring the warehouse for his quarry, or he knew where it had been stored. In the first case, he would have had to come after the gold was loaded in that morning and spent the afternoon skulking around, most likely dressed as a dock worker to blend in. In the second, he must have either been present during the process or had it described to him by someone who was. In either case, the thief was someone who knew precisely which day the crate would be brought in and when it would be taken out. It was not a crime of opportunity.

"Oy! You there!"

The voice that hailed him came from the balcony of the set of rooms, and as he looked up, Wyatt saw a man glare at him, then hurry down the narrow steps that led to the main floor. His sleeves were pushed up to the elbows, revealing muscular forearms and skin that was tough and sun-bronzed.

"Just what do you think you're doing in here?" the man asked as he approached Wyatt.

"Are you the foreman?" Wyatt replied easily. "Good. I was hoping to have a word."

"Were you?" asked the foreman with a curl of his upper lip. "And who might you be?"

"V.T. Wyatt. I work with Sir Rupert." In a sense, this was true. He'd briefly considered using an alias, but he didn't mind Sir

Rupert's being informed of his presence. The only reason he hadn't told him ahead of time was to ensure that no one at the warehouse was prepared for his visit.

"Do you now?" The foreman's voice was heavy with skepticism.

"Yes. He's busy at a house party in Derbyshire, but he's asked me to look into a few things in his absence."

The foreman's brows lifted, and some of the suspicion eased from his expression, replaced by curiosity as he looked Wyatt up and down. Clearly, Wyatt's accurate knowledge of Sir Rupert's current whereabouts had given him pause, and the evidence of Wyatt's class, seen in the tailoring of his coat and the shine of his shoes, added credence to his story.

"I won't take much of your time," Wyatt said, pressing his advantage. Using information he had gleaned from his second conversation with Sir Rupert, he added, "Sir Rupert told me you have a ship coming in tonight or tomorrow, so I'm sure you're busy preparing for that."

That seemed to have done the trick, but the foreman, not one to concede easily, said, "I'll be sending my report after we've processed the cargo, and I'll be sure to let him know how your visit went."

"You do that. I know he will appreciate having your perspective."

"What is it you want?"

"I just have a few questions about your security."

"Planning to set up your own warehouse?" the foreman asked shrewdly. "Or joining up with Sir Rupert?"

"Do you think he would have sent me if I were in danger of becoming competition?"

His question was rewarded with a laugh, and the foreman gestured for him to follow as he led him up the metal stairs to the balcony.

"Cargo comes in through there," he said, gesturing to the front doors. "It's logged and stamped with its destination, then carted off to be stored until it's time to load it on the ship."

"Is there a pattern to how the crates are stored?"

"Not so's you'd notice. It's more about where there's room. But each section has a number, and that's recorded in the log."

"Where is the log kept?"

"With me. Soon's we're done cataloging a shipment, my second brings it to me, and I lock it in my office. And before you ask, I've got the only key." He reached into his shirt and pulled out a thin chain that hung around his neck from which dangled three metal keys. "It comes home with me at night. More 'n my job's worth, that book."

"What about the warehouse itself?" Wyatt asked. "Who has the keys to that?"

"There's two doors with keys: the front door and the side." The foreman gestured to a small door on the other side of the room, hardly noticeable in that vast space. "Only Sir Rupert and I have keys to the front door. There's an extra copy of the side door key for the night guard."

"Night guard? Is there only one?"

"Only one with a key. Two altogether."

Wyatt frowned. It hardly seemed like adequate security.

"Night watchmen might be a better name," the foreman explained, correctly interpreting Wyatt's silence. "No one expects them to fight off a thief. They're there to alert the police of anything suspicious."

"And has that ever happened?"

"More often than you'd think. It's mostly drunken idiots what's lost their way, but there've been a few attempted break-ins. All stopped before any real damage was done."

"That's good," Wyatt said distractedly. "These night watchmen, they've never fallen asleep on the job?"

"That's why there's two," the foreman said with annoyance. "They keep each other awake. Patrol the perimeter every half hour or so. And they're not allowed drink on the job."

"Of course," Wyatt said penitently, kicking himself for setting the foreman's back up by his careless handling of the inquiry. "It's an ingenious system."

The foreman was not soothed by his poor attempt at flattery. "Was there anything else, sir? Only I've got work to do."

"No, there's nothing else," Wyatt said, recognizing that he would get no further help from this quarter, especially as, with Sir Rupert's insistence that no one be informed of the theft, he couldn't ask more pointed questions. "I thank you for your time."

As he descended the steps and began to make his way back through the warehouse, Wyatt considered how the theft of the gold might have occurred. There had been no break-in, or the damage would have been reported to Sir Rupert, which had to mean the thieves used a key. As it was unlikely that those with a key —the foreman and the night watchman—would continue to work at the warehouse while sitting on a large pile of gold, the logical conclusion was that the key had been taken by the thieves and returned after the theft.

"Excuse me," Wyatt said, approaching a man pushing a trolley out the main door of the warehouse. "The night watchmen, do you know their names?"

The man bent to lift a crate onto the trolley, the muscles of his back rippling under his shirt.

"Cartwright," he grunted without looking at Wyatt. "And Jenkins."

"Do you know where I might find them at this time of day?"

"Down the pub."

"Which pub?"

"Sailors' Delight."

"And that would be where?"

The man finally looked at him, irritation written across his features as he pointed with a hand the size of a dinner plate in the direction from which Wyatt had come. Wyatt thanked him and left him to his work.

To Wyatt's surprise and relief, the dockworker's vague directions were all he needed. The Sailors' Delight was situated on a corner two streets from the warehouse. When he entered the pub, it took his eyes a moment to adjust to the dimness. It was then immediately apparent that blending in would not be an option for him. Clearly a working man's establishment, The Sailor's Delight was filled with burly, sun-darkened men whose clothes were nearly as dirty as the floor under their mud-caked boots.

Knowing his welcome, if he had any, would be short, Wyatt spoke without preamble. "Cartwright? Jenkins?"

No one answered, but, even as most gazes dropped to their drinks, a few furtive looks were sent towards the front window where a man of about forty sat, hunched over with eyes downcast, mercifully alone. Wyatt made his way over to the man and took a seat across from him.

"Am I addressing Mr. Cartwright or Mr. Jenkins?"

The man eyed him with suspicion but said nothing.

Wyatt lowered his voice, keenly aware that whatever talk his entrance had interrupted had yet to resume around him. "You work at Wentworth Warehouse, do you not? As a night watchman?" When the man gave no reply, Wyatt leaned forward, planting his elbows on the table and crossing his arms. "Very well. If you won't talk, I will. I'd like to tell you a story. You let me know if I get any of it wrong." The man took a swig from his tankard and eyed him balefully. "There was once a hard-working night watchman who risked his neck every night doing a job for which he received little support from his superiors. The money he was paid for this was hardly worth the effort. Then one day, someone approached him with an opportunity to make a little extra. All he had to do was look the other way for an hour or so while a cart entered and left the warehouse. The person who approached him assured him that nothing would be discovered missing and no harm would be done. How am I doing so far?"

The man had paled beneath his tan. He set the tankard he had been in the process of bringing to his lips down with enough force that the amber liquid splashed out and onto the battered table.

"I don't know what you're talkin' about," he said quickly.

Wyatt had not been certain until that moment if the night watchman was involved in the theft or merely oblivious to it. Tamping down his excitement at discovering such a promising lead, he pressed on. "Unfortunately for you, the theft was discovered. However, it can still be no harm done if the missing items are returned."

"I don't know what they took, and I don't know where it's gone," the man said, abandoning all pretense.

"Of course not. You do, however, know who took it."

"I don't. He never said his name."

"You know what he looks like, though."

The night watchman glanced around the bar. Talk had resumed, though covert looks still flashed their way.

"He were old—grey hair, thin on top—but still strong I'd say, though his back weren't straight. It were dark when I met him, so I can't tell you what color his eyes were or nothing and his clothes was all dark."

"What about his build?" Wyatt asked. "You said he was strong. Was he bulky, thin, fat?"

Looking up at the ceiling as though trying to recall, the man said hesitantly, "I'd say thin, but it were hard to tell, it being so dark."

"What did he say to you? Could you tell anything by his accent?"

"He weren't foreign if that's what you're getting at. Not from around here, though."

Wyatt nodded abstractedly, committing the information to memory.

"Is that all?" the man asked. "I don't know what else to tell you."

"It's enough." Wyatt pushed back his chair and stood.

"You said no harm done. Does that mean I keep my job?"

Wyatt considered the matter. With Sir Rupert intent on recovering the gold quietly, it seemed unlikely the matter would come to a trial, meaning that, unless he reported it himself, no one need know about the man's involvement. He also thought it likely that, having already been caught once, the night watchman would be less likely than a new hire to take a bribe.

"You can keep your job," he said finally, "but don't expect leniency if it happens again."

"Thank you."

As he walked back to the main road where he intended to hail a cab, Wyatt remembered Mr. Smithers' parting comment to him about the old man who had been seen around the village. He had dismissed the information at the time, taking it in the spirit in which Mr. Smithers had offered it—a desire to point the finger anywhere but into the village. Yet he could not discount that he now knew of two old men connected with the case. Were they one and the same? With such vague descriptions, it was impossible to know for certain, but it was something to consider.

*****

Samantha's plans to gain Miss Wentworth's confidence were hampered by her keeping to her room for most of the day following their trip to town. She did, however, have an odd encounter with the lady's brother in the hall not long after the arrival of the post.

Oliver Wentworth was long and lanky, with a narrow face and

a mouth set in a permanent frown. He had, thus far, made little effort to ingratiate himself with his hosts or to befriend any member of the party other than Lord Linwood. Thus, it was a surprise when he appeared suddenly beside her as she exited the music room.

"Good morning," she said.

"Morning," he responded, with a stiff bow.

"You're up early," Samantha observed, for lack of anything better to say.

He grunted, then stepped around her to rifle through the post. On discovering a large, rather thick envelope, he slid it from the stack and tucked it under his arm.

"If you'll excuse me," he said, inclining his head.

He left without another word, and Samantha wondered what about that thick parcel was so important that he couldn't wait to receive it until breakfast, when the post was generally handed out.

Waiting for Miss Wentworth gave Samantha time to think. She considered everything she knew about Fanny Wentworth and compared it to all she knew of Jeremy Jones. It was not a long list for either of them, so it wasn't long before a connection appeared.

Samantha had met Mr. Jones at the abbey, and it wasn't far from there that he had been found dead. Miss Wentworth had been very interested in the abbey even before they visited it. In fact, it had been her story that had interested the others in going. Then, once there, she had wandered off on her own and been seen by Samantha and Wyatt reading a letter—a letter she was keen they not ask her about. She was so keen, in fact, that she had tried clumsily to direct Samantha's attention away from it later.

If Mr. Jones and Miss Wentworth were both involved in the theft of the gold, it would have been difficult for them to communicate in the normal course of things. What if the abbey was a meeting place for them? Or, if not a meeting place, a sort of makeshift postbox? It would have been easy to hide a letter among the stones of the ruin. It may have been that Miss Wentworth's ghost story had been a clever ruse to orchestrate a trip there so that she could pick up a letter from Mr. Jones, perhaps even leaving her own message at the same time. Moreover, if she had left a message, Mr. Jones, already dead in the river, wouldn't have picked it up, and Miss Wentworth, having just now learned of his death, wouldn't have had time to retrieve it.

The more she considered the idea, the more certain Samantha became. The abbey was the key. If she could find that meeting place or postbox, she might find a clue, be it a letter or something else, to understanding how the murder and the gold were connected. However, with her previous unwanted encounters there —first with the rude, but alive Mr. Jones and then with his corpse —she did not feel that going alone, or even with only Alice, was a good idea.

"I'm still not entirely certain I understand what we're doing here," Lord Aston said as they picked their way over the tumbled stones of the abbey a few hours later, having left the carriage at the foot of the hill with Alice keeping the driver company. "Not that it much matters, of course. Any excuse to be in your company."

Samantha smiled at his careless flattery. "I'm looking for something," she said, using the toe of her boot to upend a small slab. "And before you ask, I don't know exactly what."

"Intriguing. A mysterious treasure hunt. Is there anything in particular I should look out for?"

"Strange men lurking in the shadows with cudgels," she suggested.

"Ah, I see. Am I your knight in shining armor, then? Here to protect you from dragons?"

"Something like that."

"I would have thought you'd have asked Wyatt for that service," he said, and there was a sly note in his tone that made her avoid his gaze.

"He is away this morning," she said as blandly as she could.

"Is he? He didn't tell me. I suppose he left in the wee hours, did he? Before decent people are awake."

"I assume so."

They walked in silence for a few minutes. Samantha ran her hands along the pillars in the great hall, pushing and pulling at the stones within arm's reach.

"He thinks very highly of you, you know," Lord Aston said suddenly.

"Does he?" Her casual tone belied her thoughts, which were thrown into turmoil by his words. She was equally pleased to hear the secondhand praise and irritated that it mattered to her what Wyatt thought of her.

"Yes, I've never heard him talk so much about one lady. It's a bit annoying, actually."

She laughed to cover her embarrassment. "I'm sorry to have been the cause of any vexation to you, my lord, but it was natural for him to speak of me when we were so thrown together this summer. I'm certain he will do so rather less as our paths diverge."

"Do you think so?" She looked over at him and saw an uncharacteristically thoughtful expression on his face. "You are quite a remarkable woman, Miss Kingston."

Flustered by his directness and the seeming sincerity of the compliment, Samantha demurred. "Hardly. I am merely a woman who has been faced with some rather remarkable circumstances."

"At the risk of being called ungentlemanly, I must contradict a lady. I would argue that at least some of those circumstances came as a result of your remarkable character. But I see I have made you uncomfortable. I merely wished to point out that Wyatt has seen in you what I expect others will soon, but I wish to put in a good word on my friend's behalf before you are inundated with offers."

Samantha gaped at him. She had just wrapped her head

around the idea that Wyatt had complimented her to his friend, and now Lord Aston seemed to think he might propose. She could not believe it, though. A few odd moments aside, he hadn't given any indication that he felt more than friendship for her. At least, he had never said anything. Besides which, he knew how she felt about marriage. He wouldn't offer for her and, no matter how he might make her feel, she would never allow herself to accept him or any other man.

"If I am inundated with offers," she said finally, choosing to avoid the subject of Wyatt, "it will be because of the virtues of my pocketbook rather than my person."

Lord Aston grinned. "I am not denying that the majority of your admirers will be out to improve their fortunes rather than your own. Believe me, it is the type of admirer I am most familiar with myself. However, I think you underrate yourself if you imagine none of them will seek you out for your own sake."

"Even if that is so, Wyatt will not be among them. He is...that is...we are on good terms now, but we aren't always."

"You mean you're as stubborn as he is and neither of you will budge?"

She couldn't help but smile at his frankness. "No; that is, he is stubborn, and I suppose I am as well, but our relationship is...is not romantic in any way." It was the truth. It had to be. She put a hand to her forehead. "I cannot believe I am having this conversation with you."

He laughed. "Very well. We shall set aside the question of your and Wyatt's relationship."

"Thank you."

"For now." He laughed again as she frowned at him. "If I'm to take you at your word that there is nothing in the nature of romance between you two, I don't suppose you would mind doing me a favor?"

She narrowed her eyes. "What sort of a favor?"

There was still a playful tilt to his mouth, but his eyes had lost their mischievous twinkle as he continued, "My father has taken an uncharacteristic interest in my affairs of late and has hinted that he would like to see me married soon. It has been the dearest wish of my mother for some time now, so she supports him completely in this."

"I take it you do not."

He grimaced. "I know I shall marry eventually—the title demands it—but I cannot say I look forward to the prospect. I do think, however, that this sudden interest of my father's will be short-lived. If I could show regard for a lady for a Season, it would make him believe I was acceding to his wishes. Then, when something or other takes his fancy, the lady and I can part ways amicably. Naturally, I do not wish to lead a lady to believe I am more serious than I am—"

"So you thought of me," she finished for him.

"You are the sole lady of my acquaintance between the ages of seventeen and thirty who does not wish to marry me."

"Oh, I don't know. You are quite the prize. Perhaps I ought to consider it."

"As tempting as that is, I like you too much to subject you to my flaws. Though I doubt I'd need to worry about that, as Wyatt would have called me out long before the marriage even took place."

They were veering in a direction Samantha did not wish to go. Clearing her throat, she said, "Very well. May I think on it?"

"Take all the time you need. We have until the Season begins."

Having settled the matter foremost on his mind, Lord Aston gave Samantha space to resume her search of the abbey. She found his request extraordinary, yet at the same time, she considered how beneficial it might be for her as well. With most of Society thinking she was interested in Lord Aston, the gossip around her and Wyatt might die down, and she might also be saved from some unwanted attention from other suitors.

When she was near the courtyard she had last visited with Wyatt, it started to rain. Knowing Lord Aston would wish to leave, she decided to take a final look around. She lifted herself onto the window ledge, swung her feet around and dropped into the courtyard. Her boots crunched through the dirt as she made her way along the edge, running her hands over the stone. She heard footsteps behind her.

"I'm almost ready," she said. "Do you mind waiting just a few more minutes?"

A trickle of doubt ran down her spine when he did not immediately reply but, just as she began to turn her head to look behind her, she felt a sudden, sharp pain, and everything went black.

*****

It was mid-afternoon when Wyatt returned from Liverpool. He expected that most of the inhabitants of the house would be taking tea, so he was surprised when Bingo came hurrying into the entrance hall as he was handing Headley his hat and coat.

"There you are," Bingo said, looking relieved. "I was worried you'd be gone all day."

"Why? What's wrong?"

Bingo rubbed the back of his neck and shot Wyatt a guilty look. "There's been an accident."

"What happened?" Wyatt asked, a knot twisting in his stomach. "Is anyone hurt? Is Madge alright? Was it one of the horses?"

"No, no, Madge is fine. It wasn't a riding accident. It was..."

"What? Out with it, man!" A sudden fear that, of all the guests, there was only one who could make Bingo so worried about his reaction made Wyatt speak sharply.

"Miss Kingston was attacked." Bingo spoke the words in a

rush.

Wyatt felt as though he'd been punched in the gut. "What happened? How is she? Where is she?"

"She's in her room. The doctor has been and gone. He says she was lucky. It was a glancing blow without much force behind it. She was only briefly unconscious. She has a headache, but he thinks, with rest, she will be perfectly well in a day or so."

"How did it happen?" Wyatt asked again, fighting to calm his panic. She would be fine. No lasting damage done.

Bingo winced. "She was only out of my sight for a minute or two. We'd gone up to the abbey, you see. She said she was looking for something. I can't tell you how awful I felt when I realized she wasn't nearby and I went looking and found her lying there, looking like she was—" He broke off and rubbed the back of his neck again. "I've apologized profusely, and she says she doesn't blame me, but I cannot help but blame myself."

Wyatt couldn't help but blame him, either, but he set aside his anger in his quest for more information. "You say she was out of your sight a matter of minutes. If so, you must have seen her attacker."

"I did see something," Bingo said hesitantly. "Of course, I was mostly concerned for Miss Kingston and, what with the rain, I was likely mistaken."

"What did you see?"

Bingo opened his mouth, paused, cleared his throat, then said, "I saw—I think I saw—a ghost."

"You cannot be serious."

"I told you I didn't get a good look," Bingo said defensively. "It was raining, and I only saw her for a second."

"Her?"

"I think it was a her. It looked like a veiled lady."

Wyatt gave him an incredulous look.

"You asked what I saw, and I'm telling you." Bingo sounded

annoyed now. "I didn't claim it made sense."

With a sigh, Wyatt said, "Can I see her?"

Bingo looked confused, then understanding dawned. "Miss Kingston? No. They've given her a sedative. But you can talk to her tomorrow, I'm sure."

Rumors of Samantha's ghostly attacker had spread through the house by the time the guests assembled for supper and was the prevailing topic of conversation through much of the meal. Miss Fanshaw was convinced the ghost had been that of Evelyn from Miss Wentworth's story and that Samantha had accidentally disturbed her final resting place. Sir Rupert spoke loudly and at length of the foolishness of believing in ghosts, insisting that the attacker had been a local vagabond. His wife, by contrast, recounted stories Madge's housemaid had relayed to her about the grey lady who walked the banks of the river.

Notably absent from the speculation was Miss Wentworth, who ate in silence, giving noncommittal responses when asked for her opinions. Wyatt found her reaction intriguing, especially given that it was she who had first introduced the subject of ghosts. Was it guilt that kept her quiet? Or fear? He was fairly certain she was not Samantha's attacker, having learned from her maid that she had spent the morning in her room despite the maid's frequent attempts to get her ready to join the others. She might have sent someone to do the deed, though he was at a loss to understand why. Had she somehow learned that Samantha was suspicious of her? He couldn't imagine Samantha being indiscreet, but perhaps she had told her maid some of her suspicions, and the conversation had been overheard?

As the pudding course was served, Madge suggested dryly that it might be better to avoid the abbey in future since visits to it seemed to have irritated the spirits so.

"I cannot understand why it should have become so popular

in the first place," she said, waving away a footman who was attempting to refill her glass of claret. "I've never been able to interest anyone in it before."

TEN

When Samantha woke the next morning, the throbbing in her head had lessened considerably, though it remained a constant reminder of her harrowing adventure the day before. She hadn't been long unconscious, which the doctor said was fortunate. She had awakened in Lord Aston's arms mere minutes after the attack as he carried her down the hill. He had apologized profusely for not protecting her, but at the time, she had been more frustrated that her attacker had gotten away so quickly. Lord Aston's vague descriptions of a ghostly spectre she had dismissed as the product of some sort of guilt-ridden hysteria.

It was a mystery to her why she had been attacked at all. It was not as though she had made any significant progress in her search either for the rest of the missing gold or for Jeremy Jones' killer. She and Wyatt had just decided to work together. The only person who knew Wyatt was investigating was Sir Rupert and, as far as she was aware, no one knew she was helping. Was it possible that someone had overheard their conversation in the village? Yet, even if they had, why attack her and not Wyatt? Or was Wyatt also in danger?

She was getting nowhere by speculating. She needed to talk to

Wyatt. However, before she met with him, she wanted some useful information to share and, for that, she needed to find Miss Wentworth.

A maid directed her to the morning room, where Miss Wentworth sat at the writing desk, filling a piece of foolscap with small, tightly spaced letters. When Samantha entered, Miss Wentworth jumped.

"Oh, it's you, Miss Kingston," she said, placing a hand to her heart. "I was afraid you might be Mama. How are you feeling?"

She gestured to Samantha's head with a grimace.

"Better," Samantha assured her. Then, before she could continue, Miss Wentworth spoke again.

"It is good you're here," she said, getting quickly to her feet. She bent down to add a flourish to the end of her letter before setting down her pen and blowing on the paper. "I've been meaning to have a word with you. Would you mind accompanying me to my room?"

Intrigued, Samantha agreed and followed Miss Wentworth to her room in the guest wing of the house.

"This will sound odd, I am sure," Miss Wentworth said as soon as the door had closed behind them, "especially as we do not know each other well, but I hoped I might beg a favor of you."

"What sort of favor?" Samantha asked, watching Miss Wentworth flit about the room, straightening the bed covers and rearranging the objects on the vanity. She displayed the same nervous energy she had when she happened upon Samantha and Wyatt at the abbey.

"It may be no use now, of course. He may have found out already that I meant to ask you and be expecting it. Or he may have no idea. After all, if he had been at the abbey, he would have seen you didn't have it with you, though he may have thought you'd already delivered it."

"Miss Wentworth," Samantha said, taking hold of the young

woman's arm. "If you truly wish my help, you must stop rushing about and speak sense. Would you kindly explain what you are talking about?"

Miss Wentworth stilled, and Samantha released her arm.

"You're right of course," she said softly. "I apologize. Won't you sit down?" She gestured to a pair of armchairs by the fire, taking the one opposite once Samantha had settled herself.

"It's not easy, opening oneself up to a stranger," she began hesitantly. "Though the attack on you shows *you* to be trustworthy, at least. You are certainly not working for my father."

"Your father?" Samantha failed to hide her surprise.

"I couldn't let him know to whom I was writing, you see. He would find out if the letters were delivered in the normal way. He always checks over my post, and he is very particular about whom he considers suitable correspondents. The man who was killed— Mr. Jones—I knew him. I think you must have guessed that from my reaction to learning of his death." She smiled sheepishly. "It was just such a shock. He was our go-between, you see. The idea was that, while I was staying at Bradwell Court, I would leave a letter in a specific place in the abbey and Mr. Jones would deliver it for me. If there was a letter for me in return, he would leave it in the same place."

"I see," Samantha said, careful to hide her excitement at hearing her theory proved right. She almost asked who Miss Wentworth's correspondent was, but she didn't want to scare her into silence by seeming too eager for information.

"It was not the most convenient spot," Miss Wentworth continued. "It was hard to find reasons to visit the abbey. That's why I told the ghost story. I hoped to convince the others to form a party. I never imagined there were real ghosts in the abbey." She shuddered, and Samantha had to stop herself from groaning aloud. Had Lord Aston really told the rest of the party his ghost theory? "It was what I had to do, though," said Miss Wentworth, "not knowing whom I could trust in the house."

"What is the favor you wanted of me?" Samantha asked, though she thought she could guess.

Miss Wentworth brightened visibly. "I hoped you might agree to be my go-between. There would be no need to involve the abbey anymore, so it would be perfectly simple. You can post my letters as your own and I will tell...my friend...to write to you here at the house."

Samantha felt she could hardly be surprised that Miss Wentworth could present the favor as perfectly simple despite the murder of her first go-between remaining conspicuously unsolved. She had so far been utterly wrapped up in her own concerns, even seeing the attack on Samantha as a mere test of loyalty. Did she hope Samantha might forget the murder, or did she honestly not consider murder a risk now that there was "no need to involve the abbey anymore"?

"I have a letter ready right now."

Miss Wentworth stood and hurried over to her vanity. She opened one of the drawers, lifting several items out of the way before extracting a thick envelope. This she brought to Samantha, handing it over with the confidence of someone who was used to getting her way. Samantha took the envelope and glanced at the address. The recipient, a Mr. Smith (she somehow doubted that was his real name), lived in Manchester.

Samantha briefly considered handing the envelope back and telling Miss Wentworth she did not know her well enough to risk her own life for the dubious pleasure of becoming an errand boy, but she didn't. After the previous day's attack, she felt she could consider her safety at risk whether she took on this extra task or not, and the chance to spy on Miss Wentworth's correspondence was too good to pass up.

"Very well," she said, looking up into Miss Wentworth's eager face. "I will send it for you. You may tell this Mr. Smith to write to me."

"I hoped you might agree," Miss Wentworth said, her face breaking into a broad smile. "I included the new instructions at the end of the letter. He'll know what to do."

Then, without warning, she leaned down and threw her arms around Samantha, squeezing hard. "You must call me Fanny. I am sure we shall be great friends."

Samantha, freeing herself with difficulty from the unwanted embrace, very much doubted this assertion, but she hummed noncommittedly as she stood up.

"If you don't mind, Fanny," she said. "I have some correspondence of my own to add to this. I should return to my room."

"Of course, of course." Fanny escorted her out cheerily. "You have lifted a weight from my shoulders. I cannot tell you how happy this makes me."

Back in her room, Samantha carefully broke the seal of Fanny's letter and opened it. It took her a few minutes to decipher the cramped scrawl, but when she did, she was disappointed. The letter was cryptic, making reference to past conversations and letters with no context. Fanny's rambling prose did not make understanding any easier. What Samantha was able to glean was that Fanny was in love with this Mr. Smith. The letter was peppered with "my darling," "dearest" and "my love" to such an extent that Samantha imagined she could have saved a full penny in postage if she had cut them out. If it hadn't been that Samantha was fairly certain Madge's son did not love Fanny, this revelation might have caused her to feel sorry for him. As it was, she reflected how glad Madge would be not to have Fanny as a daughter-in-law.

It was evident that Fanny was frightened. She told of the death of Jeremy Jones (designated by the single letter "J") and begged her darling to tell her what she ought to do. She looked forward to the day they could put this all behind them and hoped that might be soon.

Lighting a candle and holding the seal over it, Samantha softened the wax, then refolded the letter and pressed it shut so that it resealed itself. When she had finished, she dashed off a quick response to the most recent condolence letter she had received from a previously unknown relation. The request for money in this one was much subtler than usual, making it even easier to ignore. Then, taking both letters, she went to find Wyatt.

Wyatt was playing billiards with Lord Godwin and Lord Linwood. He looked up as she passed the open door, and his expression lightened as he caught her eye. With a subtle nod, he returned his attention to the table and finished his shot. Samantha continued down the hall. A moment later, she heard him make his excuses and he caught up her.

"How is your head?" he asked, proffering his arm.

"Better. It is still tender, and I worry I might have a permanent lump, but it could have been worse."

"It was bad enough that it happened at all. I ought to be thankful you didn't go to the abbey alone, but I confess I'm having trouble forgiving Bingo for leaving you unprotected."

"I don't blame him. I ought to have been more aware of my surroundings. Whoever struck me didn't appear out of nowhere. I should have seen something."

"Do you remember what happened?"

Samantha shrugged. "I wish I remembered more. I was walking along the courtyard, and I heard someone behind me. I thought it was Lord Aston, so I didn't turn around. The next thing I remember is waking up in his arms halfway to the carriage."

They had reached the library. Wyatt held the door open, and Samantha preceded him inside. The library had quickly become one of Samantha's favorite rooms in the house. It was long and lined on three sides with floor-to-ceiling bookshelves complete with a narrow balcony two-thirds of the way up. Tall, mullioned windows were spaced evenly along the fourth wall, their heavy, tapestry-like curtains matching the lush richness of the room.

"What I don't understand," she said as she sank onto her favorite sofa and Wyatt sat opposite her, "is why I was attacked."

Wyatt leaned back, throwing his arm over the back of the green and gold sofa. "I believe, with ghosts, it's generally because you've disturbed their rest."

"Most amusing. If that were the case, I would have been attacked long before now. I go to the abbey fairly often."

"So you told me. That being so, why now? Why not one of those other times, especially as you were alone then and much more vulnerable?" Wyatt eyed her speculatively. "Why did you go this time?"

Samantha explained her theory about the makeshift postbox and her search for it.

"And did you find it?" he asked.

"No, I didn't, but it's a moot point, because I now know for a fact that it was a postbox."

"How?"

"Miss Wentworth told me herself." Wyatt's eyebrows rose. She thought she had impressed him. "It seems she and a mysterious correspondent had been using Mr. Jones as a courier to avoid their letters being seen by her father. She says that's why Mr. Jones was in the abbey. It was where they exchanged the letters. Also, she thinks her father might be responsible for Mr. Jones' death."

"Does she? She thinks he would kill to keep her from writing to this person?"

His expression was dubious. She didn't blame him. Murder was an extreme reaction for a problem that might be solved by half a dozen simpler methods.

"I think she's being fanciful," she said. "Her father wants her to marry for status and connections rather than love, so she sees herself as Shakespeare's Juliet."

"She's writing to a lover? She told you that?"

"She doesn't trust me quite that much. I read her letter."

Wyatt looked surprised. "How did you manage that?"

"She asked me to be her new courier—"

"After the last one was murdered?"

She gave him a wry smile. "She thinks it will be perfectly safe for me as I can simply post the letters as my own—no sneaking around involved."

"You could still be in danger."

He looked angry. Samantha appreciated his indignation on her behalf, but she sought to reassure him.

"I was attacked before I agreed to become her courier. I'm in danger either way. I may as well take her letters and learn whatever I can."

Wyatt sighed. "I wish it weren't the case, but you are probably right. Did she mention the gold?"

Samantha shook her head. "If she is involved in the theft, and I am even less convinced she is after our conversation, it does not seem to be foremost on her mind. She was more worried about her father discovering her correspondence than anything."

"If the subject of the letters is the theft, she would be." Wyatt looked thoughtful, then he said, slowly, "I still think Jones' death must be connected to the theft. He had one of the gold bars. And I can't see Sir Rupert murdering the man only because he delivered some letters for his daughter. No, there is still something here, if we could find it."

"Miss Wentworth's correspondent could be involved," Samantha suggested. "He may have ingratiated himself with her and be using her in some way to aid in either the theft or the cover-up. She may not even know, or she may be so convinced of her love for him that she doesn't care. There is certainly no love lost between her and her father. I doubt she would hesitate to steal from him."

"You said she wants you to be her new courier?" Wyatt asked. Samantha nodded. "Where are the letters going?"

"An address in Manchester. Here." She handed him the letter. He scrutinized it.

"Mr. Smith is no doubt a false name, but this address must be real enough." He handed the letter back. "I haven't the time now with the ball this evening, but when she asks you to send the next one, I think I'll travel to Manchester and see if I can meet the man who picks it up."

ELEVEN

That evening, Samantha stood before the mirror of her vanity nervously adjusting the thin white fabric that served as a veil, covering her long dark hair as it flowed down her back.

"Stop fidgeting," Alice said. "I need to put on the crown, and I can't when you're shifting your veil like that."

Reluctantly, Samantha let her hands fall to her sides. She watched as Alice lifted the gold circlet set with diamonds from the velvet-lined box and placed it on her head.

"There." Alice twisted it slightly so that it settled into her hair. "Perfect."

Looking at her reflection, Samantha hardly recognized herself, though she supposed that was the point. It had been her idea to dress as Eleanor of Aquitaine—a knowing, somewhat bold reference to the medieval queen's status as a powerful heiress. Madge had thoroughly approved and designed Samantha's dress herself from a stained-glass portrait of Eleanor she had seen while in Poitiers the previous year.

The dress itself was a brilliant blue with flowing pink sleeves that hung down past her knees. The collar was threaded with gold and shone in the light. Not quite daring enough to follow the lines of the medieval gown faithfully, Samantha had requested the skirt be made fuller so she could fit a couple of petticoats beneath it. Madge had agreed this was for the best, voicing her opinion that Samantha had a few more years before she could risk being so unconventional.

"You look lovely," Alice said, watching Samantha smooth the lines of the skirt.

"Thank you," Samantha replied. "I feel...unsure."

"Well, you needn't. Now, go down before you change your mind."

Samantha adjusted her veil one last time before heading out into the corridor. She hadn't gone ten steps when a door to her right opened and Wyatt walked out. At the sight of her, he stopped short. His eyes widened and his gaze traveled up her body, lingering on her face. If she had any doubts about the effect of her outfit, they were banished by his next words.

"You look...beautiful. Your hair..."

Samantha ran her fingers through her long dark curls. "Do you think I ought to change it? It feels strange to leave it down, but Madge said ladies did back then and..."

She stopped speaking as he reached out a hand, his eyes fixed on her hair. Then he seemed to check himself. Dropping his arm, he shook his head.

"It's perfect."

"Thank you." Samantha released the breath she hadn't realized she was holding. Then, because she felt she ought to say something, if only to disguise her confusing medley of emotions, she said, "So is yours. Your costume I mean."

He was dressed in unmistakably Tudor fashion, with a heavily embroidered, fur-lined coat, a knee-length tunic and hose, and a pair of thin slippers. On his head, a flat cap sat at an angle, and he wore a false beard so long it nearly reached his belt.

"It's atrocious, isn't it?"

"No," she said, shaking her head. "Not atrocious. I think it suits you rather well, actually. But the beard..." She bit back a smile.

"I won't have you say anything against this beard." He stroked it thoughtfully. "That is the one part of this ensemble I am happy with. It's the tunic I can't stand. I really cannot fathom how any man could have thought himself to look well in a short dress and hose."

"I daresay someday people will say the same of what we wear now," she said, adjusting her veil self-consciously.

"No doubt." He held out his arm. "My lady."

She took it and allowed him to lead her to the top of the stairs.

"Who are you meant to be?" she asked as they walked.

"Can't you guess?"

"The beard is not that of Henry VIII. Sir Thomas More?"

"Close. Sir Thomas Wyatt, poet, and advisor to the king. My ancestor and Tom's namesake." When Samantha did not immediately reply, he added, "Are you so impressed with my illustrious antecedents that I have stunned you into silence?"

"Has that happened before?"

He grinned. "Never. Though I can't say there's been much opportunity for it. Those who might be impressed already know, and I don't go around boring those who couldn't be bothered."

"I don't know that I'm impressed so much as curious. I was trying to remember what I could of Sir Thomas. Wasn't there some sort of rebellion? Wyatt's rebellion?"

"That was his son, Thomas Wyatt the Younger. He led an attempted coup against Queen Mary, hoping to bring Elizabeth to the throne. It was unsuccessful. He was executed and his lands taken away. However, when Elizabeth ascended the throne, she did restore some of the land to our family. We lost the castle forever, but we got to keep the abbey."

"And you've lived there ever since?"

"And will continue to forevermore if my mother has anything to do with it. She sets more store by the name than any of the blood Wyatts ever have."

As they started to descend together, Madge appeared in the hall below them. Samantha's jaw dropped. Madge had chosen to represent Queen Elizabeth and had so outdone herself, she might have stepped straight from the famous Darnley portrait. The tailoring on her gown of light blue silk embroidered with yellow-gold flowers was exquisite, the lace at her neck and wrists delicate, and the feathers in her fan brilliantly colorful.

"Lovely," Madge said, clapping her hands together as she looked up at Samantha. "Exactly as I imagined it. Now, come down here so I can see you better." When they were all on a level, she raised an eyebrow and added to Wyatt, "Correct me if I'm wrong, but is this not the same costume you wore three years ago when the theme was the Tudors?"

Wyatt shrugged. "Is there a rule against repeating costumes? It fits the theme again, after all."

"Hmm. It speaks to a lack of imagination I would not have expected from you."

"I'm sorry to disappoint you, Madge, dear, but I wasn't even certain I would be in the country by December, much less in Derbyshire. There wasn't time to have anything else made that would suit your refined tastes."

"You, however," Madge said, ignoring Wyatt's excuse and turning to Samantha, "have chosen well. Though it is a shame we could not find a wig of sufficient quality and length. But perhaps it is for the best. Your coloring is not suited to such a shade as Eleanor's."

"Whereas you might have been Elizabeth," Samantha said.

"With enough white face powder, anyone could wear this awful ginger wig and look the part," Madge said, patting her hair. "But, thank you, my dear."

"Margaret, there you are." Lady Chesterton's piercing voice echoed across the hall moments before she strode into view. She wore an ermine-trimmed seventeenth century gown threaded with gold. The style of dress, combined with the small crown perched atop a pile of thick, sausage-like curls led Samantha to guess that she had come as Queen Anne.

"Here I am," Madge said.

Oblivious to the resignation that lined the smile on her sister-in-law's face, Lady Chesterton barreled on. "I noticed that you had not put out the silver Charles II candelabra, so I had it brought down from the attics and displayed on the mantle in the dining room."

Samantha saw Madge's smile tighten, but her voice was light as she said, "You are always so observant."

"I also had one of your footmen move the flowers from beside the musicians, where no one was likely to see them, to the other side of the ballroom."

"Did you? You needn't have put yourself to the trouble."

Samantha could feel Wyatt shaking with repressed laughter next to her. She had to bite her lip to keep from joining him.

"It was no trouble. I helped Mama with the Winter Ball for years, after all. She set such a standard."

"Indeed. If you'll excuse me, there is always so much to do just before the guests arrive."

Madge swept from the room. Lady Chesterton, after a brief exchange of greetings with Samantha and Wyatt, followed.

"I could watch them for hours," Wyatt said with a grin.

"I doubt they would last that long," Samantha said. "Madge would strangle her within minutes."

*****

Wyatt was no stranger to the lavish nature of Madge's Winter Ball. It was one of the biggest events of the year, and the presence of the nearby railway meant guests were able to travel from all over the country. Most of the guest wing was filled with those staying overnight and the ballroom itself was packed, with those not currently dancing spilling out into the nearby rooms and corridors. The music room had been fitted out with card tables, and one of the smaller drawing rooms had been designated as a place of retirement for the ladies.

As he made his way around the perimeter of the ballroom, Wyatt took note of the variety, or lack thereof, in fancy dress. The theme that year was Famous Figures of British History, and to look at Madge's guests, one would be forgiven for thinking there were only a round dozen such figures in total. Though he spotted what he assumed to be a William the Conqueror and an Alfred the Great, among the men, the most represented period seemed to be the late 17th and early 18th centuries, with several Samuel Pepys, Sir Isaac Newtons, and King Charles IIs. The number of curly wigs on display was frankly alarming.

As far as the women were concerned, he saw each wife of Henry VIII represented half a dozen times over so that, after he was introduced to his third Anne Boleyn, he found himself wishing someone would surprise him by arriving as Boudicca.

Tom was there, having come up that afternoon from London. His Samuel Pepys was typically unimaginative—the only method of distinguishing him from the other be-wigged gentlemen was a small notebook, no doubt meant to represent a diary, sticking out of one of his pockets.

"I'm surprised to see you here," Wyatt said as he joined his brother beside one of the Corinthian columns. "I thought you eschewed all forms of entertainment."

Tom did not even turn to look at him, keeping his eyes on the dancers. "Even you must realize that balls are the most logical places to form new acquaintances, firm up partnerships, et cetera. Half the men here are only here for business. However, I likely wouldn't have come this far if Benton hadn't asked me to bring him."

"Who?"

"Alistair Benton. Over there, dressed as Sir Francis Drake. Or was it Walsingham?" Tom nodded his head to the right and Wyatt looked past him to see a middle-aged man with dark hair and a pointed beard wearing an Elizabethan ruff. He was talking to Sir Rupert, who had come dressed as Henry VIII, straight out of the Holbein portrait.

"Who is Alistair Benton, and why did he need you to bring him here?" Wyatt asked.

Tom finally looked at him, his expression withering. "He doesn't know our cousin, so he asked if he might come as my guest. It pays to have a man like him in one's debt, so I agreed. As to why he wanted to come, he didn't say and I didn't ask. He works for the prime minister. All very hush-hush."

"I would think, in that case, that Walsingham was a bit on the nose, wouldn't you?"

"No doubt he found it amusing. He has an odd sense of humor."

"I imagine any sense of humor seems odd to you."

Tom ignored him, returning his gaze to the dancers. "You wouldn't think we were standing on the brink of war to see the way people are carrying on," he said dourly.

"What did you expect?" Wyatt asked. "This is Britain. Stiff upper lip all the way."

"There's stiff upper lip, and there's turning a blind eye. The cotton industry has already been hit and we aren't even at war yet. There will be shortages all around soon. Balls such as this will be a thing of the past."

"We may as well shut it down now, shall we?" Wyatt asked wryly. "Switch everyone to mourning? We haven't even had a response from the Americans yet, have we? They may apologize."

"I wouldn't hold my breath," Tom said. He paused, then added, "I wouldn't scoff at the idea of mourning either. The prince's health has not improved."

"I enjoy our conversations," Wyatt said. "They fill me with such optimism."

"Laugh now if you like, but we are headed for trouble, mark my words."

Wyatt sighed and walked away, leaving his brother to his dismal thoughts. He supposed he ought to consider some of what Tom had said. An effect of his overwhelming desire to know the right people and gain the power to enact change was that he did usually know what was going on in the halls of government. Of course, even those in the know could but guess at the Americans' response to Britain's request for an apology regarding the Trent Affair, and Wyatt didn't see the point in worrying over an outcome that was uncertain, but Tom must be right about the prince. He had been ill before, but this seemed more serious. Was he really near death?

Turning his attention to the dancers, Wyatt saw Samantha in Bingo's arms. They looked good together. Bingo had always been a good dancer, and Samantha's grace complemented his. Wyatt felt an unwelcome surge of jealousy. He turned away, refusing to indulge it.

He could no longer fool himself that he didn't have strong feelings for Samantha. The more time he spent with her, the harder it was to imagine being without her. She was clever, witty, and endlessly interesting. She spoke intelligently on a variety of subjects. He admired her courage and her determination. Her hazel eyes drew his gaze whenever she was near, and when she smiled...

He banished the image from his mind. Yes, she was beautiful and fascinating, but she was also headstrong and stubborn. That determination he admired he also hated at times, especially when she chose to ignore his advice and go her own way. Her courage sent her into dangerous situations without thought of her safety. A life with her would be far from the scenes of domestic tranquility he had once imagined when he considered his future.

*****

At Madge's insistence, Samantha had stood next to her and Lord Bradwell, greeting the guests as they entered. She understood why Madge had arranged it so—it demonstrated clearly to everyone Madge's and her husband's acceptance of Samantha's innocence of the events of the summer and their support of her going forward. Though Madge was not a frequenter of the London scene, she was still of upstanding reputation and good family, and Lord Bradwell's people had come over with the conqueror. It was the best stamp of approval Samantha could have received, and she saw in the manner of greeting from the majority of the guests that Madge's support was enough to ease their minds and their tongues.

There were still those, however, who regarded Samantha with curiosity, suspicion, and a malicious sort of excitement. As much as she tried to ignore those people and their unabashed stares and whispers, she could not. It was exhausting to smile and dance, aware that she was always being watched, but just as aware that she could not acknowledge the attention. She could feel the energy draining from her the longer the ball went on, her smile requiring more and more effort. She pasted it on again as Miss Thorpe and Miss Fanshaw approached her.

"I must say," Miss Thorpe said, taking Samantha's arm in hers. "I am in awe of your choice. Eleanor of Aquitaine, is it not? Quite the statement."

"The color does look lovely with your dark hair," Miss Fanshaw agreed, smiling shyly at Samantha. "I could never wear such a color, I think."

"You must think me remiss," Miss Thorpe said, adopting a

somber tone and lowering her voice, "to have, as yet, neglected to extend my condolences on the loss of your aunt and uncle. Such a tragedy."

Miss Fanshaw echoed her friend's sentiments, but with more sincerity. Samantha thanked them for their kindness, privately wishing they would take their condolences and their persons as far away from her as they could manage. Sir Arthur and Aunt Victoria were dead, and anyone who'd remotely cared about the fact had been at their joint funeral in August. That she should be forced to listen to the empty words of strangers months later and act as though she were grateful for them was galling.

"You must have been so scared," Miss Thorpe continued. "Running through the city at night in naught but your nightgown. You might have been attacked or accosted by some low-born man—"

"I beg your pardon," Samantha interrupted. "In my nightgown? You think I ran through the city in my nightgown?"

"Didn't you?" Miss Fanshaw asked earnestly, her eyes wide.

"Of course not," Samantha said indignantly. Then, seeing a few heads turn their way, she lowered her voice. "Where on earth did you hear such a tale? Running around in my nightgown? It makes me sound like the heroine in some gothic romance."

"Then what did happen?" Miss Thorpe asked and, too late, Samantha realized she had fallen into a trap. She had no doubt, watching the faint look of satisfaction on the young woman's face, that the nightgown story was entirely her invention. She had said something so absurd that Samantha was bound to react to it, opening the discussion of a matter anyone could guess she would be reluctant to speak about.

"Nothing so dramatic, I assure you," she said mildly. "I was fully dressed, and I walked to the Pall Mall. It was already quite late, or rather, early, when I left the house, and I had only a few hours to wait before the clubs opened and I could ask after Mr.

Wyatt."

"You do yourself a disservice, Miss Kingston," Miss Thorpe said with an affected laugh. "When you speak so lightly of the peril you were in. Walking unchaperoned at night and then going to a gentleman's club? I don't know where you got the courage."

"Naturally, I would have brought a chaperone if I could have managed it," Samantha said. "But with my aunt and uncle lying dead on the floor, my options were rather thin."

Miss Fanshaw gasped, but her friend made a poor effort of hiding her look of glee behind her hand. She seemed the type to thrive on drama and discord, and Samantha had no doubt her words would be repeated to whatever new friends Miss Thorpe made in the upcoming Season.

"Everything that happened I described faithfully to Mr. Canard," Samantha said, referring to Wyatt's reporter friend. "If you wish to know, you may read his account."

She removed her arm from Miss Thorpe's.

"Oh, yes, in the London Inquirer, was it not?" Miss Thorpe asked, arching a brow.

"Originally, yes," Samantha said. "Though it was repeated in all the London publications and, I do not doubt, many others across the country so that I don't know what purpose there is in any continued discussion of the topic. It is old news, now, surely."

"Forgive me, Miss Kingston," Miss Thorpe said, reaching out a hand to conciliate her. "I realize this must be a painful topic for you, but you cannot be surprised by our curiosity."

Samantha wanted nothing more than to walk away, but she had to acknowledge that Miss Thorpe was right. She wasn't surprised by their curiosity, and she oughtn't to be surprised by their tactlessness, either. This was only the beginning of what was to be a long Season for her, combatting rumors and insinuations about her character until the dust finally settled or some other scandalous event overshadowed hers. So, resigning herself to the inevitable, she remained where she was.

"What do you think of the men here?" Miss Thorpe asked. "I had not realized there would be so many eligible men in the party. If I had, I might have reconsidered my wardrobe."

Considering that the gown she wore draped so low across her bosom that she was in real danger of being charged with indecency, Samantha was not sure what reconsiderations she could have made.

"Lord Godwin is quite handsome," Miss Fanshaw said, blushing becomingly.

"I prefer dark hair, myself," her friend said. "I know Lord Aston is generally considered one of the best catches, if he could be caught, but for myself, I think Mr. Wyatt just as handsome. Do you not agree, Miss Kingston?"

Samantha closed her eyes to keep from rolling them at the transparent attempts to get a rise from her. When she opened them, she saw Miss Thorpe watching her, an expression of feigned innocence on her narrow face.

"He is handsome," Samantha agreed. "Perhaps you will be fortunate enough to catch his eye this Season, Miss Thorpe."

"Perhaps I might. Particularly if you were to help me. You must know him so well after your time with him. All of his favorite things to eat, how he takes his tea. Which paper he prefers to read in the morning."

If it weren't clear enough from her words, her tone dripped with insinuation, and Samantha knew she was meant to hear the implication that she and Wyatt had been sharing a bed, not merely a house. Anger boiled up inside her, but she kept her face impassive. Beside her, Miss Fanshaw was looking askance at her friend. It was clear now why Miss Thorpe had chosen that moment to have this conversation: They were out of earshot of all the older ladies of the party, Madge in particular. She would never have dared to say such things in their hearing. And, by choosing to have the conversation in sight of the rest of the ballroom, she prevented Samantha from retaliating as she might wish which, in that moment, was by blackening the young woman's right eye.

"I'm afraid I cannot help you," she said, standing up again. "My memory for detail is not what I would like it to be."

Samantha did not give Miss Thorpe time to reply, taking her leave of both her and Miss Fanshaw. As her next dance was free, she decided to escape to the ladies' retiring room.

The small drawing room that had been converted for the purpose lay just down the hall. When Samantha entered, there were a handful of ladies making use of it. A young lady she thought she recognized from her first Season in London stood still while a maid knelt before her, mending a rip in her hem. Two middle-aged ladies sat fanning themselves and chatting amicably. As Samantha crossed the room, another emerged from behind the screen that concealed the close stool used to relieve oneself.

Samantha chose the chair farthest from the door and sat down. She let out an involuntary sigh as the pressure was lifted from her feet. Then she leaned her head back and closed her eyes.

Miss Thorpe was not unique in her assumptions, even if she was more forthright in voicing them than other ladies might be. Begrudgingly, Samantha could understand the curiosity surrounding her adventure over the summer. Anything to break up the endless cycles of Season after Season, one blending easily into the next, was a welcome change. Yet understanding the sentiment did not make her like it, nor find its manifestations excusable.

Adding to Samantha's frustration was the knowledge that, if not for her aversion to feeding the gossip, she would even now be seeking Wyatt out. She enjoyed his company. He was intelligent and engaging. He made her laugh. He treated his servants with respect, and he was the only man who had ever made her feel like an equal.

However, as much as she hated it, she felt she should be thankful for the gossip and the limits it imposed on her relationship with Wyatt because she didn't feel only friendship for him. What she felt she refused to acknowledge even to herself. She was afraid that, if she did, she would ignore her convictions and do something she would come to regret.

A voice nearby startled Samantha from her reflections, and she opened her eyes to see Eden standing above her.

"I'm sorry," Samantha said, sitting up. "What did you say?"

"I asked if I could sit here." Eden gestured to the chair next to hers.

"Of course. Please do."

Negotiating the space between them with difficulty due to the wide skirts of her eighteenth century ballgown, Eden gave a huff of frustration before sitting down with something less than her usual grace.

"You look like Marie Antoinette," Samantha said, "but that can't be right."

"Queen Charlotte," Eden said. "It seemed a good choice three months ago, but now I am regretting it. I keep bumping into people with the sides of my skirts, and my neck aches from holding up my head." She gestured to her hair, which had been built up into a towering structure embellished with flowers. "I don't think she wore her hair like this regularly. She can't have. It must have been done especially for the portrait, and I was foolish enough to copy it."

"Well, it looks wonderful. And your gown is exquisite."

Eden slid her hand over the gold embroidered silk organza. "Thank you. I love your costume as well. Eleanor of Aquitaine? It's very apropos."

"I thought so."

"I've been meaning to ask you," Eden said, glancing around the room and lowering her voice. "Has my uncle said anything to you about the man—the body—we found?"

Samantha experienced a pang of guilt when she realized that, caught up as she had been in the mystery, she had failed to check on Eden in the aftermath of their discovery. They had spoken, yes, but not about the body. As awful as the sight had been for Samantha, Eden must have been affected as well.

"I haven't spoken to him about it since I sent him that day," she said. "Have you?"

"Just once. He asked if I would speak at the inquest."

"Did he? He didn't ask me to."

"I suspect he was trying to spare you the ordeal after this summer."

"Oh." It was a thoughtful gesture on Lord Bradwell's part, but Samantha wished he had told her himself or even let her decide whether to speak. Madge must have told him about her nightmares. Did he think her too fragile even to discuss the subject?

"I wish I knew who the man was," Eden said. "Did he leave family behind? A wife? I'd like to send her flowers and some food if I may. I know how hard those first days and weeks can be."

Samantha was ashamed that the thought had never even crossed her mind.

"He wasn't married," she said, "but he had a mother and siblings. Mr. Wyatt told me. I can ask him where they live. I'll send something, too."

"That would be wonderful."

An hour later, Samantha stood near the edge of the ballroom, half-hidden behind a pillar. Her feet ached and she could feel the beginnings of a headache. She was hiding from her dance partner, a local squire she had just met that evening, hoping he would give up looking for her and choose another woman. She didn't think she could stand one more dance or the several minutes of polite smiling that went along with it. She rubbed her cheek where her muscles ached from the effort.

"I heard she ran barefoot all the way across the city."

Samantha froze as a woman's voice drifted towards her from the other side of the pillar.

"In the middle of the night," the woman continued. "And she waited outside a gentleman's club until Mr. Wyatt arrived."

"All night?" echoed a second woman, her voice breathless and eager. "A whole night outside on the streets?"

Samantha squeezed her eyes shut and kneaded her forehead. She wanted to correct the woman. It hadn't been a whole night—the murders hadn't even occurred until after midnight—but she knew that hardly made the story more palatable.

"It's shocking, I know," the first woman said. "But I'm more interested in what happened after. Though they say that everything was above reproach, I have to wonder. After all, Lady Bradwell can't have already been staying with him. He would have had to write to her. They would have been alone until she arrived."

"Most shocking," the second woman said excitedly.

"Of course, it won't matter to her prospects," remarked the first woman with a hint of disdain. "She's fortunate she turned out to be an heiress. There are plenty of men desperate enough for money to overlook such a scandalous offense, but for myself, I wonder that she can show her face. She must know we aren't fooled by her lies."

Samantha rubbed her temples, wishing she could ignore the venomous whispers.

"Still," the second woman said. "It can't have been easy for her. What she must have seen. Can you imagine? And then to learn it was Sir Charles all along."

Samantha felt a pang at the mention of Charles' name.

"I was not surprised in the least," the first woman asserted. "I never met the man myself, but Edward did, and he said he was entirely without scruples. He'd been kicked out of his clubs, and no one would take his markers anymore because he could never pay. Edward says a gentleman always fulfills his markers above anything else."

"But to be killed like he was...What an awful end."

Flashes of that horrible day came, unbidden, to Samantha's mind and she squeezed her eyes tighter, trying to shut them out.

"Oh, certainly, certainly. You know, Edward's cousin Martin was actually there."

The second woman gasped. "No!"

"He didn't see the actual shooting, because he was in the courtroom already, but he came through after, and he saw him on the ground..."

Samantha held her hands over her ears. Her breathing had become laboured, and she closed her mouth, breathing through her nose. She could see him, too, lying there in front of her, blood pooling beneath him. She squeezed her eyes tighter. Now he was turning to her. *No, no, no.* Her eyes snapped open and she scanned the room frantically, looking for something, anything to distract her. But she was facing the wall, and there was nothing about the cracking paint around the baseboard trim to hold her interest.

Her breaths became shorter. She took her hands from her ears and held one over her mouth to muffle the sound. There was silence on the other side of the pillar. The women appeared to have moved on. Placing a hand on her chest, Samantha could feel her heart beating faster. Her vision had begun to cloud at the edges. *No, not her*e. She would not let it happen here.

Samantha gripped the folds of her skirt in her hands and willed her body to calm down. She counted down from twenty and then again from thirty as she breathed slowly through her nose. Finally, when she felt she had regained some control, she relaxed her grip and smoothed the fabric of her skirt with shaking hands.

She had been away too long. People would start to wonder where she had gone. With a final, calming breath, she lifted her chin and stepped out from behind the pillar. And right into someone.

TWELVE

Hands steadied her as she stumbled, gripping her by the shoulders.

"Pray, excuse me," she mumbled.

She looked up to see Wyatt, concern in his eyes. Relief washed over her and she felt herself sag a little.

"You look as though you could use some fresh air," he said.

"That would be nice."

Taking her arm in his, he led her to the French doors that opened onto the terrace. When they reached the window, they stopped.

"I'd rather no one saw us leave," he said, looking around.

"That will be difficult," she muttered.

She saw him catch someone's eye and followed his gaze to where Lord Aston stood by the door to the refreshment room on the other side. Some secret communication seemed to have passed between them because Lord Aston suddenly grinned and disappeared through the door. A moment later, a resounding crash echoed through the ballroom and every head turned towards the door through which it had emanated.

"Come on," Wyatt whispered, edging open the door to the terrace.

Samantha followed him, and he shut it quietly behind them. Then he took her hand and led her away from the windows.

"Are you alright?" he asked.

She nodded. Though talk had once again broken out in the ballroom, the sound was muffled through the doors. In the stillness and cold of the night, the worries and frustrations of the ball seemed just as muffled in her mind. She found herself focusing on the man before her. His eyes, so dark in the low light they were almost black, searched hers. A thick lock of hair had fallen over his forehead. Almost without thinking, she reached up to brush it away.

The silence was shattered as the door swung open and the noise from the ballroom increased. With a muffled oath, Wyatt took her wrist and pulled her farther into the darkness. The terrace was not large, and they were forced to conceal themselves in a narrow alcove behind the statue of a Greek god. Samantha found herself with her back pressed against Wyatt's chest as he wrapped one arm around her waist to steady her. She could feel his breath in her ear and the rise and fall of his chest behind her. Her own breath was coming in fast and unsteady, and she was having trouble focusing on anything but the feel of his arm around her.

At the sound of footsteps, she held her breath. She could hear the heavy tread of a man and the quick, lighter steps of a woman. They came within inches of Samantha and Wyatt's hiding place.

"Do you think anyone saw?" the woman asked.

Samantha had stifle a gasp as she recognized Fanny Wentworth's voice.

"I'm sure they didn't."

The man's voice was unknown to her. He spoke with a thick, unmistakably northern accent.

Fanny giggled. "How did you get an invitation? I didn't know you knew the Bradwells."

"I don't. Lady Bradwell invited a few of your father's friends.

I was one of them."

"Why didn't you tell me you were coming?"

"I wanted to surprise you."

"You certainly did."

It was quiet for a few moments. At first, Samantha strained to hear, not wanting to miss any whispered conversation. When she realized what she was hearing was actually heavy breathing, she felt her face color and she leaned back. That merely made her bump her head against Wyatt's chest, and she began to wish she could disappear altogether.

"Has there been any news of the shipment?" Fanny asked suddenly. "Has it reached port yet?"

Samantha felt Wyatt stiffen behind her.

"No news. Your father keeps saying it's to be expected, but I fear he's learned something is wrong and doesn't want to tell the investors yet."

"How much longer will we have to wait?" Fanny's voice was almost a whine.

"Not much longer," the man assured her. "I promise. Give me a few more days to finalize a plan, and then we'll be ready."

There was a brief pause, and then Fanny asked in a voice laced with fear, "Do you think he suspects?"

"Not a chance," the man said firmly. "Don't worry. Act as you usually do. I'll send you a message when things are ready."

There followed another few moments of uncomfortable silence. Uncomfortable for Samantha, that was, and, she assumed, for Wyatt as well. She was relieved when Fanny and her gentleman finally returned to the ballroom.

As soon as the door closed behind them, Wyatt released Samantha and slipped past her. He crept over to the door and peered through the glass to the room beyond. After a moment, he stepped back into the shadows and returned to her.

"Edward the Confessor, I think," he said. Then, placing a hand at her elbow, he began to steer her away. "We should go back in another way. We don't want to risk them seeing us enter and know we overheard them."

"We could use the library," Samantha suggested. "Or I could use the library, and you could enter through the front door."

Wyatt agreed to the second plan but insisted on escorting her first. They descended the terrace steps to the lawn and had started along the side of the house when the door to the terrace opened again. Light spilled onto the lawn beside them. Samantha looked at Wyatt and, without saying a word, they both began to run.

Samantha lifted her skirts to keep from tripping over them and soon found herself outpacing Wyatt. She glanced back to see him bending down to snatch up his beard, which had fallen off, and a bubble of laughter welled up inside her. He flashed a grin at her, and the laughter spilled out.

"In here!" Wyatt said a moment later.

She stopped and turned back. She had nearly passed the library. Wyatt held up a hand for her to wait as he stuck his head through the door checking to see that they were alone. Then he reached out behind him and pulled her inside.

It was dark. Samantha tripped over a chair leg and fell into Wyatt, catching herself with her hands on his chest.

"I'm sorry," she half-whispered, half-giggled.

She looked up at him and saw the laughter in his eyes. They were both panting from their run but, as they stood in the dark and quiet of the library, something shifted. She saw it in his expression first. Then the arm he had used to catch her tightened around her waist, pulling her closer. She could feel his heart beating beneath her hands. Everything around her seemed to fade away until all she knew was the rise and fall of his chest and hers and the intensity of his gaze.

Without another thought, their lips met.

It was...wonderful. Indescribable. She lost herself in the feeling of it, thinking of nothing but the warmth of his lips on hers, the silkiness of his hair as it slid through her fingers, the heat of his hands on her back. She couldn't breathe, but that didn't seem to matter.

When they finally broke apart, they were gasping for air. Then Wyatt began to trail kisses along her jawline and down her neck. She grabbed his lapels in both her fists and pulled him closer, delighting in the new sensations.

And then he spoke, his voice breathless and low, between kisses.

"Marry me."

Samantha froze, the heady, floating feeling that had overwhelmed her moments before swept away by the shock of his words. She heard his breath catch, as though he'd surprised himself by what he said, but then he pulled back and met her gaze with a vulnerability that proclaimed his sincerity.

Their nearness, which had seemed so natural, was now suffocating. Samantha moved away from him, feeling his hands slide from her as she did. She took several steps back.

"No," she said, her voice as breathless as his had been.

"No?" He looked bewildered.

"No," she repeated in normal tones, gaining strength as unexpected anger built up in her—anger with herself as much as with him. They'd crossed a line they couldn't uncross and their relationship would be changed forever. "I am sorry if I gave you the impression, especially after..."

"After that kiss?" He gave an ironic laugh and ran a hand through his hair, turning away from her before spinning back. "You can't kiss me like that and tell me you don't feel something for me."

She felt heat rise to her cheeks, but she refused to consider the truth of his words. Her feelings were irrelevant.

"I—that's not what I'm saying."

"Then what are you saying? Because I'd love to understand how you can stand there so calmly after that...kiss when I'm—"

"I'm not standing here calmly," she shot back. "I'm anything but calm. In fact, I'm furious."

"Furious?"

"Yes, furious. Because you are one of my only friends, and you've just ruined everything!"

"I ruin—I ruined everything?" His voice rose in pitch. "You kissed me back, or have you already forgotten that?"

Samantha threw her hands up in the air. "Alright! Yes, I ruined it. Are you happy?"

"No! Why would that make me happy? What is wrong, Samantha? I asked you to marry me, and you're acting as though I asked you to throw yourself in front of a horse."

She held a hand to her forehead, feeling the return of her headache as she continued, in a pleading voice, "But I told you I mean never to marry. We talked about it only a few days ago."

"Yes," he said with an agitated laugh. "But we spoke in hypotheticals. I did not think you would apply the same reasoning to me."

"Did you not?" Her tone sharpened with her irritation at his presumption. "And how are any of my arguments changed by it being you and not some hypothetical man that would be my husband?"

He stared at her. "How are they... because it's me! Because you know me. Because I would never mistreat you or be unfaithful to you or—How can you even ask that?" He took a step towards her, and his eyes searched her face, his brows furrowed. "Is that what you think of me?"

She was startled by the hurt in his eyes, and she mollified her tone. "No. Of course not."

"Then why—"

"Not now," she said pointedly. "You are not like that now. But who's to say, in five or even ten years, you might not become that way?"

"Who's to say?" He dragged a hand through his hair and began to pace before her. "Anyone who knows me!" He gestured to her. "You, I would have thought. Every fiber of my being. How can you think I would ever...Do you truly think so little of me?"

"Can I afford not to?" She blinked away tears of frustration. "For the first time in my life, I have a say in what I do, in whom I see, where I go. I do." She beat a hand against her chest as she spoke the last two words. "I have a power I never dreamed I could have. How could I throw that all away to put myself again at the mercy of a man?"

"Not *a* man. Me." He splayed a hand over his chest. "But I see that makes no difference to you. You will persist in tying my lot to that of this hypothetical man, of ascribing all his flaws to me, earned or not." She made a sound of protest, but he held up a hand, cutting her off. "No, I see it now. And not only do you not know me as I thought you did, but it seems I do not know you. Do you value power so much that you would choose it over love?"

"Love? What love? You never even spoke the word till now."

"Of course love! Why else would I want to marry you?"

She stared at him. He had spoken with irritation, anger even, but with conviction as well.

"I...did not realize," she said falteringly.

"I love you, Samantha." He spoke in a low, earnest voice that was almost a whisper. He closed the gap between them, taking her hands in his and holding her gaze. "I have for some time now, though it's taken longer than it ought to have for me to realize it. I cannot imagine a life without you. Will you please be my wife?"

She dropped her eyes to her hands, held so carefully, lovingly by this man whose friendship she had come to value, whose presence brought her comfort, whose smile brought her joy. She thought of their adventures together, of their conversations, of their laughter. What if she said yes? What if they married? She could imagine them at his home in Knightsbridge, discussing their plans for the day over breakfast, working on cases in his study. In short, doing much of what they'd done before, only without the need for a chaperone. And she could kiss him any time she liked.

But then doubts crept in. She thought of all the times he'd tried to stop her, to keep her from joining him, to tell her what she ought not to do. She remembered a conversation they'd had when they were first acquainted in which he'd held to the absurd belief that women's brains were more suited to things of the home than the problems of the world. Would he continue to hold to that belief? Now, they might be companions, but as his wife, that would change. He would expect her to order his household, bear him children, and leave him to his work. All the things she loved about who they were, what made them a team, would be gone, and she would be trapped.

Slowly, deliberately, she slid her hands from under his. She looked back into his face and saw a flash of pain before it hardened.

"I thank you for the honor of your proposal," she began. He scoffed and turned away. "And I thank you for sharing your feelings, but I cannot return them." He stood with his back to her, one hand pressed against the wall, his head down.

"I like you very much," she continued, determined to be as honest as he had been. "I greatly respect you, nor can I deny that I...am drawn to you." His head came up sharply and, after a pause, he turned to look at her, his eyes searching hers.

"But," she went on. "Anything more, I cannot claim. At least, not to the degree that you do." He slid his hand from the wall and crossed his arms, his eyes never leaving her face and watching her with such intensity that she almost faltered.

"Perhaps I could," she admitted. "Perhaps I could love you, if I allowed myself to." She looked away, took a steadying breath, and brought her gaze back to his. "But that I will not do." His eyes darkened and she felt his anger, but her conviction gave her strength. "This power you condemn me for valuing is easy for you to dismiss because it is one you have had all your life and will always have whether you marry or not. You have never known what it is to be without it. I have only just begun to explore it, to know what it is to decide for myself rather than being forced to bend to someone else's will. How can I return to my former restrictions after tasting such freedom?"

Wyatt's jaw stiffened. She watched his chest rise and fall once, twice. "How indeed?" he said, his voice a low rumble. "I perfectly comprehend your feelings—"

"I don't think you do," she said, shaking her head.

"Well enough, I am sure, as any hypothetical man can." His voice dripped with sarcasm. "If you'll excuse me, I should return to the ball."

As Samantha watched him go, she had to stop herself from calling out to him, from telling him she had changed her mind, that she *would* love him. It wouldn't be hard. She was most of the way there already. Yet she remained silent. She had made the right decision, she knew. Perhaps one day he would understand.

However, as Wyatt's form disappeared into the night, all she was left with was an overwhelming sense of loss.

*****

He hadn't noticed the cold on their run to the library, but as Wyatt stepped outside, it hit him full force. His legs, in those ridiculous hose, felt it the most. Still, he would rather be outside than spend another moment in that stifling room.

He was angrier than he could remember being. That she had

so low an opinion of him when he had thought she knew him better than most people, he could not fathom. Of course, he acknowledged that he could have handled the proposal better. He hadn't meant to ask her at all. The words had slipped out, though, and he realized he had been considering the matter, almost unconsciously, for some time.

It took nearly a quarter hour for him to compose himself enough to reenter the house and rejoin the ball. When he did, he determined to focus on what he had meant to do before his disastrous conversation with Samantha—to find Miss Wentworth's male companion and learn his identity. Yet, even as he searched the faces of the people around him, he felt that some of his enjoyment in solving the mystery had gone now that he was back to working on his own.

"Where have you been?" Tom asked, sidling up to him. "I've been looking for almost half an hour."

"I had to step out," Wyatt said vaguely. Then, finally spotting the Edward the Confessor he had seen earlier, he pointed him out to Tom. "Do you know who that is?"

"Some cotton merchant, I believe. Name of Allerton. Really, the people our cousin invited this year—"

"Excuse me."

Leaving his brother spluttering behind him, Wyatt made his way to Allerton, a sense of recklessness prompting him to be more direct than usual.

"Mr. Allerton?" he asked when he reached him.

The man turned, his surprise morphing to confusion as he beheld Wyatt.

"Yes?" he said hesitantly.

"The name's Wyatt. I hope you don't mind my introducing myself. I've just learned we have a mutual acquaintance in Sir Rupert."

"Do we?"

Though Wyatt hadn't needed the confirmation, he was nonetheless pleased recognize Mr. Allerton's voice as that of the man from the terrace. He was a little younger than Wyatt—perhaps five and twenty—but he carried himself with a confidence that belied his years.

"I only met him recently," Wyatt admitted. "He spoke to me about a venture you were part of. Colchis Enterprises, I believe it was called."

"Did he?" Mr. Allerton's tone was casual, but Wyatt noted the stiffening of his posture.

"Would you recommend it?" Wyatt asked bluntly. "Does it pay out well?"

"It's in its infancy," Mr. Allerton said carefully. "It was my confidence in Sir Rupert that led me to invest. As far as the payout, it is a long-term investment. We won't know that for some time. But surely Sir Rupert explained as much to you."

"We didn't go into specifics; there wasn't time. When someone pointed you out to me, I thought I might see what you thought. A more outside perspective, if you will."

"I see. Well, as I said, if it's a quick return you want, you had better look another way. If you'll excuse me."

He bowed and walked away. Wyatt watched him go in some frustration.

"Wyatt!" Tom's buoyant tones, reserved for those with whom he wished to ingratiate himself, warned Wyatt that they were not alone, even before the pressure of Tom's hand on his shoulder forced him to turn around.

Sure enough, he found himself facing, not only a beaming elder brother, but the man his brother had brought with him from London. Mr. Benton, if he remembered correctly.

"Quite the social one, my brother," Tom said, smiling even as he shot daggers at Wyatt, daring him to disappear again. "Wyatt, this is Mr. Alistair Benton. Benton, my brother V. T. Wyatt."

"It's a pleasure to make your acquaintance, Mr. Wyatt," Mr. Benton said, inclining his head.

"The pleasure is all mine," Wyatt said.

"I hope you'll forgive the impertinence," Mr. Benton continued, casting an apologetic glance at Tom, "but I hoped I might have a private word."

Tom's eyes grew round with surprise, but he recovered quickly. "Of course. Whatever you need."

As he left them, he sent Wyatt a look that was both annoyed and confused. Wyatt struggled not to laugh.

"Mr. Wyatt," Mr. Benton said, drawing Wyatt's attention back to him. "I'm not sure if you're aware, but I work on behalf of Her Majesty's government in a number of, shall we say, discreet capacities."

"Like Walsingham?" Wyatt asked, gesturing to the man's costume.

Mr. Benton permitted himself a small smile before continuing. "I asked your brother to introduce us because I believe it is possible I may have need of you in the near future, and I wanted to avoid any confusion on your part as to my legitimacy."

"You may have need of me?"

Mr. Benton nodded. "At this stage, I cannot be certain, but in my line of work, it is best to consider all possibilities."

"I don't suppose you plan to explain anything now?" Wyatt asked.

"Not as yet, no, but do not be surprised if I call on you at some point in the near future."

THIRTEEN

Everyone slept late the next morning. Samantha ordered breakfast to her room, keen to avoid Wyatt as much as possible. She'd had time to consider what had happened in the library—too much time, really—and she still couldn't quite believe it. What had she been thinking kissing him like that? She hadn't been—that was the problem. She had let her emotions take over, and Charles had taught her how little she could trust those.

If only she could reverse time and return things to how they had been between her and Wyatt. Yet, she doubted that would help. If what he had said the night before was true—if he felt as he claimed he did—last night had been inevitable. Perhaps it was for the best.

Her mind drifted back to the moment he had pulled her into the library and the look on his face as he gazed down at her. She could read his every emotion. And when he bent his head...She shook her head. She would not allow her mind to go there. It would only make her regret all the more that the moment could never be repeated.

Luncheon was a somber affair, and not just for Samantha, as Wyatt avoided her gaze. The newspapers had reported that Prince

Albert's health had worsened overnight to such a degree that the prince of Wales had been called home. Lord Bradwell was particularly despondent. It felt wrong, in such an atmosphere, to enjoy oneself, and so the members of the house party spent the day reading or writing letters in their own rooms. Samantha didn't see Wyatt all afternoon. Then, although the evening papers contained the encouragement that improvement had been noted around midday, everyone retired to bed not long after supper.

Sunday morning, when Alice entered Samantha's room, her eyes were red and she sniffed audibly.

"What is it?" Samantha asked in alarm.

"Oh, miss," Alice said, wiping her eyes with the back of her hand. "He's dead. The prince is dead."

Samantha sat back down onto the bed. "Dead? But yesterday he was improving."

"It was only temporary, the papers say. He got worse sudden-like and he passed in the night."

Samantha was stunned. The prince had only been in his forties, and with access to the best doctors in the land, however sick he may have been, she had never considered he would actually die.

At breakfast, the prince's death was the main topic of conversation. Lord Linwood and Sir Rupert were interrupted in their speculations about the political implications by a few choice words from Lord Bradwell.

"The man hasn't been dead twenty-four hours," he said in a quiet voice that nevertheless carried the length of the table. "Perhaps we could save that discussion for another day."

Abashed, the gentlemen were silenced. Samantha saw Lord Linwood shoot his father an apologetic glance, but Lord Bradwell's focus had turned to his meal, and he did not look up.

As Samantha reached for her water glass, she caught Wyatt's eyes. He was watching her with one of his enigmatic expressions but, once he saw her looking, he turned abruptly to address Miss Fanshaw, who sat on his right. Samantha swallowed her disappointment and focused on her toast.

"I imagine Her Majesty must be distraught," Lady Wentworth said, speaking to the table at large. "What a comfort to know that her children are all there with her, even Bertie."

"I doubt she finds Bertie a comfort," Lord Godwin said, carrying his overflowing plate from the buffet and taking the seat to Samantha's left. "She probably blames him for the prince's death with all the headache he caused them recently."

"What headache?" Miss Fanshaw asked. Samantha saw her flush as Lord Godwin turned his attention to her.

"This is hardly appropriate conversation," Lady Chesterton said firmly, giving Lord Godwin a hard stare.

"Forgive me, your ladyship," he said, inclining his head towards her. When Lady Chesterton was looking the other way, he winked at Miss Fanshaw, who blushed even deeper.

Samantha knew what Lord Godwin referred to. The prince of Wales had become involved with an actress while living up north. It had been all over the papers, particularly The London Inquirer, which Madge had subscribed to after Wyatt's friend George Canard had interviewed Samantha for it. Mr. Canard had taken particular pleasure in speculating about the heir to the throne's indiscretion and Madge had read parts of it aloud to Samantha.

It irked Samantha that young women of her class were thought too delicate to know of the affairs of men and were expected to be virtuous, while the men themselves were encouraged to run around breaking every commandment as long as they were discreet. She did not think it was merely Bertie's lack of discretion that bothered his parents—they strove to model and instill virtue in all their children—but the British public was certainly more amused than horrified, as would have been the case had it been one of his sisters in his place.

When the Bradwells and their guests took their seats in the family's pews in the village church an hour later, the building was nearly full. Certainly there had not been nearly so many attendees of the service the previous Sunday. Many of the villagers were already in black or had at least tied on a black armband, as had the members of the Bradwell party.

The curate had spoken the previous Sunday, but for such an auspicious occasion, the vicar had deigned to be present. He spoke eloquently and at length of the virtues of Prince Albert and his position as the moral leader of the nation. Prayers were led for the good health of the queen and her children and for the strength of the nation going forward.

Samantha felt strangely outside of herself as she listened to the service. Her own concerns seemed muted, set temporarily at bay, as she looked around to see so many people, rich and poor, united in black and many in grief as well. In a day or so, they would all return to their own problems, but for this moment in time, they were alike.

"I'm leaving for London," Lord Bradwell announced when they had all returned to the house.

"So soon?" Madge asked. "They haven't even set the date for the funeral yet."

"They will, and it won't be more than a week away."

"I'll go with you, Father," Lord Linwood said.

"We'll join you." Lord Godwin indicated himself and Mr. Allen.

"Come now," Lord Aston said with a laugh. "We can't deprive Lady Bradwell of all her guests."

"I think we should all go," Madge said, waving away Lord Aston's defense of her. "Naturally, anyone who wishes to remain behind may, but I believe a strong show of support for Her

Majesty will be welcome at this time."

"We don't wish to be a burden," Lady Wentworth said. "We can stay here until you return."

"Nonsense, Clarissa," Sir Rupert snorted. "We want to be a support to Her Majesty. We'll go to London." Lady Wentworth looked as though she wanted to object, but Sir Rupert went on pompously, "It is our duty as citizens and, especially, as members of the upper classes to lead the nation by example."

"How eloquently you have put it," Madge said dryly. "Very well, I will write to Grosvenor Square and have the house made ready. We should be able to travel in a day or two."

"There is no need to make up a room for me, Mother," Lord Linwood said. "I'll stay at the club. Godwin and Allen will as well."

"I am at your ladyship's disposal," Lord Aston said when Madge raised an eyebrow at him.

"Pretty words," she said. "I should like you and Wyatt...Where is Wyatt?"

Samantha looked around. Wyatt was nowhere to be seen.

"Never mind." Madge shook her head. "I'll speak to him later. Samantha, will you come with me?"

Samantha followed Madge to the small portrait gallery where Madge kept the desk at which she wrote most of her correspondence.

"We shall need to order our mourning right away," Madge explained, pulling out a fresh sheet of paper as she sat down. "I expect there will be a run on the dressmakers as everyone puts in their orders at once. Now, I imagine we'll need at least one evening gown and two or three day dresses."

It was over an hour later that Samantha finally emerged from the portrait gallery. Unsure how long the period of official mourning would last, Madge had thought it better to be prepared than not, and there had been a lot to discuss. For Samantha, who thought she had put off mourning forever, it was draining. When they finished, she retired to her room for a rest. It was just before dinner that she emerged, running into Lord Aston at the top of the stairs.

"Did Lady B tell you if she wishes my presence in Grosvenor Square or not?" he asked good-naturedly, holding out an arm to escort Samantha down.

"The matter didn't come up," she said. "Did you find where Wyatt disappeared to?"

"Oh, yes. He was packing. Left for London some two hours ago."

"He left for London?" Samantha asked, unable to keep the shock from her voice. "Without telling m—Madge?"

She had been about to say "me" but stopped herself. Something in Lord Aston's expression told her he had not been fooled by her clumsy correction, but he accepted it, nonetheless.

"He did tell her, as a matter of fact," Lord Aston said. "I suggested he might wait to tell...other guests himself, but he said he hoped to catch the next train and couldn't be delayed."

"That's very sudden. Did he say why he was in such a hurry?"

"I don't know that he was in a hurry so much as taking advantage of the opportunity," Lord Aston said shrewdly. "Though I can't say I'm surprised. He's always been reluctant to confront conflict. It's a trait we share."

The look he gave her implied a greater understanding of Wyatt's reasonings than he was saying. Samantha sighed.

"I won't pretend to misunderstand you," she said. "But I hope you know that, however forthcoming Wyatt may have been, I feel no such obligation to share my feelings with you."

"Wyatt? Forthcoming?" Lord Aston laughed. "My dear Miss Kingston, I have been friends with Wyatt for years, and most of what I know of him I've had to pull from him piece by piece. He holds his secrets like a vault." He lowered his voice as they entered the drawing room. "However, I do have eyes, and a lifetime of studying my friend has allowed me to pick up certain clues. You are not precisely subtle yourself. The air between you is practically frigid of late."

Samantha grimaced.

"I don't know what occurred between you," Lord Aston continued, leading her to the set of chairs farthest from the entrance, "nor do I want to, but I hope you won't forget what I told you before. I've truly never heard him speak of a lady the way he does of you."

"Has he ever proposed to one before?"

Samantha wasn't sure what prompted her sudden spurt of recklessness, but the widening of Lord Aston's eyes told her he had caught her meaning. When he spoke, however, he was perfectly calm.

"I can't say he has. Leastways, he's never told me. I've always been under the impression he was waiting to be forced into it. Not as a consequence of his actions," he added hastily, noting her raised eyebrows, "but by family pressure or the like."

"So he's never associated marriage with love?"

"Does anyone?" Lord Aston asked with a hint of a smile. "Fanciful young ladies like Miss Wentworth excepted, of course. Though I would say, if he were to enter into it of his own free will, I can't imagine he'd do it for any other reason."

"I don't see why," Samantha said, uncomfortably aware of the defensiveness of her tone. "If one has to marry at all, surely it is better to do so without affection. Then there can be no disappointment when that affection fades."

Lord Aston scratched his nose. "Is affection love, though?"

It was such a thoughtful question that Samantha was momentarily struck dumb.

"I can't claim to be an expert, but I've had affection for," he hesitated, coughed, and continued, "a number of women, and I would say its greatest drawback is that it blinded me to their faults. I let myself be won over by a pretty figure or a lovely face and an easygoing personality before I'd come to know the woman herself. It was when I came to know things about her I didn't like that affection wasn't enough. But if you know the person, their flaws and their strengths, then you're going in with your eyes open."

"Supposing they change," Samantha pressed. "Supposing you think you know them and come to find you don't?"

"I don't think anyone can ever fully know another person, but I think we can know the essence of who they are. As a completely unrelated example, I have a friend whom I've known most of my life. I wouldn't say I know every one of his misdeeds any more than I know his every act of kindness, but I do *know* him. I know he's loyal, honest, stubborn as a bull, a little too full of his own cleverness, and that he'd never intentionally hurt anyone. He still employs his old nanny, for heaven's sake."

"He certainly has a loyal friend in you."

"And for good reason."

"I am surprised," Samantha said, "to hear you speak so positively of marriage. I had thought you and I were of one mind on the issue."

"Oh, I still contend that it's not for me," Lord Aston said with a laugh, "though I know I will have to marry eventually. Tis the curse of being the heir. I do think it can work for some people, however. Look at Lord and Lady Bradwell. And, strange as I view their relationship, I cannot deny that marriage has worked to an extent for my parents. I think, where there is a mutual respect and an honesty, it could be better for some people to be married than not. But it's something for each to decide for himself. Or herself." He nodded to Samantha. "When you look at your future, which do you prefer? The one with him or without?"

Samantha's first instinct was to reply that she couldn't look at her future, which was the crux of her problem. She knew what he meant though, and she didn't have an answer. Thankfully, Lord Aston didn't seem to expect one. Lord Linwood entered the room at that moment, followed by Mr. Allen and Lord Godwin. Lord Aston rose, bowed to Samantha and went to join them, leaving her alone with her turbulent thoughts.

It was three days later when the whole party was finally ready to depart for London. Trunks were loaded onto multiple carriages, which would take them all to the train station. Everything went without incident, with the exception of one of the footmen injuring his toe when he dropped one of Lady Wentworth's trunks onto it.

Grosvenor Square was one of the smartest addresses in London. Stately Georgian mansions lined all four sides of a large central garden. The Bradwell home stretched across five bays almost directly in the center of one of the sides.

Samantha had never been invited to a house on Grosvenor Square, and she couldn't help but be in awe as she walked into the spacious entrance hall with its walls covered in masterful oil paintings. From the entrance hall, she and the other guests were led by the housekeeper, Mrs. Meadows, up the grand staircase. As they passed the first floor, she explained that it contained three drawing rooms and the ballroom, as well as some private family spaces. When they reached the second floor, they were led to their rooms.

The Bradwells had fewer overnight guests when in London and thus fewer guest rooms, which meant Samantha and Eden were made to share. Samantha was glad for the opportunity to spend more time with Eden. She felt guilty for all but abandoning her after the discovery of Jeremy Jones' body and all that had come after.

Once everyone had settled in, Madge took Samantha, Lady Wentworth, and Fanny out in her carriage to visit the dressmakers. Eden had sent for her old mourning clothes from home, and Lady

Chesterton, her daughter, and Miss Thorpe had their appointments later in the day.

Madame Foussard, a petite brunette of indeterminate age somewhere between 35 and 60, welcomed them into her shop with a pinched smile, her flyaway hair half falling from its bun.

"You are fortunate to have ordered when you did," she said, snapping her fingers at an assistant carrying in several cumbersome parcels. "We are completely without the black bombazine now. It has all been sold. I have so many ladies asking me, can I make them this mourning gown or that mourning gown and I must say, no, there is no more fabric. They get angry and say they will take their business elsewhere and I tell them, do as you like, but you will not find another dressmaker with this fabric. It is all gone. Poof!"

Madge lifted an evening gown of black silk trimmed in lace from the first parcel that had been placed in front of her. "Madame, you have outdone yourself. This is beautiful! I tell all my friends you are the best, and you have proved it again."

Madame Foussard's smile became a smidgeon more relaxed as she nodded her thanks. "Always I work extra hard for my best customers."

"This is lovely," Lady Wentworth said, after glancing through her parcels. "Thank you. If you will load these into the carriage, I will settle my bill now."

"You do not wish to try them on?" Madame Foussard asked. "I had only the measurements you gave me. I usually prefer to measure for myself to be certain of the fit."

"I'm sure it will fit perfectly," Lady Wentworth said, pulling on her gloves. "Lady Bradwell has assured me you are the best, after all. I'm afraid I haven't the time for a fitting today. I have more to do before we return, and I do not wish to delay anyone more than necessary."

Pursing her lips, Madame Foussard nodded and gestured for Lady Wentworth to follow her to the small table on the other side of the room on which sat a large book of accounts. Samantha watched them go, wondering what business Lady Wentworth could have in London when the visit had been planned only a few days before.

Because Fanny wished to try on her dresses, and Madame Foussard wished to complain to Madge about the unprecedented workload the official mourning period had caused her, it was over an hour before the small group of ladies was able to follow Lady Wentworth's example and leave the shop. As they made their way to the haberdashery on foot, Samantha felt a growing sense of unease. Twice she looked behind her, almost certain someone was following her, but there were so many people about, she could not be sure.

It was possible, of course, that it was merely the strange feeling of being back in London after so many months away. Around nearly every corner, she saw reminders of the time she had spent destitute on the streets. There was the alley where she had hidden from the police after the woman she failed to pickpocket shouted for help. Down the next street was the path she had taken to her cousin Cyril's that first morning, every step excruciating in her heavily bandaged feet. A waif on the corner selling wilted flowers from a tattered wicker basket looked like a younger version of Annie, the girl who had befriended her and helped her find a place to stay when she had no one.

During all those weeks on the streets, Samantha had spent half her time looking over her shoulder, afraid of being found either by the police or by her aunt's and uncle's murderers. It may have been merely habit that caused her to feel that prickle at the back of her neck now.

They left the haberdashery with an assortment of packages that John, the footman they had brought with them, somehow managed to balance in his arms. Samantha was about to cross the street, following Madge and Fanny, when she felt someone fall into her.

"Oh! I'm so sorry, miss."

She looked down to see a bedraggled girl, one leg heavily bandaged, leaning down to pick up her fallen wooden cane. Samantha hastened to help her. She got to the cane first and picked it up. She and the girl straightened at the same time and, as they did, their eyes met. Samantha saw the girl's eyes widen in an expression she was sure mirrored her own as she gasped.

It was Annie.

FOURTEEN

They stared at each other for several long moments. Samantha could see recognition in the girl's eyes. It was Annie who looked away first, turning her attention to the stick in Samantha's hand.

"Thank you, miss," she said, reaching out and grabbing it. "So kind."

"Wait!" Samantha cried out, because Annie looked as though she meant to hurry away. Reaching into her muff, Samantha pulled out her coin purse. "Here." She shoved the whole thing into Annie's free hand, closing her fingers around it.

Annie pulled her hand away hastily, but she kept the purse.

"Thank you kindly, miss," she muttered. Then she turned and hobbled away, losing herself in the crowd.

Samantha stood frozen on the spot, watching the point at which Annie's fair hair had disappeared. It felt as though her worlds had collided and, even though she had never truly been a part of Annie's world, the sight of her former friend made her current life seem unreal. She felt foolish in her fur-lined cape and expensive gown, as though she were playing a part.

"Make haste!" Fanny called from across the street.

Galvanized, Samantha hurried after her, looking back once she was on the other side, but unable to glimpse a hint of Annie.

Lady Wentworth joined them at the carriage a few minutes later. Whatever her errand had been, she hadn't bought anything because she brought no packages with her. When Fanny expressed curiosity, her mother rebuffed her. Fanny sent Samantha a look asking for support, but Samantha was too preoccupied to do more than respond with a commiserating grimace.

She had thought about Annie since they parted last summer, often wondering where she was or what she was doing. Despite the girl's own insistence that she couldn't afford to be kind, she had helped Samantha tremendously. However, seeing Annie as she had today brought home the stark reality of their differences in circumstances. Samantha had returned to her place among the city's elite, living in beautiful homes with servants and plenty of food to eat, and Annie was still working the same schemes, trying to earn the pennies to feed herself.

Samantha's whole life, she had been taught that the impoverished were so because of a combination of loose morals and poor work ethic. And, though Samantha's mind had been opened to the possibility that this idea was not entirely right when she read *London Labour and the London Poor* by Henry Mayhew, it was meeting people like Annie that had made her question what she had been taught. Annie was one of the hardest workers she knew and, beneath a rough exterior, she had a good heart.

A poke in the ribs jolted Samantha from her thoughts, and she frowned at Fanny, who shrugged and pointed to Madge.

"Are you feeling alright?" Madge asked.

"Yes, why?"

"I asked you a question, and you didn't respond."

"I'm sorry, I—"

"Never mind that. There is clearly something on your mind. Was it the girl you ran into? Did she say something to you?"

"No, nothing of consequence."

Madge hummed but did not pursue the matter until they had reached Grosvenor Square. Then, when Samantha had removed her hat and gloves, she hooked her arm, steered her up the stairs and into one of the drawing rooms on the first floor.

"Now," she said, depositing Samantha in a chair. "Tell me what is on your mind. I can see it is troubling you."

Samantha sighed. "It's really nothing."

"Nonsense. Out with it."

Samantha hesitated a moment longer and then bowed to the inevitable.

"I feel guilty," she said. Madge gave a satisfied nod and sat down across from her, fixing her with an attentive stare. "That girl in the street—she had nothing and I have...so much."

"There is nothing new in that," Madge said practically. "Even before you came into your fortune, you had a good deal more than a street urchin. What has brought on this sudden feeling of guilt?"

"I knew her," Samantha said. With a glance at the door, she lowered her voice. "When I was on the street, before I found Wyatt, she helped me."

Understanding lit Madge's eyes and her expression softened. They hadn't ever spoken of Samantha's time on the streets even though it was the reason for Madge entering her life. It was Wyatt who had explained the situation, though he had omitted the sordid details of Samantha's time breaking the law in the employ of Skinny Jim. The fewer people who knew about that, the better.

"It isn't only that," Samantha continued. "I was almost ruined. If you and Wyatt hadn't helped me and cleared my name, I might have been that girl."

"Nonsense."

"Is it? I had no family, no friends willing to champion my cause. Even if I hadn't been wrongfully accused or convicted, where would I have gone? To whom could I have turned?"

Madge looked thoughtful and Samantha pressed on, "What makes me so different from her? Why should I be so fortunate when she is not?"

Madge sighed. "I wish there were a simple answer to that question, my dear, but there isn't. Yet, the why is much less important, in my mind, than the what."

"'The what'?"

"Yes. What do you plan to do about it?" When Samantha merely stared blankly at her, she continued, "There's not much point in bemoaning what cannot be changed. Even if you were to give all your money to that girl, you could not simply change places. It is not only your money that makes you different, but your families, your upbringings, your circumstances. So, short of throwing your money in the air and disappearing into the streets forever, how do you plan to address your guilt? The inequality?"

"I don't know," Samantha said. "That's just it. What do I do?"

Madge eyed her shrewdly. "I have a friend. Not an especially close friend, but a friend, nonetheless. Her name is Angela Burdett-Coutts. Perhaps you've heard of her?"

The name struck a chord but Samantha could not be certain, so she shook her head.

"She is, or she was, at any rate, before all that business with his wife, a good friend of Charles Dickens'. They did a great deal of charity work together, including creating a home for unfortunate young women. I think it might be a good idea if I were to invite her around for tea sometime. After the official mourning period for His Royal Highness, naturally. You may find you have much in common."

"Thank you," Samantha said in some surprise. "I think I would like that."

"I am certain you will," Madge said, getting briskly to her feet. "Now, no more moping about. We are in even more confined quarters with the same insufferable people. I need you to help me keep my sanity."

She left Samantha to her thoughts, which were marginally more pleasant. She liked the sound of Madge's friend, and the possibility of finding some good use for her fortune eased her guilt somewhat. She hoped she might find a way to help Annie in particular.

As her thoughts returned to Annie, however, a realization hit her. She had been right about Annie. She had felt, instinctively, that she could trust her, and her instincts had proven true. She had been right about Wyatt, too. She had not opened up to him immediately, but she had trusted him to keep his word and then to protect her secrets. In fact, her instincts had served her well throughout her adventures of the previous summer.

She had been thinking, ever since learning of Charles' betrayal, that her judgment was at fault—that she couldn't trust herself—because she had fallen for his lies. And yet, had she fully trusted him? Though she had initially meant to go to him for help, once she met him, she hadn't told him her full story. She had kept back a lot of it from him. Wyatt alone had known the full truth. And when Wyatt told her of Charles' treachery, she may not have wanted to believe it, but she didn't entirely discount it, either. There was a part of her that recognized it as truth. She had beaten that part back in her determination to see Charles as he had been, but she wasn't entirely fooled.

A palpable weight seemed to lift from Samantha's shoulders. She hadn't realized how much she had lost when she thought she couldn't trust herself. She looked back on everything that had happened since she met Jeremy Jones in the abbey. She had blamed herself for that. Yet, what had she done wrong? It had been logical to assume the abbey would be empty at such an early hour. It had been for weeks, and it was on Madge's property. It was not her fault he felt he had the right to attack her, and Alice's defense of her had been just that—a defense. It was also the right decision for them to leave him alone while they sent someone to check on him, for their own safety.

Samantha's thoughts turned to Fanny. Her instincts were telling her that Fanny was innocent, if not of the theft, at least of planning it. If she were involved, it was either in ignorance or through a misplaced sense of loyalty. And, while Samantha may consider the young woman silly and self-centered, she could not, in good conscience, leave her to face the consequences of her actions alone. After all, a man had been murdered, and whoever did it had already proved they had no qualms attacking a woman. With a solidifying sense of resolve, Samantha decided it was time to be open with Fanny.

She found Fanny in the second drawing room just across the hall.

"Could we talk?" she asked. "Somewhere private?"

Immediately alert, Fanny glanced at her mother, who sat in the corner, absorbed in reading a letter, then back at Samantha, and nodded. They descended the stairs and found the library empty. Samantha shut the door behind them and joined Fanny at a set of chairs by the window.

"What is it?" Fanny asked, her brow furrowed in concern. "Have our letters been intercepted?"

Samantha shook her head. "No, your letters are safe. However, I have a confession to make. I overheard you speaking with your gentleman friend at the ball. Out on the terrace."

Fanny's mouth fell open. "What do you mean? We were alone. I...I mean, we weren't...I didn't..."

Samantha held up a hand to stop her sputtering protestations. "I have no interest in ruining your reputation or telling your father."

Fanny looked visibly relieved.

"Though I do think you should tell Lord Linwood."

"I know." Fanny winced. "And I will, just not right away. Once

I tell him and it's clear there will be no engagement, my father will want to know why. I cannot risk that yet."

"It doesn't concern you that Lord Linwood—" Samantha began, but Fanny interrupted her.

"He won't be upset. I made certain when Father insisted I encourage his advances that his heart was not engaged. He is only hoping to further his ambitions, and he will be perfectly able to do so another way."

Surprised by Fanny's astuteness, Samantha did not pursue the matter further. Instead, she steered the conversation back to her real purpose. "How soon do you think you'll be able to tell your father? It's not that I wish to pry into your personal affairs, but I am somewhat involved now. I overheard you say something about a shipment?"

"How much did you overhear?" Fanny asked, flushing slightly.

"I wasn't trying to hear anything," Samantha said. "And I didn't see anything."

Fanny turned even redder, but when she spoke her tone was normal. "The shipment is my father's. He convinced some men to invest in a new venture. It was quite expensive and a bit of a risk, or so Henry says. My father does not approve of Henry as a suitor for me. It isn't that he dislikes him particularly, but he has such hopes for me to marry into the aristocracy. He's very ambitious, my father. It's all he's ever wanted, to be accepted in Society, and he sees me and Oliver as a means to that end. So he wouldn't like me to marry Henry, who is merely a plain 'mister' and hardly much different from Father when it comes to social background."

"And how does the investment venture factor in?" Samantha asked.

"Oh, yes. Forgive me. You see, Henry had the idea that, if he showed faith in my father and not only invested but brought others in as well, he would show Father what an asset he could be to him, and Father might overlook his lack of title. However, it will only truly work if everything goes well with the venture. The money was shipped overseas some time ago and we are waiting to hear if it was received."

"I see." The explanation sounded plausible, and her experience with Fanny's poor attempts at subterfuge made her inclined to believe it to be true.

Fanny nodded. "That is why it is so important that Father knows nothing of our intentions at this point. That would only put him out. He must be in a fantastically good mood before Henry can ask his permission. You won't tell him about us, will you?" She held her hands together in front of her in a pleading gesture. "You have been such a help to us since that Mr. Jones died and I thought all my hope of ever communicating with Henry again was lost."

"I won't tell," Samantha assured her. Then she braced herself as Fanny threw her arms around her and hugged her.

"Thank you!" she exclaimed.

"You're welcome," Samantha said, rubbing her ear where Fanny had shouted into it.

"Would you be able to post a letter today? I want to let Henry know of my new address."

Samantha agreed, and Fanny hurried off to retrieve her letter.

When she had gone, Samantha considered what she had revealed. It may still be that this Henry was playing her false, but she couldn't see why he would. How would carrying on a secret liaison with Sir Rupert's daughter help him to steal the gold if she was completely unaware of its existence? He hadn't used his influence on her to persuade her to sneak information for him, and she seemed unlikely to have come across anything useful by happenstance.

Samantha thought his plan, as communicated to Fanny, was likely genuine. It would explain their interest in the status of the shipment and his reassurances to her that it would all be over soon. It seemed as though neither of them were involved in the theft, nor was it likely that they had killed Jeremy Jones. And yet, if that were the case, how had Mr. Jones come into possession of a gold bar? And who else had motivation to kill him?

*****

Wyatt had never considered himself a coward before, but now, sitting alone and idle in the lounge of the Oxford and Cambridge Club, he wondered how much cowardice had influenced his recent actions. It was true that he had business with his solicitor and that he'd wanted to ask Inspector Whicher what he might know about Sir Rupert's closest business partners, but there had been no real need for him to rush off to London so precipitately. He might have done both of those things after arriving with the rest of the party. He had convinced himself at the time that there was urgency, at least to his meeting with the detective, but he had known, even then, how much he wished to avoid Samantha.

Her rejection of his proposal had surprised him, and her assessment of his character had angered him, but he knew, upon reflection, that it had been his pride hurt more than anything. He had thought she felt the same way about him that he did her. Their kiss had convinced him of that as nothing else had. It was what had spurred him to rash action. To learn that, not only did she not love him, but she refused to even consider the idea, had stung. He didn't want to be around her after that, to see the anger in her eyes, or worse, the pity.

"Mr. Wyatt?"

Startled, Wyatt looked up to see the small, bearded man he had met at Madge's ball—the one Tom had been so keen to do a favor for—who had told Wyatt he might have need of him soon.

"Mr....Benton, wasn't it?" he asked, standing and shaking the man's hand.

"That's right. I called at your house, but your housekeeper said you were here. Might I have a word?"

"Of course." Wyatt gestured for him to take the seat beside him and sat back down. "I must say, I didn't expect to see you again so soon."

"I wish it hadn't been necessary," Mr. Benton said, sitting down and leaning across the arm of his chair towards Wyatt. "What I need to speak with you about is of a delicate nature. I need your assurance, before we go further, that you will not repeat what I tell you to anyone. It is a matter of national security."

"You have my word," Wyatt said.

Mr. Benton looked around to assure himself they were alone. The room was empty but for themselves. Then, he scooted forward in his chair and lowered his voice.

"I know Sir Rupert has asked you to discover his missing gold, gold that was part of an investment scheme known as Colchis Enterprises."

Wyatt's eyebrows rose involuntarily, but he kept silent.

"There is no need to confirm it, and I applaud you for your discretion, but the matter is rather more complicated than it appears. I have been monitoring Sir Rupert for some time. Many of our cotton manufacturers have expressed frustration with the prolonged war in America and its effect on their industry. Its impact will certainly have far-reaching consequences. However, Sir Rupert has been more vocal than most."

Mr. Benton cleared his throat, then went on, "As Britain has stated her position as neutral, any significant action taken by a British citizen to influence the course of the war could be interpreted as an attempt to subvert that neutrality."

"And you believe Sir Rupert has taken significant action?"

"I don't just believe it, I know. Colchis Enterprises does not exist. It is merely a vehicle for Sir Rupert and his collaborators to collect money—money that was intended to be sent, via the Caribbean, to leaders of the Southern Confederacy, to pay for weapons and supplies."

Wyatt was momentarily stunned.

"The idea was, so I understand," Mr. Benton went on, "that the war would be ended sooner and that, in exchange, Sir Rupert and his top investors would receive special privileges and significant discounts on the cotton produced for the next half dozen or so years."

"How do you know all of this?" Wyatt asked.

"As I said, I've been monitoring Sir Rupert for some time. He does not hold onto servants well, and I've managed to get one of my own onto his staff."

"But the gold never left England," Wyatt said, recovering himself. "So what is the concern? Unless, did you steal it?"

Mr. Benton shook his head. "We were not aware of its purpose until after it had left port, or rather, when we thought it had left port. As for the reason for our concern..." He sighed. "Relations between America and Britain are tenuous. If Prince Albert's letter is received well and peace is restored, it will be a fragile one. We don't know who stole the gold or why. If that person chooses to reveal Sir Rupert's plan, the Americans will have reason to renege on whatever agreement we come to. And with the prince dead, those in our government who seek reconciliation will be without an influential ally. We may likely find ourselves at war."

Wyatt ran a hand through his hair. "Why are you telling me this?"

Mr. Benton tilted his head to the side, considering Wyatt a moment before answering. "I have several reasons but, I suppose, the primary one is that my resources are limited. You are already investigating the theft of the gold on your own. I would like to take advantage of that. You needn't change anything you are doing, only inform me of your findings before you tell Sir Rupert. That will give us time to act."

"I have only your word that any of this is true," Wyatt said.

"Why should I trust you?"

Mr. Benton smiled grimly. "I had your brother introduce us at the ball so that you would know who I was before this conversation became necessary."

Wyatt nodded. "I know who you are—someone who deals in secrecy. That hardly makes you trustworthy."

Mr. Benton shrugged. "I will concede that. If you prefer to trust Sir Rupert, I cannot stop you. I had hoped we could work together; it would certainly make my task easier." He stood up.

"I'll consider it," Wyatt said, standing as well.

"I hope you will."

They shook hands, and Mr. Benton handed Wyatt his card. "I move around a lot, but if you need me, someone here can usually find me."

"Thank you."

After Mr. Benton left, Wyatt sat down heavily. He had no real reason to doubt Benton's word. He had never truly liked Sir Rupert but, treason? He put his head in his hands and dragged his fingers through his hair. One thing was certain, no matter the outcome, he would recommend to Madge that she steer Linwood clear of Miss Wentworth and the whole Wentworth family.

Wyatt was still reeling from Benton's revelations when he met George Canard for lunch an hour later. His preoccupation must have shown, because George asked, sardonically, if he wouldn't rather be alone with his thoughts.

"And miss out on your company?" Wyatt asked, cutting into his steak and kidney pie.

George snorted. Then, winking at the barmaid across the room, he said, "I could find other uses for my time."

"You're having quite the banner year," Wyatt said, ignoring him. "First a sensational murder, now the death of the prince."

George shrugged. "The prince's death is a tragedy, of course, and there's plenty of opportunity in future for speculation about the state of the nation and the queen's bereavement, but for now, people want to read saccharine posts about what a great man he was and how we must come together as a nation and support the royal family. Not my idea of an interesting story."

"I'm sorry the people's grief has inconvenienced you," Wyatt said.

"Charles Prescott's death, however, was a gift for a while there. Until I was told to stop reporting on it, that is." Wyatt looked up, and George grinned. "I thought that might get your attention."

"You were asked to stop reporting on it?"

"I was. After the major papers carried that farce of a story about how the killer had been gunned down in a shoot-out with police, I started digging around. I found out that several witnesses to the original shooting had gone missing or emigrated all of a sudden. My editor was thrilled. Then, after I published the first in what would have been a great series of stories, I got called into his office and told I wasn't going to be allowed to publish any more."

"I wouldn't have thought there was any limit to what your editor deemed appropriate."

"Neither would I, but there it is." George shrugged, but Wyatt could see he was agitated.

"Do you think the police—" Wyatt started to say, but George interrupted him.

"Not a chance. Stubbins has never let Scotland Yard's disapproval influence him before. It would have to be someone he was really afraid of. Which, until now, I would have said was no one."

Wyatt nodded, thinking he was fairly certain who that person was.

George leaned forward and lowered his voice. "You still talk to Whicher, right? You're still friends? I can't imagine he bought into that humdrum about the shootout. What's he say?"

Wyatt raised an eyebrow. "Do you expect I'd tell you if I knew?"

George eyed him shrewdly, then leaned back. "No, but I expect I'd be able to tell if you knew. And you do. You know something. And I'm going to figure it out."

"How?" Wyatt asked skeptically.

"There'll come a day when you want something from me again. I'm telling you now, that's the price."

Wyatt laughed. "What would you do with the information? You can't print anything."

George shrugged again. "I'll think of something. No one shuts me down."

"Or up," Wyatt muttered.

George grinned. "Or up. I won't apologize. I never stop until I find the truth. It's why you like me, isn't it?"

"Honestly," Wyatt said, standing, "there are times I can't remember why."

George's laughter followed him out of the pub.

As he stood waiting for a cab, Wyatt thought back to the conversation he'd had with Whicher a fortnight ago. There seemed no doubt Whicher had been right and Skinny Jim had ordered Charles' murder. Who else could scare a sleazy penny press editor into suppressing a story that was sure to earn him a lot of money?

With coldly brilliant expertise, Skinny Jim was ensuring that Charles' murder would never be connected to him. How many times had he used these same methods? It ate at Wyatt to realize that, though he might know exactly how and why Charles had died, he would never be able to prove it.

And then he remembered Whicher's response when he asked what he ought to tell Samantha. *Do you think she can handle another disappointment?* He hadn't been sure at the time, but when she had asked him about Charles' death, she had seemed so fragile that he'd decided the answer was no. He'd misled her. It had been for her benefit, or so he thought, but now he wondered if he had overstepped by answering that question for her.

When she rejected his proposal, she told him she feared losing her freedom in marriage. He had balked at the idea that she could imagine he would take it from her, but as he thought about what he'd done, he considered that she may have been justified. After all, had she been a man, he wouldn't have hesitated to tell her the truth, but something about her femininity and his desire to protect her had led him to mislead her.

It wasn't until the cab had arrived and Wyatt had grabbed hold of the handle, prepared to step inside, that he noticed a familiar figure some way down the road. It was the thin Irishman—the one who dogged Wyatt's steps every time he was in London. He had been leaning against a pillar, but as Wyatt reached for the handle, he'd pushed himself off and begun to walk towards him.

All of Wyatt's frustration resurfaced, creating a reckless energy within him that begged to be acted on. Without thinking, he let go of the carriage and stepped back.

"I've changed my mind," he told the driver. "I think I'll walk."

Turning his back on the Irishman, he adjusted his hat and continued down the road. He walked until he reached a crossing, where he turned right and ducked into the first alley he could find. Reaching into the pocket of his coat, he extracted his pistol.

When the Irishman appeared moments later, Wyatt sprang forward and grabbed him by the arm, shoving the barrel of the pistol between his shoulder blades.

"Don't call out," he said harshly, pulling the man back into the alley.

"There's no need for the barking iron," the man said, a hint of laughter in his voice. "I'd've come quiet-like if you only asked."

He stood lax in Wyatt's grip. Wyatt spun him around, his pistol aimed at the man's chest, and was annoyed to see a lopsided grin on the man's thin face.

"I suppose there's a point to all of this?" Wyatt asked testily. "Not that I don't enjoy looking over my shoulder and seeing you dogging my every step, but I admit I am curious."

"He said as you might be. He's been waiting for you to ask."

"Skinny Jim, I suppose?"

"He was hoping you'd've guessed. Saves time that way." The man grinned again. Wyatt could see a gold tooth among his dingy, yellowed ones.

"Well?" he prompted.

"He says he hopes you've noticed as how there ain't no point pinning any murders on him as he didn't do. He also says he knows what you've been up to, and he hopes you'll be smart enough to see he makes a better friend than an enemy."

"Does he now? He thinks I might be friends with him?"

The man shrugged. "He's got a lot of friends in high and low places. I wouldn't say as he needs another, but it's easier to make new friends than enemies. Less messy, if you get my meaning."

"Tell him I'm flattered," Wyatt said, lowering his pistol deliberately, his eyes watching the man for any sudden movements. "As it happens, I don't need any new friends, either, and surely a man as intelligent as he can see that I don't have the resources to make a formidable enemy."

"That's your answer?"

"That's my answer."

The man nodded thoughtfully.

"Are you done following me then?" Wyatt asked, stepping back and gesturing towards the street beyond.

The man eyed him shrewdly, then shrugged. "Let's just say, you shouldn't stop looking over your shoulder."

With that Parthian shot, he winked at Wyatt and exited the alley.

FIFTEEN

That evening, Wyatt arrived early for dinner at Madge's, determined to find an opportunity to talk to her about the need to disassociate herself from Sir Rupert. When he entered the front hall, however, it was the man himself that he met with first.

"Lady Bradwell said you'd be here this evening," Sir Rupert said genially, clapping Wyatt on the back. "I can't tell you how happy I was to hear it. Any news on my little problem? I thought there might be after you rushed off to London as you did."

Bristling under the man's overly familiar manner, Wyatt gave him a tight smile. "Oh, I've had some news."

"Excellent. Let's talk in here, where we might enjoy some privacy."

Sir Rupert led the way to the library, just off the hall. Once they were inside and a glance around had assured them of their solitude, Sir Rupert turned to Wyatt. "Well?"

Though a part of him hoped to be proven wrong, not only because he found the whole business distasteful but also because he hated to think he had been even tangentially involved, Wyatt had found Mr. Benton's story more credible the more he considered it. He decided to go on the offensive.

"Did you think I wouldn't find out?" he asked.

"Find out what?" Sir Rupert asked, nonplussed.

"Colchis. Enterprises." Wyatt bit the words out. "It's not a simple business venture, is it? It's an underhanded scheme to fund the war efforts of another country."

Sir Rupert's jaw tightened. "How did you find out?"

Wyatt's mood soured as all remaining hope fled. "You aren't denying it, then?"

"Why should I?" Sir Rupert asked, beginning to pace the room. "I have done nothing wrong."

"'Nothing wrong'?" Wyatt echoed angrily. "You sent money to aid in a conflict Britain had sworn to stay out of. You acted in direct opposition to your government's wishes. If it is discovered, it may be hard to convince the Americans that the government was not aware of and tacitly approving of your efforts. Your actions could be construed as treason."

"Bah!" Sir Rupert raised a hand and batted away Wyatt's remarks. "You sound like my wife. Treason? If anything, I acted patriotically. The manufacture of cotton fabric is one of this country's major industries. What do you think will happen to the economy if this conflict in America is allowed to drag on for months or even years longer?"

"If you were so convinced of your righteousness, what reason was there to hide it from me? No, you knew what you were doing was morally grey at least, and you didn't want anyone to find out."

"I didn't tell you because there was no need for you to know," Sir Rupert retorted. "I wanted the gold found, not an analysis of my business plan."

"When you ask for my help, you don't get to decide what's relevant and what isn't," Wyatt said, his voice rising in pitch. He paused, and regained control of his emotions, continuing in even tones, "It is entirely possible that the theft of the gold has everything to do with why it was being shipped. It may have been taken by someone who wished to stop your efforts. It may not have been greed at all. It adds an entirely new layer of motive to the theft. You may have sent me on a week-long wild goose chase and wasted my time and yours."

Sir Rupert had stopped pacing. His face purpled.

"I'll need a list," Wyatt said, "of everyone who knew the real purpose behind Colchis Enterprises, whether they were investors or bankers or servants."

"I'll have to think about it."

"If you want your gold back, I need that list. You can hand it to me after dinner. Otherwise, I'm done. Good evening."

Without waiting for a reply, Wyatt left the room.

*****

Samantha paced the small anteroom by the stairs on the first floor. Ever since Madge informed her that Wyatt would be dining with them that evening, she had resolved to speak to him. She needed to tell him what she had learned from Fanny, but for the first time since their initial meeting at his house that summer, she was nervous to talk to him. She did not regret her refusal of his proposal—at least, not when she set aside her emotions and concentrated on her reasoning—but she had come to regret how she expressed herself.

When she finally heard muffled footsteps ascending the carpeted stairs, she hurried to the doorway. Wyatt was always well turned out in evening dress, but the elegant tailoring of his jacket contrasted sharply with the ruffled nature of his hair. He'd clearly been running his hands through it vigorously. If that hadn't been enough of a clue as to his state of mind, his ferocious scowl certainly was. She hesitated a moment before stepping forward and making her presence known.

"Samantha!" He stopped abruptly, looking startled. Samantha took advantage of his silence to speak.

"Might I have a word?" She gestured to the anteroom. He followed her in but, before she could begin the speech she had been rehearsing, he recovered his own.

"There's something I need to tell you," he said. "It's something I ought to have told you a week ago, but I didn't. I thought I was doing what was best for you, but I've come to realize that wasn't my decision to make." He took a breath before continuing, "You asked me about Charles and the search for his murderer. I didn't lie about what the newspapers reported. Neither, however, did I tell you everything I knew." Samantha felt her stomach tighten. "Inspector Whicher and I had been tracking down witnesses to the shooting, but every time we found one willing to talk to us, he would disappear or move to another country without warning. The inspector told me that such things have happened before when Skinny Jim is involved."

"Skinny Jim?" Samantha interrupted. A spike of fear shot through her as she remembered the cold, calculating face of the man who controlled half the criminals in London. Charles may have been the one to pull the trigger, but Skinny Jim had been almost as responsible for the deaths of her aunt and uncle. He had made Charles desperate. He had sent his men to kidnap her, forcing the family into hiding, and he had been the one to hunt them down.

"Whicher thinks Skinny Jim hired someone to kill Charles in order to stop him from testifying about Skinny Jim's part in the murders of your aunt and uncle and your attempted abduction. I think he's right, especially as I've just learned that George—you remember my friend George Canard—was told to stop reporting on the missing witnesses when someone strong-armed his editor into it."

"So it wasn't a random killing related to Charles' gambling?"

"No, it wasn't."

Samantha nodded and looked down at the floor as she

marshaled her thoughts. She had been surprised when Wyatt told her the lies from the newspapers. It had seemed strange for Charles' death to be so mundane after everything he'd done. It was a relief to learn that, again, her intuition had been right. And yet, she could not ignore the fact that Wyatt had lied to her.

"I made a mistake," Wyatt said. She looked up to see him watching her earnestly. "I didn't think I was lying—or at least, I convinced myself I wasn't—but I did deceive you, which is the same, and for that, I apologize. It was unforgivable."

"I thank you for the apology," she said after a moment. "And for telling me the truth. You are right; it wasn't your choice to decide what I could handle. Nor do I like to hear that you thought I was so weak."

"Another mistake. I ought to have known better."

"Yes, you should have." They stood in silence for a moment. Then Samantha sighed. "I owe you an apology as well. I was surprised by your proposal, but that's no excuse for how I reacted. I should have been kinder. You're a good friend, and I don't want to lose your friendship."

He regarded her for a moment. Then he said, "I accept your apology. As for the friendship, it's something I'd like to discuss further, but now is not the time. Was that what you wanted to talk about when you asked for a word?"

"No, or rather, not entirely," Samantha said, careful to hide her disappointment. "I have some new information about Fanny— Miss Wentworth—and the man she's been writing to."

"Allerton."

"I beg your pardon?"

"The man she's been writing to. I met him at the ball. His name is Allerton."

"Mr. Allerton, then. His Christian name is Henry. I spoke to her about the conversation we overheard between the two of them." She proceeded to relay the basic facts of the interview, concluding, "I don't think Fanny is involved at all, and I'm inclined to believe that Mr. Allerton isn't, either. However, I'm at a loss to understand how their emissary, Mr. Jones, found himself in possession of that bar. It seemed such an obvious connection."

Wyatt had begun to pace as she spoke. He now stopped and turned to her. "I did learn who bribed the night watchman, or, at least, I got a vague description of him. He was an old man who, judging by his accent, wasn't from Liverpool."

"That's not especially helpful," Samantha said. "Although, depending on what one considers old, it could eliminate anyone we have discussed thus far."

"There was a strange old man seen in the village. Mr. Smithers, the constable, told me."

"There was? Why did you not tell me so before?"

"I had other things on my mind when I returned from the warehouse." He looked at her pointedly. "And when we did have the chance to talk, your news about Miss Wentworth and her letter took precedence. To be honest, I forgot."

"Very well. Will you be traveling back to Derbyshire then? To speak with the villagers about whether Mr. Jones was seen with this old man?"

"I suppose I will. I had intended to before now, but with the prince's death, it hardly seemed appropriate to walk around interrogating people."

They were silent for a moment. Samantha didn't know how Wyatt felt, but she was growing frustrated. Fanny and Mr. Allerton and Jeremy Jones had been such a promising trio. It felt as though they were starting over again.

"Perhaps we are looking at the problem from the wrong angle," she said musingly.

"What do you mean?"

"Well, we've been focusing on who stole the gold as a means to find it. However, it is a lot of gold—in bars, you said—which must be bulky, heavy and, therefore, not easy to hide. I doubt whoever took it hid it somewhere where it might easily be traced to them if found, but neither would they wish to be far from it. And yet, Jeremy Jones, who lives miles from where it disappeared in Liverpool, had a brick of it."

Wyatt looked thoughtful.

"What if," Samantha said, beginning to pace in her growing excitement, "Jeremy Jones is not connected to the theft at all? What if, instead, he found the gold after it had been hidden? You said he was telling people he had come into money? What if he found a stash of gold and was arrogant or foolish enough to think he'd discovered his own personal treasure? Then, when he went to retrieve more, the person who stole the gold saw him and killed him?"

She turned to Wyatt, flush with exhilaration.

"It makes sense," he said, nodding, "especially if the old man from the warehouse is the same who was seen in the village. Yet, why bring it all the way from Liverpool to Bradwell? We know he was a stranger in the village. Unless there's someone Sir Rupert has failed to tell me about, which is entirely possible, the only people in Bradwell connected to the gold are the Wentworths. I can't imagine Sir Rupert would steal his own gold and then draw attention to it by asking me to find it, and if we take it that Miss Wentworth is innocent, whom does that leave? Lady Wentworth? Oliver Wentworth?"

"I did see Oliver Wentworth with a mysterious parcel a few days ago," Samantha said slowly. "He was keen that no one should see him with it. But what would be his motive? He doesn't strike me as desperate for money now and he will inherit his father's wealth. Surely he would want its investments to prosper."

"He may have had another motive," Wyatt said hesitantly. He grimaced. "I don't mean to be oblique, but I've been sworn to secrecy."

"By Oliver Wentworth?"

"No. Suffice it to say, Sir Rupert has not been entirely honest with me about the purpose of the investment. The truth is a matter of national security."

"Oh." Samantha blinked. "Do you think the purpose of the investment might be the reason for the theft?"

"It might be."

"So Oliver Wentworth is a strong possibility as the thief."

"I wouldn't say strong..."

"What about Lady Wentworth? I can't see what benefit it would be to her. If she stole the money, or hired the old man to, what could she do with it? How could she hide her sudden inexplicable wealth from her husband?"

"I don't know," Wyatt said. Then his eyes widened. "But she did know about it. She knew about the purpose behind the investment."

"She did? Sir Rupert doesn't strike me as the type to confide in his wife."

"Just a moment ago, when I was tasking Sir Rupert for keeping secrets from me, and I told him what he might be accused of, he said I sounded like his wife. It didn't strike me at the time, but it sounds as though they had an argument and she accused him as I did."

Samantha set aside her irritation at Wyatt's roundabout way of speaking. She supposed she ought to consider him honorable for keeping confidences, but she wished he would stop mentioning it.

"Then Lady Wentworth is also a possibility."

"I would say so. But more importantly, where is the gold? Not at the Court, or Jones wouldn't have gotten ahold of it."

Samantha gasped as realization hit her. "The abbey!"

"Possibly," Wyatt agreed, nodding.

"No, think about it," she said eagerly. "Mr. Jones traveled to and from the abbey to deliver letters for Fanny and Mr. Allerton.

That must have been why he was there the day I met him. And his body was found not far from the abbey."

"You were attacked at the abbey," Wyatt said, "when you were with Bingo."

"That's right. The thief must have been there and been afraid I might find the gold."

"The veiled woman?"

"Yes, although, Lord Aston did say he couldn't be certain if it was a man or a woman."

"We need to go back to the abbey."

Samantha looked at Wyatt, surprised as she realized they had both spoken at the same time.

"You want me to come with you?" she asked. "I thought I'd have to convince you."

"I want you to come," he said. "Also, I need you to come. You can show us where you were when you were attacked."

"Us?"

"There's someone I need to contact. Someone who needs to come with us."

"Is he the one who swore you to secrecy?"

"Yes."

"Very well. I'll go change while you get him."

"Now?"

"Why not? Is this not a matter of national security?"

"That's true," Wyatt said slowly. "But what about dinner?"

"Madge didn't tell anyone but me that you were coming, and no one will be shocked if I miss one dinner. Go, hurry." She shooed him with her hands.

"Very well. I'll be back as soon as I can."

As Samantha followed him out the door, she thought she heard quick footsteps heading in the opposite direction of the one in which Wyatt had gone. Lifting her skirts, she followed the sound, but the chase was short-lived. Around the corner, the hall was carpeted and, though she strained her ears, she could hear nothing further. With a prickling of unease, she wondered if their conversation had been overheard and, if so, by whom.

SIXTEEN

Back in her room, Samantha rang for Alice. While she waited for her maid to arrive, she leaned against the wall and looked out the window. Her room faced the mews. It wasn't the best view, but she sometimes enjoyed watching the comings and goings in the stable yard.

The soft click of the door closing drew Samantha's attention as Alice entered.

"Are you ready to change for dinner?" her maid asked.

"Not for dinner," Samantha said. "For travel. We're taking a quick trip to Derbyshire."

"Derbyshire?"

"Yes, but I'd rather the rest of the household didn't know."

Briefly, Samantha outlined her plan to go to the abbey with Wyatt and his mysterious friend. As Alice knew nothing of Sir Rupert or the missing gold, Samantha merely explained that it was related to Jeremy Jones' murder.

"I don't know," Alice said, frowning as Samantha finished her story. "I don't understand why you have to go. Aren't you worried what people say about you and Mr. Wyatt?"

"It's not as though we'll be alone. I'll have you, and his friend will be with us."

"But you were attacked at the abbey the last time you went and that was with Lord Aston accompanying you. Aren't you worried something might happen again?"

"Not particularly. There will be two witnesses rather than one. If the same person tries to attack me again, it will be all the easier to arrest her. Or him."

Alice looked unconvinced. Nevertheless, she set about helping Samantha into a traveling gown and her sturdiest boots. Samantha was tying the ribbons of her cloak when a noise in the mews below drew her to the window.

A carriage had pulled up to Madge's back door, and a footman was carrying trunks from the house and strapping them to the back of the carriage. The driver climbed down from his seat and began conversing with a woman in a dark cloak. Though her hood was pulled up to conceal most of her face, when she turned to gesture to her trunks, Samantha caught a brief glimpse of a pointed nose and auburn hair that was so like her daughter's. It was Lady Wentworth.

She appeared to be negotiating the price of passage for, a moment later, she passed a handful of coins to the driver and he returned to his seat. Samantha had just begun to wonder what Lady Wentworth could possibly be doing, entering a hackney via the back door with what looked like all her belongings when the footman dragged out the final trunk. It was clearly heavier than the others and, as he struggled to lift it, Samantha recalled how another footman had dropped one of Lady Wentworth's trunks and injured his toe the day before.

Half-formed thoughts raced through Samantha's mind. Did that trunk contain what she thought it did? Had Lady Wentworth been the person Samantha heard running down the hall? If she was —if she had heard Samantha and Wyatt's conversation, then she knew they suspected her.

As Samantha watched, Lady Wentworth handed a folded-up paper and a coin to a small boy. He tipped his cap and ran off down the mews. Then, she climbed into the carriage with the assistance of the footman. Knowing she had mere moments, Samantha spun round and raced to the door, calling over her shoulder for Alice to follow her.

"What is the fastest way to the back door?" Samantha asked as they entered the corridor. "The one that leads to the mews?"

"Follow me."

Alice led her to a small door at the end of the passage. It opened onto a narrow staircase, which they descended as quickly as they could, their footsteps echoing loudly as they went. When they reached the bottom, another door led them into a wide, unadorned corridor. As they raced down it, Samantha could hear the clanking of pots and pans and the sounds of voices from a passage to their right.

At last, Alice opened a door that led outside. Samantha ran out after her just in time to see the black carriage clattering down the mews. Spinning on the spot, she saw the footman who had been loading the carriage.

"Where is that carriage going?" she asked.

He looked surprised and a little disconcerted, but he answered without hesitation. "I heard her ladyship ask to be taken to St. Pancras Station."

Samantha turned to Alice. "I need you to find Mr. Wyatt. He should be returning with his friend soon. Wait for him out front. Tell him it appears Lady Wentworth overheard our conversation and has fled to St. Pancras and that I've gone after her."

"Gone after her?"

"There's no time to explain. Just tell him to hurry."

Without another word, Samantha took off in the direction of the departing carriage. She caught up to it before it turned onto the street and grabbed the post of one of the rear lanterns, using it to lift herself onto the footman's ledge at the back. She clung on for she knew not how long until the carriage was forced to come to a stop at a crossing, at which point she jumped down and flung open the door.

Lady Wentworth let out a little scream as Samantha slid into the seat across from her. At the same time, the driver shouted "Oy!"

Reaching into the reticule she had earlier tied to her waist, Samantha extracted several coins and stood, sliding open the window in the roof, and handed them to the driver. He took them, grunted, and nudged the horses forward.

"What are you doing?" Lady Wentworth asked indignantly as Samantha resumed her seat.

"I could ask you the same."

"We're not prisoners in Lady Bradwell's house," Lady Wentworth said, evidently trying for bravado, though her voice shook. "I simply wished to take a drive."

"In a hackney? Why not take one of the Bradwells' carriages?"

"I had no wish to be an inconvenience."

"Is that why you have brought all your luggage?" Samantha asked innocently. "Do you wish so strongly not to be an inconvenience that you are removing yourself entirely from the house?"

Lady Wentworth opened her mouth, then closed it. She frowned at Samantha. "Perhaps I do. After all, when Lady Bradwell invited us to her home, she did not expect we would so soon be removing to London, where she has far less space for so large a party."

"How very thoughtful of you," Samantha said blandly. She paused and then, thinking she might get further by more direct speech, added, "It is a pity you were not quite so thoughtful when you took advantage of her hospitality to hide a quantity of stolen gold on her property."

Lady Wentworth went white. "I didn't...How can you...It's not..." She sputtered.

"There is no use denying it," Samantha said. "Your reaction has given you away."

Lady Wentworth clasped velvet-gloved hands in front of her and leaned forward, fixing Samantha with a pleading look. "You must allow me to explain."

"What explanation can possibly justify murder?"

Lady Wentworth winced. "That wasn't supposed to happen."

"No doubt," Samantha said dryly. Then curiosity overcame her. "What was supposed to happen?"

Lady Wentworth sighed and sat back, pulling back her hood. She looked tired, and the lines on her face seemed deeper in the shadow of the carriage.

"It should have been simple," she said softly. "The abbey was deserted, and the legends of spirits ensured it was rarely visited, especially at night. I needed to make fairly regular visits, and it seemed an ideal place to go unnoticed."

"Why did you need to make regular visits if you thought there was so little chance of someone stumbling upon your stash?"

Lady Wentworth raised an eyebrow. "You don't suppose I could have escaped to the continent with a pile of gold bars, do you? I was exchanging them—using the gold to purchase jewelry. A middle-aged lady traveling the continent and using her family jewels to fund her lifestyle is so much less suspicious than a lady paying for everything in gold bars."

"You were planning to flee the country?" Samantha asked. "Without your husband and children?"

Lady Wentworth was silent for a moment, watching Samantha thoughtfully as the carriage swayed and bumped.

"You are young," she said finally. "So was I, once. I believed: in the promises of others, in the hope of a future. I never loved Rupert—our marriage was arranged by our fathers—but I believed we would get along well enough. He told me he respected my opinions, and for some time I think he did. We grew the business together, you see." She sighed. "But Rupert was ambitious. Not in business so much—that would have been fine— but socially. He saw the aristocracy as something to be desired. He wanted to be accepted into that life of luxurious indolence.

"In pursuit of his goal, Rupert was determined we should all fall in line. He would no longer speak to me about work. A *lady*" – she pronounced the word with distaste— "must not concern herself with such matters. She must turn her mind to the problems of the home. She must train the servants and host dinner parties with progressively more important acquaintances.

"My children were taken out of their schools and placed in new schools where they were likely to form friendships with those of good breeding. Fanny was to be prepared to have a London Season when she came of age, for she must marry a title, and Oliver must get into parliament. My children became strangers to me."

"I am sorry," Samantha said, and she was. She was uncomfortably aware of the echoes of her own fears in Lady Wentworth's story.

Lady Wentworth smiled grimly. "We cannot all control our destinies. I endured. But then the war in America began, and the cotton industry suffered. It was all anyone spoke of, even the ladies. And one night I overheard my husband discussing a plan with his closest friends—a plan so risky it would undoubtedly implode, and we would all be damaged by it. I confronted him with it. I tried to reason with him. I appealed to his greatest desires and fears, pointing out how he would be ostracized from those he had strove for so long to join."

Her face darkened with the memory. "He laughed at me. He said it was appropriately womanly of me to care so much for his well-being, but that I must see that he had a greater understanding of such matters." She twisted the fabric of her cloak in her lap, scowling. "I spent days worrying what would happen to us. And then it came to me—I could put a stop to it. I knew when he planned to load the cargo on the ship. I could remove it before anyone was the wiser. What's more, I could take the cargo for myself and start a new life, far away from here."

"But you didn't remove the cargo," Samantha interrupted. The smile that had begun to form on Lady Wentworth's face at the memory of her epiphany vanished. "It wasn't you who stole the gold—at least, not from the warehouse. It was an old man. Who was he?"

"There was no one else." The words shot from Lady Wentworth's mouth like bullets. "No one. I acted alone."

"Did he kill Jeremy Jones?" Samantha asked. "Or was it you?"

The color drained from Lady Wentworth's face once more. "I acted alone," she said slowly. "So it was...me that killed him."

"Why?"

"He saw...me...in the abbey one night. He'd found the place where the gold was hidden and come back for it. We struggled, and he hit his head on a stone. It was an accident."

Samantha's skepticism must have shown because Lady Wentworth leaned across the carriage and grasped Samantha's hand between hers. "It was an accident," she repeated. "You must understand that."

"What about when you attacked me in the abbey? Was that an accident, too?"

Lady Wentworth dropped her hands and sat back. "It was bad enough when my daughter organized that big excursion, but at least then I felt fairly certain none of you would be digging around, dressed as you were. When you found the body of that young man, I thought the one good to come of it would be that it would scare you all from returning. But then I heard you and Lord Aston planning a trip to the abbey and I worried. I thought perhaps you had seen something before and decided to investigate further.

"While you were getting changed for the journey, I ran to the abbey and waited for you to arrive. I know it well, and I knew how to remain unseen. You were searching for something, and I couldn't let you find the gold. When you separated from Lord Aston, I took my chance. I only meant to stop you looking and to frighten you away from returning. I wouldn't have done any worse than that. Lord Aston seeing me in the veils I used to disguise myself and taking me for a ghost was a serendipitous addition."

"You didn't frighten me away," Samantha said, a little more defensively than she meant. "I was looking for something completely different in the abbey, and I didn't return because I learned something that made finding it irrelevant."

The carriage came to a sudden stop, and Samantha looked out the window. They had reached the train station.

"I'm sorry for attacking you," Lady Wentworth said. "It wasn't personal—I've always liked you, even before I met you. When I read about you escaping from those murderers and finding a way to endure, I admired you tremendously. You took charge of your own destiny and now that you've inherited your fortune, you have the power to continue directing your own steps. You have a chance. That's all I wanted. You understand, don't you?"

Samantha understood that Lady Wentworth was trying to make her feel guilty and, much as she hated to admit it, it was working. She knew she was fortunate, unique in the opportunities her grandfather's money afforded her.

"You cannot deny me that chance, can you?"

Samantha hesitated. She thought of the life Lady Wentworth had been constrained to—the lot of many women of her class—with its restrictions and rules, without choice. It did seem unfair for Samantha to deny her something she herself had, to an extent. And yet...

"I don't believe you killed Jeremy Jones," Samantha said. "I think you are trying to protect the person who did, though I don't know why. But even if that does not bother your conscience, surely you cannot deny that most of the people who invested in your husband's scheme were innocent. They invested in good faith. Will you take their money?"

"Investment schemes are always a risk. They knew when they put the money in that they might not get it back."

"But not because they thought someone would steal it."

Lady Wentworth shrugged. "They had enough to sacrifice some. I have no money of my own."

"You believe that justifies taking what is not yours? Simply that you have none?"

"I will not be lectured to by you," Lady Wentworth snapped. "You, with your unlimited resources."

"I haven't always had them," Samantha argued. "I know what it is to live at the mercy of a difficult man, to feel that your options are limited. It doesn't justify theft, and it certainly doesn't justify murder."

Lady Wentworth recoiled. "I said it was an accident."

"You also said you did it, though that is clearly a lie."

There was silence for a moment, broken by a tapping on the door.

"You getting out?" the driver asked, his voice muffled.

Lady Wentworth nodded, and he opened the door. As she moved to step out, she turned to Samantha.

"Do not think I don't regret that man's death," she said, a rare hint of vulnerability in her expression. "It's a regret I will carry with me for the rest of my life. But it's a life I intend to take charge of, and I won't allow you to stop me."

Samantha waited until she was out of the carriage, then stepped down herself. The sounds of the busy train station, which had been quieted in the confines of the carriage, surrounded her.

People shouted to one another over the hiss of steam engines and the clatter of carriage wheels. From the far end of a platform, a whistle sounded.

The driver was helping Lady Wentworth to unload her baggage. Samantha trained her gaze around the station, searching for Wyatt. She wasn't sure how long Alice would have needed to wait for him—if she could even expect him yet. She wondered if she might be able to ask the assistance of a police officer in delaying Lady Wentworth, though she doubted she could find one who would believe her. Then, as the driver climbed up and took the reins again, urging his horses forward, an idea occurred to her.

Lady Wentworth's trunks had been loaded onto a trolley. She was standing beside it, adjusting her cloak when Samantha pushed confidently past her and took hold of the handle.

"What do you think you're doing?" Lady Wentworth said as Samantha turned the trolley in the opposite direction of the ticket booth.

Samantha ignored her, continuing to walk away with purposeful strides.

"Give me that!" Lady Wentworth ran after her and grabbed hold of the trolley.

Samantha gasped aloud and tightened her grip. "What are you doing? Let go!"

A man walking nearby looked over at them in surprise.

"You let go!" Lady Wentworth exclaimed, now shoving Samantha with her elbow.

Samantha raised her voice. "Madam, control yourself! Release the trolley!"

A crowd began to gather around them as they wrestled over the cart. The onlookers shouted a mixture of questions and words of encouragement.

"What's going on?"

"'Ere, there's no call for this!"

"Leave her be!"

Lady Wentworth became more frantic at the attention. She stamped hard on Samantha's foot and, when that didn't work, she elbowed her in the nose.

With a gasp, Samantha let go of the trolley, putting both hands to her nose, which had immediately begun to stream blood. In triumph, Lady Wentworth yanked the trolley away and began to turn it back.

"What's all this?"

A blue-uniformed police constable, drawn by the site of the crowd, had joined them. Immediately, the onlookers began to call out explanations. Shaking his head, he turned to Samantha, who had been handed a handkerchief by one of the watching ladies and was using it to stem the flow of blood.

"What happened, miss? Who hurt you?"

"It was her what did it!" said a squat woman standing behind Samantha. She pointed to Lady Wentworth, who had been trying, with difficulty, to navigate the crowd with her trolley.

The constable turned his attention to Lady Wentworth. "Did you attack this young lady?"

"Don't be ridiculous," Lady Wentworth said. She attempted to sound haughty, but her eyes darted all around, looking for escape.

"She's lying," said a man in the crowd.

"She stole t'other one's trolley," another man said helpfully.

"Did you steal her trolley?" the constable asked.

"No!" Lady Wentworth shouted. "This is my trolley."

"Madam?" The constable turned to Samantha.

Not wanting to start by lying to the constable when she needed him to believe her about Lady Wentworth, Samantha said merely, "She's a thief."

"I think we'd best sort this out inside," the constable said as Lady Wentworth protested.

Taking charge of the trolley, he called one of his colleagues over to help him escort both ladies to the station master's office nearby. Lady Wentworth protested that she was going to be late for her train, but the constable merely assured her that he would do his best to resolve matters swiftly.

To Samantha's relief, the constable's desire for swiftness was thwarted almost immediately—first by the station master's insistence on having the whole situation explained to him before he would allow the use of his office and then by his refusal to allow any questioning to take place until everyone had been provided with tea and Samantha's nose had been seen to.

Once extra chairs had been located and everyone had sat down with their cups of piping hot tea, there was a knock at the door. A small, middle-aged man with a pointed beard entered, followed by Wyatt.

"Good evening," the small man said pleasantly. His eyes scanned the room, quickly taking everything in.

"If you'll wait in the hall," the station master said, standing and gesturing to the door, "I'll be with you in a moment. I'm busy now, as you can see."

"Quite. As it happens, we are here to see this young lady." The small man gestured to Samantha before addressing her. "I presume you have some charge against the lady beside you."

Samantha glanced at Wyatt, who nodded.

"I do," Samantha said. "She's a thief."

"I see. Do you have any proof of this accusation?"

"The ladies were fighting over a luggage trolley," the constable said. "We were just about to discuss the matter."

The man didn't even glance at the constable, continuing to fix his attention on Samantha. She found herself wanting to squirm under the intensity of his gaze, but she resisted.

"I'm sure it was a misunderstanding," the man said, "hardly worthy of the attention of the station master."

"They were causing a disturbance," the constable said,

frowning at the man. "I brought them here to preserve the peace, as is my duty."

"Of course," the man said. "And now that peace has been restored, perhaps they might be allowed to go on their way."

"I'm sorry, who are you?" the station master asked. "What concern is it of yours?"

"Mr. Wyatt here is a friend of the young lady's. He was concerned when he could not find her where he expected to, and I offered to help him."

"As the young lady is the one doing the accusing—" the station master began.

"I dare say he's right," Samantha interrupted. She could see that Wyatt and his friend wanted to keep the constables and the station master ignorant of the true situation. "I must have been mistaken." She turned to Lady Wentworth. "My apologies."

The station master threw his hands in the air and sat heavily back in his chair.

"You're saying she didn't steal your trolley," the constable said to Samantha in disbelief.

"That is correct."

"She did punch you in the nose, though."

Wyatt looked at her sharply.

"It's of no consequence," Samantha said.

The constable muttered something under his breath that sounded suspiciously like, "Women" before shoving to his feet. "Very well." He turned to the station master. "My apologies for wasting your time."

With a glare at Samantha and Lady Wentworth, he left the room, followed by his colleague.

"Allow me to escort you, my lady," Wyatt's friend said, holding out an arm to Lady Wentworth. She eyed him warily, but took it, and they exited.

"Thank you for the tea," Samantha said to the station master.

"And for the handkerchiefs. Would you like me to—"

"Keep them," he grunted, and he gestured for her and Wyatt to leave.

"What happened?" Wyatt asked as they re-entered the smoky air of the train station.

"I had to stop her from leaving somehow. I took her trolley and, when she tried to take it back, I made a scene, as the constable said."

"Did she really punch you in the nose?"

"Don't be ridiculous. It was her elbow."

Wyatt snorted.

"She has surprisingly sharp elbows," Samantha said, touching her nose and wincing. "I presume that man is your mysterious friend?"

Ahead of them, the man, who had a firm grip on Lady Wentworth's elbow, was muttering something in her ear while gesturing to a waiting carriage.

"He is. Luckily, he was at the address he gave me, and I didn't have to track him down across the city. Otherwise, we might have been too late."

"As it was, your timing was perfect. They might have insisted on opening the trunks, and I'm fairly certain she didn't get all the gold converted into jewelry."

"What?"

Samantha started to explain, but she was distracted by the sight of an old man pushing through the mass of people and trolleys towards Lady Wentworth, worry sketched across his brow. Lady Wentworth saw him and gasped. She began vigorously to shake her head, but the man persisted, coming to stand beside her and Wyatt's friend.

As one, Samantha and Wyatt moved closer to hear.

"You can't take her," the old man was saying in heavy northern accents. "It weren't her. I'm respons—"

"No!" Lady Wentworth shouted. "He's lying. I did it. I did it all myself."

"Now, lass." A sad smile stretched the old man's wrinkled face. "I won't have you taking the blame for what I did."

"It was my fault," Lady Wentworth choked. "It was all because of me."

"Who is this?" Wyatt's friend asked, his voice polite, as though he were asking to be introduced to a mutual acquaintance.

"Colm Jeffords, sir," the old man said. "I'm the one what killed that man and stole tha—"

"If you'll come with me, Mr. Jeffords. I know a place we can talk about this comfortably."

Lady Wentworth had begun to sob, her breath coming out in choking gasps. The old man patted her back and climbed into the carriage.

"That must be the old man," Samantha said. "She wouldn't admit he existed when I asked her about him. Why do you suppose she's trying so hard to protect him?"

"I have no idea."

They watched as Wyatt's friend helped Lady Wentworth into the carriage.

"I should get you back to Madge's," Wyatt said.

"I brought my reticule." Samantha opened the small bag and deposited the soiled handkerchiefs in it. "I can take a hackney back."

Wyatt raised an eyebrow at her.

"I know you feel you ought to escort me," she said, "but I also know you would like to go with your mysterious friend to learn what is to become of Lady Wentworth and, to be frank, I would like you to, so that you may tell me later. Besides, hardly anyone is aware I am gone. If I arrive at the front door with you and no other escort, will that not look odd? Much better that I sneak back in the rear entrance." When Wyatt still looked hesitant, she added,

"If it would make you easier in your mind, you may hail the cab yourself and hand me into it. That should discharge your sense of chivalry."

He gave her a small smile that did not reach his eyes. "If chivalry were my sole motive, your solution would do nicely. However, you are correct, it would look odd for us to arrive together. Wait a moment, and I will hail a cab."

When the cab pulled up, Wyatt spoke to the driver. Samantha saw money exchange hands, and she frowned at Wyatt when he came to help her into the carriage.

"I know, you said you would pay, but I hope you will allow me this one extra moment of chivalry, if that is what you wish to call it, when I am deprived of the opportunity to accompany you home. I will try not to make it a habit."

"See that you do not," she said, holding back a smile.

He took her hand to help her up. In her haste to follow Lady Wentworth, she had neglected her gloves and, at the touch of his skin against hers, she started. An odd sensation, at once familiar and strange, welcome and unwanted, spread through her. Almost involuntarily, she glanced up. Their eyes met, and she thought she saw a flash of vulnerability in his before his all-too-familiar enigmatic expression arrived to shield his thoughts from her.

"I won't come to dinner after all," he said. "Give Madge my regrets. But inform her and Lord Bradwell that I will see you all this evening to report what I learn."

SEVENTEEN

It was later than he had intended when Wyatt finally returned to the Bradwells' London residence. Under ordinary circumstances, he would have waited until morning to call, but he knew they would be still be awake, eager to hear what he had to say.

Headley, who had traveled with the family from Derbyshire, took Wyatt's coat and hat with a valiantly suppressed yawn.

"I'm sorry to have kept you up, Headley," Wyatt said, handing over his cane.

"It's of no consequence, sir," Headley said, hanging Wyatt's coat on the hook. "They're waiting for you in the front drawing room."

Taking the stairs two at a time, Wyatt ascended to the first floor. The drawing room door stood ajar, the light of the crackling fire spilling into the hall.

"Finally!" Madge exclaimed as he entered the room and shut the door behind him.

A long divan had been drawn up to the fire and it was on this that she sat, beside Samantha, with Lord Bradwell in a high-backed armchair across from them, his back to the door. On Wyatt's entrance, Madge rose to her feet and came to him, taking his arm and pulling him along with her.

"You have thrown us into chaos this evening," she chastised, leading him to a chair beside Lord Bradwell and depositing him into it. "My table was completely off, and I can't tell you the complaints I had from Monsieur LaPointe when he discovered that three of the anticipated guests would be absent—four, once Sir Rupert was called away mid-meal. The capons had already been cooked, it seems. And then, I hear from Samantha that you have known for some time that all was not right with Sir Rupert and yet have neglected to inform me, the very person who asked you to investigate him in the first place."

Wyatt glanced at Samantha, who grimaced and shrugged.

"I apologize, my lady," he said solicitously to Madge. "I merely wished to be certain before I brought any accusations against the man."

"Pish," Madge said, resuming her seat beside Samantha. "You merely wished not to look a fool if you were wrong."

Samantha grinned at him, and he pretended to look abashed.

"I do hope you plan to enlighten us now," Madge said, smoothing her skirts and looking at him expectantly.

Wyatt inclined his head. "I do. I extracted permission to inform the three of you of the true circumstances of the case with the understanding that the information will go no further."

"I hope," Lord Bradwell said, setting aside the newspaper he had been reading, "that you also extracted an explanation that I might give to the village and the members of Mr. Jones' family as to the cause of his death?"

Wyatt sighed. "I did. It is, more or less, the truth."

"Well?" Madge prompted.

"I assume Samantha has informed you of what she knows?" he asked, looking to Samantha for confirmation.

"I thought it would save time," Samantha said. "When you said you would speak to the three of us, I presumed you would wish us to be on the same page."

Wyatt gave her a grateful nod and continued. "The old man, Mr. Jeffords, has been Lady Wentworth's partner from the beginning. On her information, he stole the gold and drove the majority of it to the abbey, where he hid it in anticipation of Lady Wentworth's stay here. Since the theft, they have taken it in turn to visit jewelers in a variety of locations, purchasing jewelry with the gold. Though, once Lady Wentworth came to Bradwell, it had been solely Mr. Jeffords who performed this action. He would then secrete the jewelry in another part of the abbey for Lady Wentworth to pick up."

"But who is he?" Samantha asked. "Why did he help her? Why not just take the gold for himself?"

"He was Lady Wentworth's gardener, it seems. He came with her from her family home when she married. He is himself unmarried and childless, and I received the impression that he regards her in a fatherly way."

Samantha looked doubtful. "I remember her talking about him once, and I did think it odd when she said he'd been her family's gardener when she was a child. Do you remember, Madge?"

"I do," Madge said. "She certainly seemed fond of him, and I suppose, if they'd known each other for so long...She did say she employed him after he was fired by her father, but still, it is odd."

"Was it this Mr. Jeffords, then," Lord Bradwell asked, "who killed Jeremy Jones?"

"It was. Mr. Jeffords had returned to the abbey with his most recent purchase and was stashing the jewelry. He found Mr. Jones with a large sack, attempting to remove most of the remaining gold. Sneaking up behind him, Mr. Jeffords hit him over the head with a heavy chunk of fallen masonry. He then dragged the body to the river, hoping it would be carried far enough downstream to draw attention away from the abbey. He did not realize how low the river was."

"Then it wasn't an accident?" Samantha asked. "He meant to kill him?"

"I think he felt he had to, to protect his and his lady's secret."

"What will happen to her?" she asked hesitantly.

"Ah," Wyatt said, and all three of them looked at him with interest. "That is where the complications arise. You see, Mr. Benton—my mysterious friend, as Samantha calls him—says that Her Majesty's government is not eager for the full truth of these events to be made public. They fear reprisals from America if it is known that Sir Rupert was attempting to fund the Confederate war effort. Therefore, they have struck up a deal with the Wentworths."

"A deal?" Madge repeated. "What sort of deal?"

"Mr. Jeffords will be prosecuted for the murder of Mr. Jones. He has admitted to it, so there ought not to be any complications. He will be delivered to Lower Bradwell to stand trial. No mention is to be made of the gold. Mr. Jeffords will be portrayed as a degenerate wanderer who killed Mr. Jones over an accusation of cheating at cards."

"And Mr. Jeffords has agreed to this portrayal of his character?" Lord Bradwell asked skeptically.

"He has," Wyatt nodded, "because it allows Lady Wentworth to go free."

"She is to go free?" Samantha asked in surprise.

"She must return what she stole," Wyatt explained. "Sir Rupert will ensure the money is returned to the original investors, explaining that the venture fell through but he was able to preserve their capital."

"Sir Rupert does not strike me as one likely to admit a mistake," Madge said scornfully. "Is he willing to comply?"

"More than willing. In return for his compliance and his silence on the matter, as well as his assurance to refrain from further communication with his co-conspirators in America, he is being given a coveted post in India."

"What?" Samantha gasped as Madge said, incredulously, "India?"

Wyatt nodded.

"So then," Samantha said indignantly, "not only does he receive no penalty for his actions, but he is to be rewarded?"

"Benton considers that he is being sent where he can do no more harm," Wyatt said, "but, yes, I suppose Sir Rupert may construe it as a reward."

"This is why I loathe London," Madge said, taking a sip of tea from the cup beside her. "All the secrecy, the veiled insults, the pettiness. It is not merely in the ballrooms, but in the government as well."

"Will Sir Rupert and Lady Wentworth be returning here?" Samantha asked.

"Absolutely not," Madge said, setting down her cup and getting to her feet. "And I shall be having a word with Linwood about Miss Wentworth as well."

"We cannot betray any knowledge of their wrongdoing," Wyatt cautioned. "Remember, as far as the public is concerned, nothing at all has happened with them but Sir Rupert's promotion. However, with that in mind, they will be returning home soon to prepare for his departure."

"I don't think you need concern yourself about Lord Linwood," Samantha said. "I would guess that Sir Rupert is in just the right sort of mood for which Miss Wentworth has been hoping. She has an understanding with another man, you see."

"Well, that is a relief," Madge said, sitting back down. "I don't suppose Linwood will mind terribly."

"He'll be sorry to see Sir Rupert go," Lord Bradwell said. He folded his paper and rose to his feet. Leaning down to kiss Madge's cheek, he said, "Next time our son gets it into his head to pursue a girl for her father's sake, let him invite them to his own house. I'm going to bed."

Samantha stood up. "I think I will, too. It's been a long day." She flashed Wyatt a tired smile.

"Of course, dear," Madge said. "Goodnight to you both."

Lord Bradwell allowed Samantha to precede him from the room. Wyatt stood as well but was kept from following them by a militant look in Madge's eye.

"There's something else you've been keeping from me," she said when the sound of footsteps had receded.

"Is there?"

"Of course, you may say it is none of my business, but I do have to live around you both, so I am affected, if nothing else."

"Whom are you talking about?" Wyatt asked, feigning ignorance.

Madge rolled her eyes heavenward. "You know perfectly well whom, and if you thought I wouldn't notice the way you look at each other, you must imagine me a perfect simpleton. What I want to know is what you plan to do about it."

"I don't plan to do anything."

"I hope this idiocy is not on account of your mother," Madge said, narrowing her eyes at him. "Knowing her, I am certain she has seen an opportunity to increase the family wealth and has made the perfectly foolish choice to attempt to direct you rather than simply wait for the natural course of things. And you, being you, have put up your hackles and refused."

Wyatt found himself both annoyed and amused at this assessment, but he spoke with civility when he said, "This idiocy has nothing to do with my mother. She will not have me."

"You've asked her? When?"

"At the ball."

"Ah." Madge nodded thoughtfully. "That would certainly explain...What reason did she give for refusing you?"

Wyatt snorted. "What reason did she not give? She does not wish to give up her freedom, she does not trust me, she does not love me, or rather, she will not love me, though that is much the same thing."

"How did you ask her?" Madge asked, her voice suddenly sharp.

Wyatt ran a hand through his hair and looked down at the floor, feeling unaccountably flustered. "I...we...well..."

Madge raised her eyebrows. "May I assume by your eloquence that there was some exchange of affections beforehand that you would rather not divulge?"

"She certainly gave me reason to believe her answer would be yes," Wyatt said defensively. "I had not intended to ask her, but it sort of...slipped out."

"Just the sort of proposal every woman dreams of," Madge said dryly.

Wyatt frowned, but she ignored him, clasping her hands behind her and beginning to pace.

"So she told you no, and you, offended, demanded to know why."

"I hardly demanded—"

"Had you spoken of marriage with her before?"

"I...yes, actually, I had."

"And she told you she did not intend to marry?"

"I...how did you know?"

Madge stopped pacing and gave him a withering look. "Because she told me the same. I told her I perfectly understood, because I do, though I see you do not."

"She is comparing me to that fiend, Charles," Wyatt said dourly. "She will not even consider me on my own merits."

"She is not only comparing you to Charles, my dear boy. She is comparing you to every man she has known, all of whom have disappointed her in some way, as I have no doubt you have as well."

"If she is seeking perfection, she will be sorely disappointed," he said bitterly.

"But that is just it," Madge said. "She *isn't* seeking perfection. She is anticipating the opposite and bracing herself against it. She is protecting herself, both physically and emotionally."

Wyatt threw up his hands in frustration. "It comes out the same either way."

Madge sighed. "My dear Wyatt, you may be my favorite cousin and very nearly my favorite relative, but you can be remarkably dense at times. It is not at all the same."

"How?"

"The very fact that she is protecting herself shows that she has something to protect. She is not a heartless flirt seeking an impossibly perfect man. She is a vulnerable young woman with a good heart who, in the right environment, could be very open to love. That is not to say that I feel she ought to marry. If it were not that I sensed something between the two of you, I would be perfectly happy to champion her desire to remain unmarried. After all, she is correct in much that she says about the role of women in marriage, legally speaking. I would even stomach a Season in London for the mere pleasure of watching those predatory fortune-hunters get their just desserts when she rejected them one by one."

She paused. "But I see I am letting my thoughts run away with me. The point is, there is something to be said for a marriage of true minds, and I believe you two have the potential to have such a marriage, if you can only learn to disregard your pride and give her time to trust you."

"How am I to do that when she refuses to even consider the idea?" Wyatt asked, half in despair, half in hope.

"You cannot expect me to do everything for you," Madge said, waving his question away with a touch of irritation. "You are an intelligent man, most of the time. I trust you will think of something. Although, to be quite honest, I am surprised at you. I've never known you to give up so easily."

*****

For almost two full days, Sir Rupert and Lady Wentworth did not return. Their children were told they'd been called away unexpectedly but not to worry. Unfortunately, Fanny did worry, and—as her new, dear friend—it was Samantha who had the privilege of listening to her litany of concerns. Whenever she could, Samantha escaped to the library and, more often than not, was joined by a sympathetic Eden. Wyatt had not been back since the night of Lady Wentworth's detainment.

Samantha was in the library with Eden on Friday evening when there was a knock at the front door, and she heard Headley welcome back Sir Rupert and Lady Wentworth.

"The roads were congested as usual," Sir Rupert boomed in response to a murmured question from Headley. "I must say, I certainly won't be missing that part of London."

Samantha went to the door and opened it. She could see Sir Rupert handing his coat to Headley and, just behind him, Lady Wentworth was untying her cloak. At the sound of footsteps coming from down the hall, Lady Wentworth looked up. Her gaze swept the room and landed on Samantha. She froze. Samantha was frozen, too, struggling to reconcile the woman she saw standing calmly before her with the one who had admitted her part in a murder, elbowed her in the nose, then stood sobbing over her gardener.

The footsteps grew louder, and Madge entered the room.

"There you are. What a relief that you are able to join us once more," she said with only a hint of sarcasm. "Ought we to expect any more sudden departures?"

Sir Rupert laughed good-naturedly. "Not sudden, no.

However, we will have to cut short our visit. We must return to Manchester after the funeral."

"How disappointing. Rest assured, you will receive all the assistance you need to expedite your departure. I would hate for you to feel you cannot leave as soon as you might."

"Thank you, my lady." Lady Wentworth gave a little curtsey.

"Headley," Madge said, turning to the butler, who had just finished hanging Sir Rupert's coat.

"Yes, your ladyship?"

"Have supper set back an hour so our guests can freshen up."

When the ladies retired to the drawing room after supper, Samantha settled herself on the settee. Fanny joined her almost immediately.

"I have news," she said in a hushed voice, a light of excitement in her eyes. She clapped a hand over her mouth as a giggle nearly escaped her.

"What news?" Samantha asked, though she thought she could guess.

"Father has given his consent to my marriage," Fanny said, grabbing Samantha's hands from her lap and squeezing them. "He says I may marry Henry as soon as I wish!"

"How wonderful," Samantha said, extricating her hands carefully. "I am happy for you."

Fanny beamed. "It is even better than I hoped. He was in such a good mood when I spoke to him that he even agreed to purchase a whole new wardrobe for my trousseau!"

Samantha could imagine Sir Rupert's mood was as cheerful as it had ever been. His lost gold had been recovered, he had avoided any appearance of scandal or legal repercussions for defying Britain's neutrality, and, at a time when his primary business was set to experience an extended period of loss, he had been given a plush position abroad without any effort on his part whatsoever.

Samantha's expression must have reflected her disgust because Fanny's smile seemed to dim. Summoning an energy she did not feel, Samantha smiled. "It's the best news."

Fanny's face relaxed. "It truly is," she said. "Though I expect Ollie would not say so. He has had good news of his own."

"Oh?"

"Yes," Fanny said. "It seems he had also been working behind Father's back, and I must say I am glad Father is so very happy because, if not, Ollie's scheming might have put him in such a state as never to sanction my marriage."

"What had he done?"

"Applied for university. Oxford, it seems, to study the classics. Not, as Father wished, to Cambridge for politics. He has some money of his own, you see, and he planned to go whether Father liked it or not, destroying Father's plans for his future. Can you imagine how angry Father would have been? Only, now he just says that Ollie has time to learn what he likes and ten to one he will hate the classics and come round." She laughed. "I am not sure that he will, but it's of no matter, for I will be married by then and Father will be far away in India. Isn't it funny how things work out? Now, if you don't mind, I would like to ask Lady Chesterton where she procured her fourth daughter's wedding gown. I hear it was exquisite."

With Fanny gone, Samantha searched the room for her mother, finally spotting her near the window.

"I suppose I owe you an apology," Lady Wentworth said when Samantha joined her, her eyes fixed firmly on a point outside. "It was silly of me to imagine I could escape, and I ought not to have injured you."

"Not so silly, it seems," Samantha said.

Lady Wentworth pulled her gaze from the window and turned to look at Samantha. There was a heaviness, a sadness behind her eyes that had not been there before. "Colm Jeffords was so much more than my family's gardener—he was more of a father to me while I was growing up than my father ever was. After I married, my father discovered love letters between my mother and Mr. Jeffords, proving that they had conducted an affair around the time I was conceived."

Samantha's eyebrows rose.

Lady Wentworth sighed. "It was why my father terminated his employment. There was no knowing whose child I was. Even my mother could not be certain. But since the revelation, my father has barely spoken to me. Mr. Jeffords, however, has always treated me as his own. I brought him into my plans because there was no one I trusted more. And now, because of me, he will be executed."

She turned back to the window. Samantha saw a lone tear spill from the corner of her eye and travel down her cheek before she brushed it away.

"No doubt, you believe I ought to be in Newgate for the part I played in that young man's death and the theft of the gold, but I assure you I am very much a prisoner. Regret binds stronger than any chains of steel can hope to. I have lost the most loyal and steadfast of friends and have not even the comfort of imagining it to have been God's will, for I know it was on account of my own folly. So trust me when I tell you, Miss Kingston, that I have been sufficiently punished for my actions and in a manner from which I shall never be freed."

Lady Wentworth excused herself to bed not long after their conversation. Samantha watched her go with conflicting emotions. She had expected a sense of relief to follow the discovery and arrest of Mr. Jones' killer and a sense of accomplishment at solving the mystery of the missing gold, yet she felt neither. If only the villain had been motivated purely by greed, there might have been some pleasure gained in hunting him down.

There was no joy in seeing the broken woman before her or in imagining the death of her friend and gardener. Yet neither could

Samantha feel only pity for them, as they had chosen paths that harmed others, stealing the life of one man and the livelihoods of unknown others.

EIGHTEEN

Eight black horses in royal escutcheons pulled a black-draped carriage down the nearly silent street late Monday morning. Despite the presence of hundreds of mourners, crowded onto the pavement on either side, the clip-clop of the horses' hooves on the cobblestone road was the loudest sound for miles. Standing beside Madge near the edge of the street, Samantha scanned the somber faces around her. Every mourner had put an effort into their dress so that it was nearly impossible to tell the rich from the poor as they all stood together as one.

As the carriage passed in front of her, Samantha heard the distant sound of cannon fire from one of the half-masted ships on the Thames saluting the dead. Its reverberations were echoed in the bells of St. Paul's, which began their mournful tolls.

When Prince Albert's casket turned down another street on its way to St. George's Chapel in Windsor, it was several minutes before anyone moved. It was as though they had all been waiting for someone to tell them what to do, and finally, upon the realization that they were on their own, they began to wander off in all directions, no one in a hurry, speaking in whispers.

Samantha and Madge walked back to Grosvenor Square with

the other ladies of the party. Only Lord Bradwell had been invited to the actual funeral, but the other gentlemen had chosen to go to Windsor as well, in order to be among those waiting outside the chapel, the last to pay their respects before the prince's internment.

Once they had left the path taken by the prince's carriage through the city, the ladies came across few people. All of the shops were closed. There were no costermongers' stalls or market stands. There were not even many carriages on the roads. It seemed as though the city itself mourned the passing of one of its most prominent residents.

Supper that night was subdued. Of the gentlemen who went to Windsor, only Lord Aston and Sir Rupert had returned in time, so everyone ate informally but mostly in silence. Even Sir Rupert, who had been almost jubilant since his return, was affected by the mood.

After supper, no one dared approach the piano or suggest a hand of cards so, following some desultory conversation, everyone went to bed.

Christmas came two days after Prince Albert's funeral. As any celebration could only be considered in bad taste, it was the strangest Christmas Samantha had experienced. No carols were sung, no gifts were exchanged, and there was no holly or mistletoe to be seen.

After a dismal Christmas dinner with no goose and no pudding, Samantha took refuge in the library. She had intended to find a novel to distract herself from her melancholy, but, unable to focus on the page before her, she spent the better part of an hour staring out the window, watching the carriages trundle around Grosvenor Square.

The door opened, startling her from her reverie, and Wyatt entered, the smile he bestowed on her not quite reaching his eyes. Any happiness she might have felt at seeing him again after so many days apart evaporated. They still had yet to talk about their relationship, as he had promised they would, and if he'd decided that now was the time, his expression did not bode well.

"Might I join you?" he asked, closing the door behind him.

"If you like."

He sat beside her on the window seat, but rather than speak, he turned to look out the window.

"Was there something you wished to say?" she asked. She did not want to draw out the unpleasantness.

"There was." He turned back to her with another forced smile. "Though I'm not sure that I should say it."

"You know I don't like it when you speak in riddles."

"I know. And I'm sorry. It's just, I want to get this right."

Samantha felt a sudden jolt of panic at the thought that a second proposal might be coming.

"Don't worry," Wyatt said, palms raised in placation. "I'm not asking you to marry me again. At least, not yet."

Her heart skipped a beat. He didn't give her time to consider what he meant or how she felt about it.

"Before you begin your myriad objections," he said. "I beg you would hear me out. I am well aware that, if we were to marry, the advantages would be entirely on my side. You have no material reason to marry and almost every reason not to. You do not even, by your admission, have love to sway you in my favor. And yet, while you may not love me, I think I am right to say you like me, and I have experienced for myself your attraction to me."

She gasped and made to hit his arm, but he caught her hand. "If you disagree, I am happy to give you the opportunity to prove your indifference." He leaned closer, his eyes dropping to her lips.

She shoved him back and scooted away. "I never attempted to deny the attraction between us," she said defiantly, trying to ignore how tempted she had been by his offer, "but mutual attraction is not a solid basis for a marriage."

"On its own, no," he agreed, a grin playing around his lips. Lips she was now struggling not to look at. "Though it certainly makes it more enjoyable, I should imagine." In spite of herself, she smiled at this. "But mutual respect, friendship, an enjoyment of each other's company, the ability to challenge each other to improve—are they not good reasons for a marriage?"

Samantha sighed. "Perhaps. But so is trust. In fact, I think that is the most important aspect of a marriage."

Wyatt nodded, his face solemn. "I know I lost what trust you had in me when I hid what I knew about Charles' killer from you. I cannot tell you how much I regret it. I could swear to you right now that I will never deceive you again, no matter the circumstances, but I know it would be pointless. Trust is not recovered in a moment." He held her gaze as he continued, "All I'm asking for is a chance—a chance to prove to you that I'm worthy of your trust. Beyond that, well...I have no expectations."

Samantha looked out the window as she considered his words. Could she trust him again? Enough to put her whole life in his hands? She didn't know. She didn't know if that much trust was possible. Then she thought of the question Lord Aston had posed to her. *When you look at your future, which do you prefer? The one with him or without?* She turned back to Wyatt. "No expectations?"

"There would be no point," he said. "How could I have expectations when I never know what will come out of your mouth next?"

She pursed her lips to hold back a smile, but it escaped her, nonetheless. "Very well. You may have your chance."

He smiled.

"No expectations," she said firmly.

"No expectations."

He stood and held out a hand. She took it, and he pulled her to her feet. Then, still holding her hand, he leaned forward and spoke quietly, his breath tickling her ear, "Yet, I will continue to hope."

Samantha turned to him. Their faces were inches apart. She could see a fleck of shaving soap on his jaw that his valet had missed. She reached up to brush it away. As her fingers touched his skin, he drew in a breath. Their eyes met. She watched his drop to her lips.

The sound of a throat clearing broke them apart. Headley stood at the door, an impassive expression on his face.

"There is a...young person...here to see you, Miss Kingston."

"Oh?" Samantha asked, blushing and avoiding looking at Wyatt. "Will you not send her—or him—in?"

"That will not be possible. She is waiting for you in the kitchens." As Samantha's brow furrowed, he added, "We would not have bothered you, only she was most insistent, and she is in a bad way."

Completely nonplussed, Samantha exchanged a look with Wyatt.

"Did she give her name?" Wyatt asked Headley.

"I believe it was Amy, sir," Headley said. "She was in a state of considerable agitation, and I confess I could not quite make out her words."

"Amy?" Samantha repeated. Then, as realization dawned, "Could it have been Annie?"

"It may have been."

"Annie?" Wyatt's expression told her that he remembered Annie's role in her previous adventures.

"I will see her."

"Would you like me to come?" Wyatt asked.

"Yes." A mixture of fear and trepidation churned in Samantha's stomach. "I think something is very wrong."

A great confusion of noise in the working portion of the house ceased almost abruptly as Samantha and Wyatt entered the large, airy kitchen behind the butler. Half of Madge's staff seemed to have converged on the room, but they all, save Mrs. Meadows, the housekeeper, stepped back as Samantha approached the long, wooden table.

Mrs. Meadows stood with her hands submerged in a bowl of some red substance. Beside her, seated in a sturdy wooden chair, was the bedraggled form of a girl whose tangles of dirty-blonde hair hung to her elbows.

"Annie?" Samantha ventured softly.

The girl looked up, and Samantha gasped. It was indeed Annie, but as Samantha had never seen her. One eye was swollen shut, and her face was so covered in bruises that her skin was a mottled purple. Mrs. Meadows lifted her hands from the bowl, which Samantha now realized contained water tinged with Annie's blood, and wrung out the cloth she had been rinsing. She then applied the cloth to the cut on Annie's lip.

"What happened?" Samantha asked, squatting beside the girl.

Annie reached out and grasped Samantha's hands in her own, her grip painfully tight.

"I have a message for you," she said in a hoarse whisper, leaning forward and speaking into Samantha's ear. "Skinny Jim sends his greetings."

Author's Note

In early 1861, Britain declared itself neutral in the American Civil War despite attempts on both sides to gain its support. Hoping to persuade the British to change their minds, Confederate President Jefferson Davis selected two ambassadors—John Slidell and James Mason—to plead his cause. While the ambassadors were aboard the British ship, RMS Trent, it was boarded by Captain Charles Wilkes of the USS San Jacinto, who claimed them as contraband. He took the men, over the protests of the British captain, onto his ship and brought them to Boston as prisoners of war.

While Wilkes was hailed as a hero in the northern states, the British were outraged. Only fifty years previously, seizure of neutral ships had been one of America's gripes against Britain which led, in part, to the War of 1812. Many of the British saw Wilkes' actions as not only hypocritical, but tantamount to a declaration of war.

Before researching for this book, I had never heard of the Trent Affair, but the more I read about it, the more fascinated I became. From what I discovered, military preparations began almost as soon as news of the capture reached Britain with many considering war with America inevitable. The sudden death of Prince Albert in the midst of it all only added to the strain. The prince was buried two days before Christmas. We have the Victorians to thank for many of our modern Christmas traditions, but I can't imagine that Christmas of 1861 was anything but bleak.

Thank you for reading *Ghosts in the Abbey*! If you liked it, please consider posting a review. If you would like to read more of Samantha and Wyatt's story, join my newsletter at www.emilylfinch.com to be notified when the next book releases. You can also follow me on Facebook or on Instagram @writer_elf.

Acknowledgements

First, I would like to thank everyone who read my first book and, especially, those who left reviews. Your response has been so positive, overwhelming and humbling. It was a long journey to publishing for me and I am so thankful for your support.

To Brandon, my biggest champion, thank you for once again being my sounding board. Thank you especially for those weekends at crunch time when you watched the kids to give me time to edit. None of this would have been possible without you.

Thank you to my editor, Meredith Spears, for slogging through a much rougher draft than I was hoping to send. Pregnancy brain is real.

To my beta readers, Jen, Mer, and Aunt Cindy, thank you so much for your time and your feedback.

Thank you Mom for taking time from your busy schedule to copyedit for me and for pointing out my overuse of certain words.

Finally, thank you to all the family and friends who lent their support to the sales of my first book, either by sharing on social media or telling people they knew. I feel very loved.

Printed in Great Britain
by Amazon